THE ROSE MUDDLE MYSTERIES

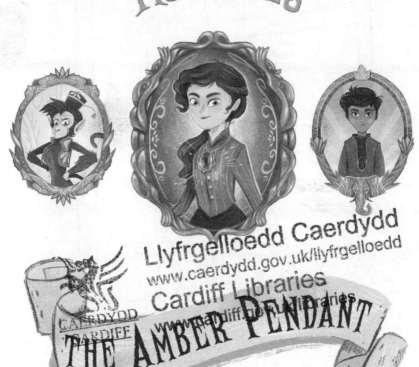

THE AMBER PENDANT

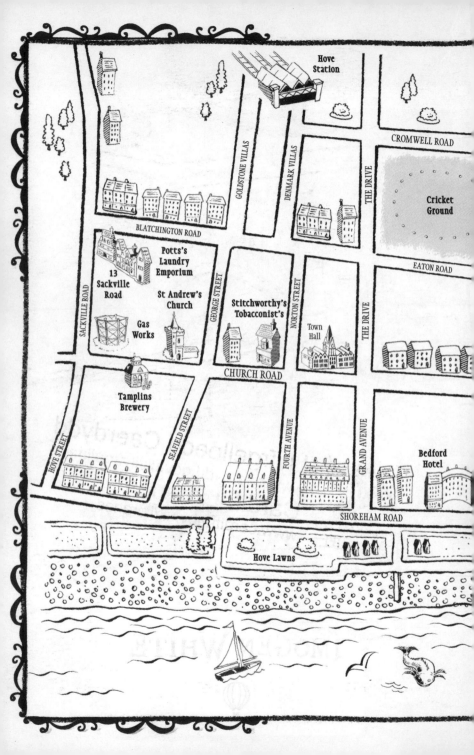

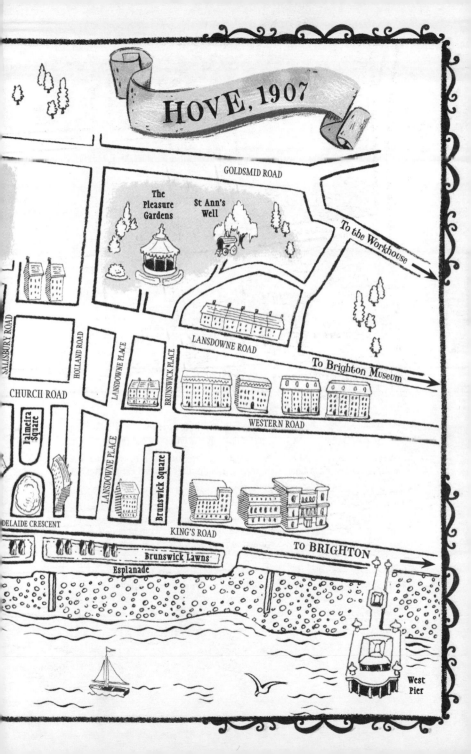

For Bobbie, 1928 – 2015

First published in the UK in 2017 by Usborne Publishing Ltd., Usborne House,
83-85 Saffron Hill, London EC1N 8RT, England. www.usborne.com

Text © Imogen White, 2017

Cover and inside illustrations by Davide Ortu © Usborne Publishing, 2017

Artwork for map by David Shephard © Usborne Publishing, 2017

The right of Imogen White to be identified as the author of this work has been
asserted by her in accordance with the Copyright, Designs and Patents Act, 1988.

The name Usborne and the devices ♀ ⊕ are Trade Marks of
Usborne Publishing Ltd.

A CIP catalogue record for this book is available from the British Library.

ISBN 9781474927291 04337-1 JFM MJJASOND/17

Printed in the UK.

Thirteen Sackville Road

Hove, 1907

"ROSE MUDDLE! Miss Templeforth has requested your company in the library."

Rose fell off her stool, sending it clattering across the kitchen. Drawing a sharp breath, she scrambled to her feet. Mr Crank, the butler, snarled at her from the doorway.

"M-me?" she stammered. "In the library?" She felt the colour leaving her cheeks. "But I ain't supposed to go in the library."

"Stop your braying, and get over here!"

Adjusting her frilled headpiece, she rushed over to the butler. Straight-backed in her maid's uniform, she tried to stand every one of her twelve years to a regimented attention.

The butler gripped her arm, and pulled her close. "As you know, Miss Templeforth has been interviewing a number of young girls this afternoon and she is extremely tired. Once this last girl leaves, it will be your turn. I suggest you go in quietly and listen to her very carefully," he smirked. "One may hope that she's reconsidering her act of charity in having you here, and is shipping you back to the workhouse where you belong. Imagine being replaced after just one week. Ha! I never understood why they brought you here in the first place."

Rose scrunched up her face against his hot cabbage breath. She decided his liver-spotted bald head looked like a quail's egg under the glare of the lamp.

Egghead! Rose thought, her slate-coloured eyes flashing at him.

The butler winced as if he'd detected her unspoken insult. Squeezing her arm even harder he opened his mouth to speak, but was cut short by a bell from the library upstairs.

With a sigh, he let go of Rose and set off up the creaky servants' staircase that led to the lobby above.

"Stay put. I'll be back to get you, Rose Muddle."

Shuffling from one foot to the other, Rose waited until the sound of the butler's footsteps had faded. Then she squeezed her eyes shut and wished really hard that she could vanish into thin air. But it didn't work – it never did. She slumped onto her lumpy bed in the corner of the kitchen.

Rose hadn't met her mysterious mistress yet; she'd only heard the strange, haunting moans coming from the library. Miss Templeforth was ill – tuberculosis, so Rose had been told. She lived in the library, which remained out of bounds to everyone but the butler, the physician and the family lawyer. Until today that is, when a stream of girls had arrived to see her. They'd been sent in there, one by one, but had all come away screaming, or so struck down with fear they'd had to be carried out.

Rose did not want to visit the library – what if she *was* to be sent back to the workhouse? Thoughts of barred windows, turning the rotten mangle, Miss Gritt's punishments and the icy cold of the dormitory filled her mind. She shivered. This place was a piece of cake compared to there. In fact, working as a scullery maid at Sackville Road was more than Rose Muddle had ever dreamed of.

From her bed, Rose looked over the heavy table to where the stockpot bubbled merrily on the stove. Above it copper pans, arranged according to size, lined the wall. Everything here felt toasty warm.

And a shilling and threepence a week. Rose smiled. This

was a proper job. All her board and lodgings included, and she even had every other Sunday off – free as a bird to do whatever she fancied. Her smile faltered, as the words of the housemistress at the workhouse came to her. "They'll never keep you, Rose Muddle. Mark my words. You'll be back," Miss Gritt had said. And now the butler wanted shot of her too. A thread of alarm stitched itself inside Rose's heart. She wiped her sweaty palms on her apron. *I won't go back there, not ever.*

Voices carried from the servant's staircase, as the day maids headed back down to the kitchen.

Rose panicked, her tummy in ribbons; she needed some fresh air, and somewhere alone to think. Heading to the door, she freed the latch softly and slipped into the basement yard.

The October chill gnawed through her black floor-length dress and apron. She sniffed, wiping her nose on her sleeve and clapping her arms with her hands as the basement yard pressed in around her.

At four thirty it was already getting dark. The evening light made the yard, which had a grey stone floor, feel even smaller, just a few feet across. Rose looked at the tall brick wall that stretched up to the roadway above. She could hear the carriages rattling past on Sackville Road.

Scared stiff, she paced back and forth, still hoping she

could wish the situation away. She spotted the coal-hole and stopped, chewing her nail.

Maybe if she hid for a while she wouldn't have to see the mistress after all. *And what with the mistress so tired from all them interviews, and being as ill as she is…she could have a little nap instead. Yes,* Rose convinced herself. *I'd be doing her a blessed favour.* She jumped down in front of the hole.

"Oi, Rose! Is that you?" A scruffy head peered over the wall from the neighbouring yard, eyes hidden beneath a heavy fringe. "What's been happening to all them girls leaving your place looking like they seen a ghost or summin'."

"Shh, Jack Billings," Rose said, tugging with all her might at the barred door to the coal-hole. "I ain't got time to talk to you now."

"So, how's life treating you in the big house?" he pressed on, though it was taking all his effort to hold himself up.

"Bloomin' marvellous," she muttered, forcing the stiff bolt.

"Rose, what you up to?" he giggled.

"Miss Templeforth" – Rose looked up – "wants to see me in the library." She fell back to rest on her hands as the door groaned open. "But I fancy stopping inside there." She pointed into the sooty cavern of the coal-hole.

"Them girls," Jack said, clawing at the wall to get a better grip, "the ones leaving with the collywobbles. Them's the ones what answered to the advert in yesterday's local rag."

"Advert?" Rose got to her feet, dusting herself off. "What advert?"

She climbed onto an upturned pail and stared at Jack's dirt-smudged face as it hovered over the wall, his feet still dangling over Potts' Laundry Emporium next door. The Templeforth premises was the last of the smart townhouses on this side of the street; next to it crouched a line of shops and businesses.

Jack Billings beamed down at Rose amid the sweet-scented steam drifting up from the basement washroom behind him.

"What you on about, Jack Billings?" she asked, throwing him a sharp look. She'd known Jack from the workhouse – he collected the surplus laundry that Nanna Potts paid the workhouse to wash. He was always full of mischief and a rumour-mongerer to boot. But this particular snippet of information had well and truly sparked Rose's interest. "Well?" she asked.

"Look, I got it here." Jack's tongue balled in his cheek, pleased to have gained her attention. He fished something out of his pocket. "You workhouse lot can all read, can't ya?

So take a look for yourself, Rose." He thrust forward a crumpled piece of paper.

Rose flattened the newspaper cutting against the wall.

SEARCH FOR A TEMPLEFORTH HEIR

The esteemed Miss Lucile Templeforth, being of ill health and in fear of death, is without an heir for the Templeforth family estate. She is compelled to undertake...

Rose shot a nervous glance at the house. She could hear the two day maids bashing about in the kitchen. She squinted back at the small print that trailed into a long article.

"Jack Billings, I ain't got time to read all that." She passed it back. "Do you know what it says or not?" she asked, knowing he would. He seemed to know everyone's business before it even happened.

"Yep." He winked, scrunching the paper back into his pocket. "Nanna Potts told me. Everyone's talking about it."

"Well? Spit it out then."

"Nanna Potts says of all the funny goings-on in that house, this is the oddest of all. Your mistress is dying, right? And coz she ain't got no family she knows of, she's asked in *The Evening Argus* for girls – girls what are not older than thirteen – what might be related to her, to come today to be interviewed."

"Why only girls?" Rose asked. "And why just that old? What is it they'll get?"

"Well that's just it. Everything! When she snuffs it, they'll get the lot: the spooky house, all her dosh, and some old pendant what's been in the family for ever. Can you imagine getting all that? Some days I just wish I was a girl…" He eyed the grand townhouse and shook his head. "Nanna Potts thinks the old lady's batty. She must have had half the girls from town in and out of there today trying their luck."

"Well, I never!" Rose exclaimed. "But that don't explain why all them girls have been leaving in such a state…"

A thud, followed by a scream, cut her short. Rose looked up, but the projection of a bay window obscured her view. The noise came from the main doorway on the street above.

Rose turned to Jack, a finger pressed to her lips. Leaving him behind, she crept up the steps that led to the pavement gate.

High above, the front door crashed open, sending the fist-shaped knocker into convulsions. The outline of a feeble young girl hovered outside.

Rose ducked out of sight as the girl zigzagged down

the steps and swayed between the stone lions flanking the entrance. She wore a starched white frock, tied in the middle with a blue sash, and her hair was set in tight blonde ringlets. Like the others leaving that day, she looked delirious and wretched with fear. The girl staggered towards a waiting carriage. Its door swung open, allowing her to crawl inside.

Rose jolted as the carriage door slammed. The driver, high up on his bench – collar up and hat low – cracked his whip hard. The two black mares whinnied before jerking forward. They turned sharply in the street and headed back towards the junction at Church Road.

An emblem on the luggage hold flickered into view under the street lamp, a black sun with a face at its centre. In matt relief against the sheen of the carriage, it glared back at her before vanishing into darkness.

Rose gulped. *It's my turn next.* Awful memories of the workhouse stacked one on top of the other. The penance cupboard. The hunger. Ten of the best from Miss Gritt's rod. She swallowed. *If I'm discharged from here Gritt will have it in for me… I can't go back, I won't!* Rose fumbled with the latch on the gate to the street but it was no use; it was locked. She stared longingly up into the darkness outside.

"ROSE MUDDLE. It is time!" The butler's voice boomed from the kitchen doorway below.

Rose's heart tripped over itself. She snatched back her hand from the gate as icy dread flooded her body. *No good can come of this. I don't want to be sent back.*

"Sir, I were just...urm...I heard another scream and I..." she spluttered, rushing down the steps.

"Move it!" he spat, as she dashed past.

Inside, Rose felt the maids' eyes pinned to her back like daggers, but she ran on.

She climbed up the wooden staircase from the kitchen and hurried along the corridor into the imposing lobby, stopping outside the closed library door to catch her breath. Mounted animal heads and stuffed birds in glass domes leered from the walls, and the grandfather clock ticked away her final seconds before her fate would be sealed.

Rose yelped as the butler appeared behind her. Pushing her to one side, he opened the library door wide.

"Rose Muddle, as you requested, Ma'am."

Rose blinked up at him. "For pity's sake, don't send me in there. I can do better...work harder," she whispered. "I'll scrub the floors all night if you want." She willed him to change his mind. But the butler's thin lips crept into a twitching smirk as he nudged her inside.

The Library

The heavy library door closed behind Rose, plunging the room into silence. Her heart jiggered like a bee trapped in a pill pot as she stared across the vast, brooding room. Exotic skulls hung between the bookcases. Their shadows danced in the firelight, making phantoms which seemed to reach out for her.

"Do come and sit with us a while, Rose." The lady's voice echoed across the dim room. Rose traced it to a winged armchair positioned by the fire. The fifteen paces separating them seemed to swell and extend.

"Yes, Ma'am," Rose heard her own quivering voice reply.

She edged across the library, while the woman in the

grand portrait mounted above the stone mantelpiece sneered down at her from behind an open fan.

As she reached the fire, Rose swayed, feeling like a Christmas goose ready for the chop. Steadying herself, she took her first look at her mysterious employer.

The fire picked out a motionless body, dwarfed by the massive chair. Haggard, with hollow cheeks and skin like parchment, Miss Templeforth stared unblinking into the hearth.

So this is the frail old bird? A vision of grey and white: high-necked nightdress, grey plaits to her waist and a thick blanket covering her legs. The only colour on Miss Templeforth was a circular orange pendant, edged in gold and suspended on a chain around her neck.

The woman's pinched lips parted to take a rattling breath. Rose flinched. This woman looked closer to death than anyone Rose had ever seen. This place, this woman – everything felt wrong.

Footsteps sounded behind her. Rose gasped as a new figure emerged from the shadows.

It was Miss Lee – the woman who'd collected her from the workhouse a week ago. *Why's she here?* Rose thought. It felt as though the floor beneath her was about to be swept away. *What if she's here to take me back, like the butler said?*

Rose's gaze locked with Miss Lee's. She was a strange, quiet woman. Her clear blue eyes shone like searchlights from under a bob of black curls. She wore the same maroon shawl she'd had on before, fringed with golden discs. Rose forced a smile.

"Hello, Rose dear, do sit down." Miss Lee nodded, indicating the stool close by. "Miss Templeforth has just experienced another dark visitation. I need to administer some medicine. This shouldn't take long."

Rose nodded mechanically, as she perched on the edge of the stool. *Dark visitation?* Did that have anything to do with those haunting moans that had filled the house all week? And what exactly had so terrified all the girls leaving today…? Her heart galloped.

Miss Lee tucked the blanket around Miss Templeforth's body and produced a hip flask from her dress pocket. Popping off its stopper, she held it to the old lady's trembling lips for a moment. She poured some more of the red liquid into a tumbler, the firelight dancing across her gaudy rings, and carefully placed the glass on the table before settling in the chair next to Rose. "There," she said, her face falling into an easy smile.

Miss Templeforth coughed and Rose turned to her.

"Enna," Miss Templeforth managed, gesturing to Miss Lee, "is keen to discover how you are finding domestic life here at number thirteen? It must be quite a change from the workhouse. I do so hope they treated you well there? I've been desperate to speak with you, but…we have had to be cautious."

The old woman's manner had changed and she seemed suddenly so full of life. Rose glanced at the glass of strange liquid Miss Lee had given her. *What is that stuff?* she wondered.

Looking up from the table, Rose saw both women staring at her and realized she was meant to be saying something. "H-hum. Well, Ma'am…and Miss Lee, of course," she twisted her hands in her lap. "The truth is, I am so thankful for the kindness you've shown me, giving me this chance and—"

"Not at all. It is we who are thankful," Miss Templeforth interrupted, shooing the comment away with her hand. "Now, the visitors you may have seen earlier were all those who responded to my advertisement in yesterday's *Evening Argus*. It requested girls from my maternal line to present themselves to me. My time on this earthly plane is drawing to its end…" Miss Templeforth paused to take another sip of her fortifying drink, leaving the statement about her death dangling between them.

"The advert unearthed every charlatan and gold-digger from Piddinghoe to Portslade." The old woman shook her head with a sigh and stared into the fire. "This was to be expected. They got a whiff of the inheritance, you see – just as we imagined. Even those with genuine links to the family have proved to be weak-spirited, entirely unworthy, or worse. But it was a carefully planned diversion, Rose. To stake out the enemy. To put them off the scent."

Rose glanced at Miss Lee, who was smiling. It was the same strange smile she had given when she'd chosen Rose from all the other girls lined up at the workhouse to come and work here in the big house. The one she'd had when she'd said, *"I'll take this one, the one with the unusual eyes."*

"Rose, we wanted to speak to you about values," continued Miss Templeforth, waving her long knotted fingers as she spoke. "What do *you* value?" Her face hardened in the firelight as she examined Rose through a pair of circular spectacles suspended on a long stick.

"W-well, Ma'am," Rose stammered, noticing how the glasses made the old lady's eyes look freakishly large. *Think, Rose Muddle, say what they want to hear, don't mess this up.* "I don't own much to value. That ain't to say I don't value much what I own, it is to say I don't own much. I value the people what are kind to me – oh, and I value this job of course." Her words spurted out like water escaping a cracked pipe. She flashed an apologetic smile just as an image of Miss Gritt tapping her leather rod against her palm, welcoming Rose back to the workhouse, formed like a spectre in her mind. "P-please don't send me back to the workhouse." Rose gulped.

"We were never going to send you back there. Whatever gave you that impression?" Miss Templeforth said sitting forward in her big chair. "Goodness me, we've only just found you!"

Rose's mouth opened and shut, but all her words had run away. Instead, her mind performed somersaults, trying to work out what the giddy aunt was going on here. *Maybe Nanna Potts is right, the Mistress really is barking!*

"Now, I would like to show you something of personal value to me," Miss Templeforth said slowly, and Rose blinked. The old woman unfastened the chain from around her neck and held out the large orange pendant for Rose to see. It had a black disc inlaid in its centre. Rose felt a rush of cold run through her and the lights in the room flickered.

And as she looked at the pendant, she couldn't explain how, but something deep inside told her that this moment was about to change her world for ever.

Miss Templeforth's Pendant

The pendant swung in the space between Rose and Miss Templeforth, its gold rim glinting in the firelight. The orange disc seemed to be illuminated from within, *like a bit of glass from a church window*, Rose thought. In a trick of the light, the black dot in the middle looked to be throbbing.

"Whatever is it made from?" Rose murmured.

"Amber," Miss Lee answered. "Ancient tree sap, hardened over millions of years. Some pieces have prehistoric insects or plant matter trapped inside them. Inclusions they are called. Some people believe amber can preserve stranger things. Dark things."

Rose's mouth ran completely dry. *Dark things?*

Miss Lee nodded, encouraging Rose to take the pendant. Miss Templeforth held out the chain, her eyes peering, owl-like, from behind the lenses clasped in her other hand.

As Rose's fingers touched the pendant, the fire in the grate roared into mighty flames, filling the hearth, but she did not notice, for she was somewhere else entirely.

Loud noises crashed around in her mind, voices blurred, falling in and out of earshot. Blackness. She strained to see. A small room fell into focus. The heavy smell of peppermint clawed at the back of her throat. Her body rattled up and down.

No, *she thought,* it ain't a room, it's a carriage, with crimson curtains drawn across all the windows.

A hand reached up in front of Rose. Her hand? No, not her hand at all. Skeletal and shrivelled, with thick veins stretched across crooked knuckles.

I'm in someone else's body. Seeing through someone else's eyes, *Rose realized. Fear whispered through her bones.*

The aged hand, whoever it belonged to, reached forward and twitched the curtains, exposing a tattoo on the wrist. A blazing blackened sun with a face in its centre – the same design Rose had seen on the back of the carriage earlier. The inky face stretched like rubber across raised tendons.

"What news do we have of our foreign visitor?" rasped the owner of the hand. It was the voice of an elderly man. A streak of lamplight burst through the parted curtains as the carriage

halted. *The man blinked and Rose felt herself blink with him. He lifted a pendant into the dusty channel of light.* A pendant? *Like the one she'd been given in the library, encircled by the same band of gold, but with the colours in reverse; the amber of this pendant was much darker, but for a small circle of luminous orange right in the centre.*

"I have received confirmation he's travelling from the East, via London, and will be arriving tomorrow, Sir," *a gruff voice replied from the shadows.*

"Indeed," *the old man hissed. She could feel his hunger in her, as if they were one. The horrid craving swelled as he examined his pendant. The intruding light transformed the dark amber into a glowing, luminous red, which seemed to bubble deep inside. Rose's heart beat faster as distorted faces started churning within the pendant, otherworldly creatures with mouths that stretched one into another. She stifled a lurching nausea, as the old man's head shifted from side to side, studying the morphing beings. He chuckled.*

"And the book travels with him?" *the man spat.*

"It does, Sir," *replied his hidden companion.* "And the Amber Cup awaits him at the museum."

Two pendants, a cup of amber and a book? *Rose's thoughts hurried, trying to make sense of it all, but she couldn't.*

"She's controlling it!" *Miss Templeforth called from far away, like a whisper.*

"Whose is that voice?" the man shouted. *Snatching the pendant into the ball of his fist, he stiffened.*

"Sir?" his companion said.

"Damnation! Someone's in my mind. How is this possible?" The man moaned, grabbing at his head. "I order them gone!"

At his words, a grey smog instantly blanketed Rose's view. Thin, black shapes appeared, shooting in and out of focus, obscured by the mist spinning around her. Voices chattered in a strange tongue. A desperate surge of fear sprang up inside Rose as the mass swarmed closer. She felt a cold breath on her neck as something sniffed her, and out of the corner of her eye, a black shape twice her size shifted off. A helter-skelter of panic twisted in her chest. The sound of gnashing teeth encircled her.

"Get away!" Rose shrieked, gripping her head.

On her command, the hidden things broke into a high-pitched squeal. Rose covered her ears – the sound was like a hundred cats being drowned all at once. The screams faded inside the fog, shrinking away to silence.

"ROSE?" Miss Lee shouted close by. Cold fingers touched her arm. "Come back to us. NOW!"

Belonging

With a jolt, Rose found herself back in the library. The bookcases swayed and then stilled. The whispering voices had gone, but her heart still raced. "What just happened?" she panted, looking at the two women.

"What did you see?" Miss Lee asked, clutching Rose's arm.

Speechless, Rose studied the pendant wedged in her palm. Glowing like a living thing, it throbbed in time with her heartbeat. A part of her. A deep calm took hold, a sense of total belonging that made her feel like everything was somehow going to be all right. Rose had never really belonged anywhere or to anything before and despite everything she had just witnessed, this felt…*lovely*. Her fear evaporated, the memories of the shadowy creatures and all that had just happened faded to nothing. A new brightness shone inside her, right in the very heart of her. It grew bigger and bigger until every cell of her body hummed with it. She sighed and leaned back, wanting the moment to last for ever.

"Look at the way the amber is glowing," Miss Templeforth said. "It's her, we can be certain. Thank goodness. But I need the pendant back…PLEASE!" Miss Templeforth's eyes looked desperate.

Rose hesitated, not wanting to part with it.

"My dear Rose," Miss Lee spoke in a hushed voice. "We must pass back the pendant to its rightful owner. She needs it."

Reaching over, Miss Templeforth loosened Rose's fingers and prised the pendant out of her hand.

"Thank you…" the old lady said. "It strengthens me."

Without it, Rose at once felt empty. Whatever it was, she yearned to hold it again. It was as if, by giving away the pendant, a piece of her had been removed.

Rose watched as the old lady fastened the pendant around her neck. The nice feelings had been washed away, replaced by a bubbling anxiety in her chest. *What kind of witchcraft is this?*

"Can you tell us what just happened, Rose?" Miss Lee asked again.

Her heart pounded as both women stared at her, their eyes full of wonder. Rose placed her hand to her throat and tried to concentrate. "I saw stuff what I don't understand. When I held that," she pointed to the pendant, "I were inside someone's head. An old man...it were horrible – he were horrible. We were in a carriage. He had another pendant, like yours but different. It had...faces inside of it. The two of them talked about a cup in a museum and about a book. I dunno."

"You saw the other pendant!" cried Miss Lee. "What did the man look like?"

"I couldn't see him, I saw things like what he saw. I were in his mind. I felt...his hunger...it were awful. And he had a tattoo on his wrist of a black sun with a face in its middle and—" She stroked her apron.

"The black sun!" Miss Lee interrupted, and turned in her chair to face Miss Templeforth. The old woman appraised Rose like a butterfly under a magnifying glass.

Rose's mind flashed from the tattoo to the image of the black sun she had seen on the carriage collecting the girl with ringlets earlier. She opened her mouth to speak but Miss Templeforth cut in.

"In-credible...how could *you* do that?" Her eyes narrowed.

"I dunno, Ma'am," Rose answered truthfully, her mind still reeling from everything she had seen.

"I've never been able to see into the mind of the other pendant holder. Extraordinary." Miss Templeforth looked at Miss Lee and then back to Rose. "Have you ever seen the Amber Cup at the museum in Brighton?" The old woman craned forward, her watery eyes searching Rose's face. The dusty library hushed to just the crackle of the fire.

"No," Rose shot a look between the two women, "I ain't never been to any museum, Ma'am." Rose shook her head. *Me, rubbing shoulders with all them fancy folk what go there? Chance would be a fine thing.*

"What else did you see when you held the pendant, Rose?" Miss Lee urged. "You seemed distressed."

"A nasty fog came, I couldn't see and there were black things in it. Hateful creatures...and I screamed at them to go and they...did." Rose squeezed her eyes shut. *Did they go just because I told them to?* She frowned, trying to recall the rest. "That was it. You called me back." She stared without blinking at the pendant. "Please, tell me what it is."

The two ladies remained silent for a moment. With a glance at Miss Templeforth, Miss Lee leaned towards Rose.

"Mrs Templeforth's pendant is very old and magical.

It requires a guardian at all times, and when the time is right, it chooses a new guardian. That time is now, Rose, and it has chosen you."

Guardians

A *magical pendant? A guardian? Me?* Rose's heart beat
faster. Despite the horrible things it had shown her,
the pendant had felt a part of her. She couldn't explain
how, but since she'd held it, Rose somehow felt different.
Her grey eyes shone.

"But why would that pendant pick me?" Rose muttered,
not meaning to say it aloud.

Standing, Miss Lee threw another log on the fire, and
the flames licked around it. The portrait of the lady with
the fan watched from the mantelpiece as Rose shuffled on
her stool next to the old woman.

"Your connection to Miss Templeforth's pendant is

strong. Actually, from what we've just seen, it's stronger than any other before you. Do you know why this might be?" Miss Lee asked.

Rose shook her head repeatedly. "I haven't a clue!"

"Well," Miss Lee said, with a smile. "I believe it is your identity that makes it so."

My identity? Rose stilled. She'd never really had one of them. In the workhouse she'd been a nobody; most of the time she'd been called by a number. *People have names, paupers have numbers* – Miss Gritt's words rang through her.

"We have searched for so long –" Miss Templeforth's voice drew her back – "and last week, we found you. That was when Enna brought you here as a scullery maid so we could keep you close and introduce you into the household without arousing suspicion."

"Yes," Miss Lee paced in front of the fire and the floorboards creaked, "and at the same time, we set about drawing everyone's attention to our search for an heir. We made sure the pendant was mentioned in the paper, to underline the fact we were without a new guardian. We have successfully diverted them from you. For now."

"Them? From me?" Rose mouthed, trying desperately to take it all in.

"You only became visible to us after the turning of your

twelfth birthday. It has always been so," Miss Lee explained, taking her seat again. "When I found you, Rose, I knew you were the one. There is a likeness about you." She grinned.

It was true that she'd been taken from the workhouse the day after she'd turned twelve. Rose remembered the curious smile Miss Lee had given when she first saw Rose, lined up with all the other workhouse girls. How it had made her tingle. And how Miss Gritt had seemed especially wary of Miss Lee.

"It's your eyes," Miss Templeforth purred, appraising Rose once more through her spectacles. "Such an unusual grey. They are like my father's."

My eyes? Her father? I ain't related to her!

"What do you know of your parents?" Miss Templeforth asked.

Rose's shoulders dropped and she looked down. "My ma died" – her voice shrank to a whisper; she fiddled with her fingers – "when I was born." She looked up. "I'm workhouse born and bred." The two women exchanged a glance. Rose carried on, "I was told my pa was a seaman who sailed to the South Indian Ocean and never came back. That's what the workhouse governess told me, Ma'am." *See? A nobody. I ain't nothing to do with any of this,* she thought.

"Dear Rose." Miss Lee kneeled beside her, and a slight smell of lavender hung in the air. "You look so confused. I will do my best to explain things to you." She cleared her throat. "Now, I have known Miss Templeforth since she was a child."

The skin on Rose's arms goose-pimpled. *Did I hear that right? Known her since she was a child?* Rose studied Miss Lee's fresh face, covered in a splattering of freckles. She looked young enough to be the mistress's daughter.

"The pendant has been closely following the Templeforth bloodline for many generations," Miss Lee explained. "She was chosen by the pendant some fifty years ago – chosen as you have been tonight – to undertake the role of guardian."

Miss Templeforth nodded, and sank back into her gigantic chair with a faraway look in her eyes.

"But what d'you mean, guardian?" Rose sat forward. "What's one of them?"

"To explain this, Rose, I must start with some history," said Miss Lee, gripping hold of her hand. Rose stared into her sparkling blue eyes. "There is an Amber Cup," she began, "displayed at the museum in Brighton. It contains something…something—" She struggled to find the right word.

"EVIL!" Miss Templeforth cut in. Rose jumped.

"Yes," Miss Lee carried on. "Something terrible –
something of great evil is trapped inside the amber of the
cup."

Miss Templeforth took over. "And there are two
pendants, which, if used together, can release this evil
from the cup. One of them is mine." The old lady held her
jewel aloft. "And the other belongs to the hidden person
you miraculously saw tonight."

*The old man in the carriage with the other pendant and
the tattoo.* Rose shivered, concentrating with all her might.

Miss Lee spoke again. "The pendants have been kept
apart for thousands of years. And the cup remained safely
buried. But fifty years ago, in 1856, it was exhumed – dug
up from the ground."

"And put in the museum?"

"That's right, Rose…and now the other guardian is
here somewhere in Hove with his pendant. He seeks Miss
Templeforth's – to use it together with his own to release
the evil trapped inside the cup. He wants to use this evil to
make himself powerful. These three objects, the cup and
the two pendants, you see, contain mysterious and ancient
magic of incredible strength."

"How d'you know Miss Templeforth's pendant is in
danger now, after all this time?" Rose asked.

"They have been sending shadow creatures… Creeplings,

they're called, to torment her in dark visitations." Miss Lee moved behind Miss Templeforth and rested a hand on the old lady's shoulder. "They sense she is weakening."

Miss Templeforth nodded. Reaching up, she gently squeezed Miss Lee's hand.

Dark visitations? Creeplings? The words conjured images of the horrid black shapes she had seen snaking around her in the fog when she'd been inside that man's head. A sense of unease grew within her. Rose pointed at Miss Templeforth's pendant. "Hang on. Is that pendant e-evil too? Like what the cup is?" she asked, her pulse quickening. "It showed me bad things. But...it never felt evil when I held it. It felt...right. And—" Rose shook her head, trying to untangle the words she wanted to say.

"Dear heart," Miss Templeforth smiled. "This pendant is a force of great good, you must not fear it. It will protect you, and offer you much comfort. It contains strong magic and a memory of all those who have guarded it. You will become a part of it. A part of a special family, if you like."

Family? Rose gripped the edge of her stool, remembering the way it made her feel like she belonged. "Yes," she whispered.

"It bonds with each new guardian in different ways," Miss Templeforth pressed on. "It warns me of danger. It has kept me strong for many years; offered me great well-being.

But now I am dying – and it seeks the next guardian –" she looked directly at Rose – "YOU."

Miss Templeforth gave Rose a quick smile that spoke a thousand words. It spoke of relief, delight and something else – of finding something really precious they'd thought lost for ever. The smile of someone who knew they could finally die in peace. The old lady held her hands in front of her lips and rubbed them together. "And you, Rose Muddle, will do us very nicely."

"Me? But I was just getting used to being a scullery maid and—"

"Hush now, Rose." Miss Lee tapped her hand. "Miss Templeforth and I are here to guide you. You are not alone. You are very special."

Special? When Rose had held that pendant it *had* felt like a part of her, she knew that wasn't imagined. Impossible though it might be, she found herself wondering if it *could* be true. *What if I am someone special after all?* A bolt of adrenaline rushed through her.

Rose straightened. "If I am the guardian," she looked between the two ladies, "like what you say I am, what is it that I'm s'posed to do?"

"Excellent question, Rose!" Miss Templeforth clapped her withered hands. "The most pressing issue at the moment is that the pendant will become vulnerable when it switches from being mine to being yours. It needs time to bond with you once I have passed away. We fear the other pendant holder will try to take it during this period of transition. It is vital as the new guardian that you prevent this from happening – you *must* keep the pendant safe."

Rose's fingers flexed. The old lady knew she was dying, and yet she was being so brave. Miss Templeforth's final earthly wish was for the pendant to be protected by Rose. And even though it was the biggest responsibility anyone could ever give her, Rose wanted it. If that pendant was hers, she knew she'd keep it for ever and ever. Her gaze fell to the curious orange disc once more, longing to feel its energy again.

"Rose," Miss Lee's blue eyes electrified as she spoke, "you have been chosen by the Templeforth pendant. Which means you, like Miss Templeforth, are part of an important bloodline that stretches back over thousands of years."

Rose nodded, catching her breath.

Miss Lee continued, "I will help you to learn how to control it, Rose. Together we can discover more about your powers over it. About who you are and why it chose you. And about the identity of the other pendant holder. We need your help. The evil in the cup must stay contained. Without you…I fear all is lost."

All is lost without me? Rose swallowed, scarcely able to believe what was happening. Then she asked the question nagging at the back of her mind. "But...what *is* inside the cup?"

Miss Lee walked over to the fire. The portrait of the woman with the fan still stared at Rose. Miss Lee turned. "It's everything together that creates the problem, Rose. If the pendants are held back to back in the presence of the cup, a gateway is formed. The dominant pendant – the one placed on top – will cover its twin and draw the other's energy into itself. Creating a powerful force."

"The pendants held back to back. Gateway?" Rose mumbled to herself.

"Yes, a gateway to somewhere...terrible. Together they would allow an unimaginable evil to escape onto this earth. You need to protect the pendant with your life once it belongs to you."

"Right." Rose gulped, her mind exploding into a thousand pieces. All she'd ever wanted was to be free from the workhouse, to be a name, not a number, to be needed. And now here she was. After all those years of being told she was worthless. The stray pieces of herself had begun to fly back together. Her grey eyes glistened. Rose felt different, she realized. For the first time ever she felt... real. A new fire was burning inside her.

"Are you all right, Rose?" Miss Lee asked squeezing her arm.

Rose nodded with a grin. "I can do it!" At that moment Rose felt she could do anything.

"Good. It is vital your presence here is not met with suspicion." Miss Lee spoke in urgent whispers. "No one must know that you are to be the next guardian. You are in terrible jeopardy should the other guardian find out."

"So," Miss Templeforth continued, "I have a new job planned for you. Important visitors are arriving at noon tomorrow and I should like you to take on the role of companion to one of them."

"Important visitors? A companion?" Rose lifted her hand to her chest and leaned forward. "Me?"

Miss Templeforth smiled. "It will mean that we can spend more time together without people asking questions give you the freedom to leave the house. And at the same time we can do some more work with the pendant."

Rose nodded. More than anything in the world she wanted to hold that pendant again, to learn about the magic inside it, and find out why it had chosen her.

The old lady went on. "It is important you learn to control it, and with your extraordinary power over it, perhaps we can work out exactly who this other guardian is..." she trailed off, then brightened. "And, as for your new companion, I would trust him with my life."

Rose sank her nails into her arm, and it hurt. *This really is happening.*

"You must take the attic room as your quarters, Rose," Miss Lee interrupted. "The kitchen is no longer suitable."

"A room…of my own?"

"Indeed!" Miss Lee beamed. "And I have taken the liberty of depositing a package up there. Just some clothes and a bit of money."

"Thank you, Ma'am, Miss Lee," Rose gasped.

Things were happening so fast she could barely keep up, but to be given her own room – not just a bed in the corner of the kitchen – a place just for her. No one had ever treated her so kindly. From the workhouse, to a scullery maid – to *THIS*. Tears stung Rose's eyes. She couldn't find words to express how much it all meant.

"We are dependent on you now, Rose. We will talk more tomorrow. The pendant is to be yours on my death, which is not far off, I fear." Miss Templeforth sighed. Lifting the back of her hand to her forehead, she slumped further into her chair. "That is quite enough for today. I need to rest; we all do."

Rose bobbed her head and turned to leave, wonder shining in her eyes, but Miss Lee gripped her arm. "From now on you must call me Enna. If you ever need me, you can find me at the Pleasure Gardens in St Ann's Well, up near the furze. I work there telling fortunes and I go by the name Gypsy Lee. Dark forces are penetrating this world; if the pendant falls into the wrong hands we will all be in mortal danger. You, Rose Muddle, have been chosen to stop them."

A Room with a View

It's got to be a load of old cobblers, Rose thought the following morning. She stared out of her attic window at the chimney pots merrily chuffing away. Any thoughts of pendants, guardians and evil things stuck in cups seemed a million miles from reality.

She'd been delivered a tray of buttered toast earlier, and even had a bath prepared for her. But the day maid had not smiled once. News of Rose's promotion surely caused quite a stir downstairs. Mr Crank must have been spitting enough feathers to stuff an eiderdown by now.

From this high up, Rose could see from the English Channel right across to Blatchington Windmill and the rolling South Downs beyond. Closing her eyes, she drew a deep breath, her mind buzzing with all that had happened the evening before.

She couldn't forget the way that pendant had made her feel – and she longed to hold it again, despite the scary visions it had given her. *How comes I could see inside that man's head? And who was he anyway?* Question upon question stacked in her mind like jars about to topple. And in the midst of it all, Enna's words came back to her about ancient things trapped inside amber: "Inclusions they are called. Some people believe amber can preserve stranger things. Dark things."

And they think I'm somehow related to the mistress! Rose's nose crinkled. *But how can I be?* She'd never questioned anything she'd been told about her past; she'd had no reason to. But now things were different. She closed her eyes and tried to remember the story she'd had from Miss Gritt.

Her mother had been a workhouse child too. Rose knew that much. *Patricia Martha Flitch.* Rose smiled, she liked that name. She'd always imagined her ma was kind and smelled of flowers.

They'd told Rose that Patricia had left the workhouse when she was old enough, and got a job at the docks in Shoreham. There she'd met Rose's pa, got married and become a Muddle. Rose liked to think they were madly in love.

After Rose's pa had left on a sea voyage and never returned, her mother discovered she was carrying their baby; she was totally penniless. *She'd had no choice but to go back to the workhouse to have me...and that's where she... died.* Rose swallowed the lump in her throat. No matter which way round she looked at it, Rose couldn't see how she could be a Templeforth. Unless Miss Gritt had lied to her – but why would she bother to do that?

Rose settled herself down at the dressing table. "Ma would be proper proud of me now though, wouldn't she? A companion!" Smiling, she rested her chin on her hands and examined the attic bedroom through the reflection in the oval mirror in front of her. The sloping whitewashed ceiling shone in the morning sunshine.

Her smile faltered as she remembered the rest of the girls, back at the workhouse, sleeping in that freezing dormitory, dreading the sound of Gritt's jangling keys as she patrolled outside, just waiting for the chance to give one of them a good hiding. She knew she was lucky to be out, and that the ones still living in that wicked place would want her to make this work.

Taking a deep breath, Rose stood up and patted down the green velvet dress she had found inside Enna's brown paper package. It fitted well enough. The boots she'd discovered pinched her toes a little, but they were new and looked expensive, she thought, pointing her toe from beneath the hem of her dress. She'd also been given a nightdress and a kid-leather pouch containing five shillings. Five whole shillings! More than a month's wages. More money than Rose had ever held before. She jingled the pouch and grinned.

She spun around to look at herself in the mirror again. Leaning forward she studied her face, her clean, clear skin, wide slate-grey eyes and small lips. She had tried to dress up her hair by pinning it at the front and leaving it to hang long at the back. She hardly recognized herself at all.

Well, I look the part all right. Her nerves tingled as she wondered about the visitors, and who she would be a companion to. She just hoped that they would like her… and not ask too many questions. She decided to stick to talking about the weather or better still, to saying as little as possible, just nodding and smiling instead. *After all, how hard can it be?* she rallied. *I'll be absolutel—*

RAP-RAP-RAP.

The front door. *Midday?*

And as if to confirm it, the grandfather clock in the lobby began to chime – twelve times.

She jumped over the maid's uniform that lay discarded

at the side of her bed and, lifting her velvet dress to her knees, charged down the narrow wooden steps and along the landing. At the top of the grand staircase – the same one she'd spent the previous morning polishing – she could see Mr Crank striding past Cook and the grim-faced day maids, who were already lining up. Rose nearly threw herself down the remaining stairs, and, taking the last three steps in one huge leap, she landed with a clap on the tiled floor.

Mr Crank spun round and scowled.

"Sorry, Sir," Rose mouthed, her chest tight.

"Phff." His thin lips curled as he turned away. But he didn't say a word.

Raising her chin, she smiled inwardly. *I'm a companion now. He can't have a go at me so easy any more.* She positioned herself by the clock, next to the others and looked nervously at the front door.

Mr Crank dabbed his temples with a folded hanky. Then he opened the heavy door and stepped aside. Rose balanced on the balls of her feet, trying to see past him. She spotted the grand carriage parked outside and nearly squeaked.

An old Indian gentleman, wearing a cream silk turban set with a large central ruby, strode into the lobby. His face was as wrinkly as a walnut with a long, grey beard covering his chin and a well-coiffed moustache finished with waxed twists hanging over his upper lip. He clasped a thick gilded book covered in ornate patterns in one hand. But most striking of all was the metal hook that protruded from his sleeve where his other hand should have been.

Rose bobbed a curtsey, but the gentleman didn't notice her, he just swept past. His silk tunic shifted noiselessly about him. A *visitor from the East?* The words of the strange man from her vision in the library slipped into her mind.

The visitor stopped next to the entrance to the library and considered the many stuffed creatures adorning the walls – they stared straight back at him.

Coach hands were busy lugging carved wooden trunks through the front door. They stacked them up one on top of the other in the lobby. The breeze from the open door carried a faint and unfamiliar smell. *Sweet and smoky*, Rose thought, as she shut her eyes and breathed it all in.

On opening them again, she noticed another guest had appeared at the entrance, a boy of about her age. But he was like no boy she'd ever met. His embroidered golden coat reached the floor while his matching slippers turned up at the toes. He strode forward. Intelligent brown eyes fringed with dark, thick lashes flashed beneath his turban. Rose gawped; never in all her days had she seen such fancy folk.

The sound of shattering glass and jeering cries from the

street outside suddenly broke her train of thought, but just as Rose craned her neck to see what was going on, some kind of animal tore across the lobby. She stepped backwards. *What the—?* A monkey skidded to a halt in front of her. *A monkey?* It wore a red, cup-shaped hat and a waistcoat. Arching its back, it hissed and patrolled the ground between Rose and the new arrivals. Knee-high and agile, it spun round, its fierce little eyes pinned on her.

Before she had a chance to react, the creature stood on its hind legs. It waved its miniature hands above its head manically, snarling and extending its jaw – loaded with oversized teeth – to reveal a thick wedge of gum. Rose shrieked, pressing herself against the clock.

"No, Bahula!" The boy stepped forward, pulling the creature away by the scruff of its waistcoat.

The monkey whimpered. Falling back on all fours, it scuttled over to its master. The old man scowled at Rose and rubbed the creature's chin.

Not the best of starts, Rose thought, with a dry swallow.

Mr Crank coughed and everyone turned towards him.

"Gentlemen, this way, please. Miss Templeforth is expecting you."

The boy left Rose with a backwards glance and Mr Crank knocked on the library door before making his grand introduction.

"Ma'am, I have the great pleasure in announcing the arrival of Rui Singh, nephew to the Maharajah of Jaipur, his tutor and chaperone, Mr Gupta and their...erm... monkey?"

The nephew of a maharajah! Rose's eyebrows flew up. *What's one of them anyway? It don't matter, they look like royalty. ROYALTY!*

Mr Crank jerked his head at Rose as the visitors disappeared inside. With a deep breath she hurried in behind them, wobbling just a little on the heels of her new boots, and totally unprepared for what might happen next.

7

All Teeth but no Smile

The library looked more friendly in the daylight than it had the evening before. Sunshine streamed through the trio of sash windows creating stretches of light, thick with floating dust particles. The animal skulls seemed less menacing too, with their shadows tucked beneath them. But the lady in the portrait still eyed Rose suspiciously from behind her fan. Rose looked away, towards the guests.

"R-uiii?" Miss Templeforth's voice trailed off.

The boy dashed across the room in a haze of gold, and hurriedly kneeled next to the winged armchair. "Miss T," he began. "My favourite—" He stopped mid-sentence, his brow buckled.

He weren't expecting her to look so ill, Rose thought with a pang of pity.

"Governess," he managed through a forced smile. He cradled her withered hand.

"The water, John," Miss Templeforth croaked to Crank, who scurried around the back of the armchair. Rose edged forward so she could clearly see Miss Templeforth.

"Fear not, I am here, Ma'am," Crank crowed, rushing forward.

The mistress's face looked drawn of all blood. Rose's eyes moved down to the pendant. Today it looked dark and ordinary – as lifeless as its owner.

Mr Crank lifted a tumbler filled with the strange red liquid. Miss Templeforth sipped some, allowing the butler to wipe her mouth with a folded napkin.

Rose noticed how gentle and caring Crank was towards his mistress. She'd never imagined he had it in him to be kind to anyone – but he clearly doted on her.

Nodding her gratitude, Miss Templeforth turned to the boy, her pinched lips suddenly breaking into a generous smile, her eyes at once alive and glistening.

What is that stuff? Rose stared at the glass.

"Rui, you have grown so!" she began, her vigour renewed. "Why, you are nearly a man. The last time I saw you in Jaipur you were no bigger than a yardstick.

Your journey from London was agreeable, I trust?"

"We travelled by train, Miss T. The stations are like palaces and the trains shiny, and everything runs on time!" The boy spoke English very well, with just the slightest accent.

Miss Templeforth reached up and cupped his face with her hand. "Now, tell me, how is your uncle the Maharajah?"

"He is in London visiting the King. He's brought two enormous urns the size of elephants, full of holy water – from the Ganges river in India so he doesn't have to use the English water."

"How extraordinary…but you managed to come down to see me here in Hove. I feel extremely honoured, Rui," Miss Templeforth said with a slight bow of her head.

"Miss the opportunity of visiting you," he gushed, "and experiencing an adventure of my own in Hove, like the stories you told me? Never."

Miss Templeforth's laugh broke off into a fit of coughing. Mr Crank stepped forward once more, but she shooed him away. Taking a couple of deep breaths, she composed herself.

"Now, Rui. This is Rose Muddle." All the eyes in the room switched to Rose and her skin bristled. "She is to be your companion during your stay here. I am sure you will find you have a lot in common."

Lots in common! Doubt wedged itself in the pit of Rose's stomach. *Well he has lots and I'm just plain common, I suppose.* She caught Crank's scowl and was suddenly aware of the ridiculous fixed smile slapped across her face.

"Delighted to make your acquaintance, Miss Rose," the boy said, striding forward, pressing his palms together. He nodded his head and put out his hand to shake hers. Rose swiftly wiped her sweaty palms on the back of her dress, then offered her hand. He shook it firmly.

"Miss T and Miss Rose," the boy continued. "I would like to introduce my tutor, Mr Gupta, eminent archaeologist and curator of the Jaipur Museum."

Mr Gupta stepped forward, his monkey stalking his shadow.

"Ah yes, I am most grateful you have chaperoned Rui for this visit, Mr Gupta. I trust your stay here will be a comfortable one," Miss Templeforth finished with a quick smile.

Mr Gupta held his hook in front of him and executed a low bow, his other arm outstretched to the side. "Greetings, Miss Templeforth," he said, in a deep voice. He flashed a toothy grin, which was instantly mirrored by his monkey.

All teeth and no smile, the both of 'em, Rose deduced with a shiver.

"A curator. How fascinating, Mr Gupta. You must make

a point of visiting our humble museum in Brighton town. I am sure you will find some curiosities of interest to you." Miss Templeforth leaned away to take another sip of her medicine.

"As a matter of fact, I was in communication with the curator at the Brighton Museum prior to my journey here," Mr Gupta mused, his eyes glaring at Miss Templeforth's pendant. "They have a cup on display that I am particularly keen to handle."

The room charged with invisible tension and Rose's eyes rounded to saucers.

Butterfly Magic

"A cup!" The word flew out of Miss Templeforth's mouth amid a splutter of water as she leaned forward and tucked the pendant inside her lace collar.

Rose's ears pricked. *He's on about the evil cup at the museum.* She glanced at the boy. He'd sensed the changing atmosphere too she was sure, but his face was difficult to read.

"Yes, I have a certain passion for mythical cups," Mr Gupta offered. The monkey dived behind his legs and peered around them.

"How very intriguing, Mr Gupta. Pray do tell us more." Miss Templeforth tried to hide her surprise, but Rose could see the barbed interest flashing in the old lady's eyes.

Mr Gupta began to pace in front of the fireplace. "Well, I have dedicated my working life to studying magic, myths and legends from across the globe. I find ancient objects fascinating, you see. And there are some who believe that certain relics and places contain great mystical powers."

"Is this what you believe too, Mr Gupta?" Miss Templeforth held up her spectacles. Her other hand clung on to the pendant, now hidden beneath her blouse.

"Well, that is a matter of personal conjecture," Gupta waved his good hand in the air, "but—" He spun round, his index finger raised.

The boy remained respectfully silent, but Rose could see he watched everything very closely. Gupta pulled free a book from his tunic pocket, the one he'd been carrying earlier. "My lifetime's research is contained in this journal." He held it aloft.

As thick as a bible, the journal's cover was bound in silver. A swirling design was pressed into the metal, surrounding the central detail of an enamelled human eye. It looked so real that Rose shivered; it was quite the creepiest thing she'd ever seen. Gupta's hook held the book in place as he flicked through the pages. It was full of strange-looking handwriting and pictures.

"Here! To demonstrate," the old man announced, drawing a length of silk ribbon to mark out a chosen page.

He turned the book round to show Miss Templeforth. "An amber cup, recorded within some ancient scriptures I discovered and reputed to be a mythical vessel of great power. Could it be the very cup located in your humble museum?"

Rose strained to see; she didn't want to miss any of this.

The page showed what looked like a glowing red cup, with black shapes cascading out from inside it. The pages seemed stained brown and the corners blackened – as if the book had been burned. Rose edged closer to get a better look, but Mr Gupta snapped the book shut and slipped it into his pocket.

He spoke again. "This cup is thought to be capable of giving its owners great knowledge and power –" he paused – "some even say it might give eternal life, or have the potential to open gateways…to other worlds."

Miss Templeforth's fingers clenched the arms of her chair so tightly that her knuckles turned white.

Gupta suddenly snatched a fistful of air from in front of his face. Rose blinked and stepped back.

"When the magic of the cup is harnessed," Gupta said kissing his clenched fist, "it is to be like the caterpillar… transformed!" He unfurled his fingers. A blue butterfly rested in the centre of his palm, its wings parting gently. A satisfied smile formed in the midst of Mr Gupta's grey beard as he searched the faces of his audience. He blew the butterfly off his hand. The butterfly took flight, rising and falling as if suspended on a length of invisible string.

Rose drew a quick breath. *How'd he do that?* she thought, watching the butterfly dancing across the room.

"Very good, Mr Gupta." Miss Templeforth clapped slowly. "Rose," she continued, without looking in her direction, "please show Rui to his quarters. Rui, we will speak later. I need to discuss some matters privately with Mr Gupta. I will send for you shortly."

Unwelcome Deductions

As Rose stepped into the lobby, Rui shot to her side, resplendent in his golden gowns. He looked her up and down. "So here we are, Miss Rose."

Rose gave a quick nod. *How am I going to pull this off?* she worried. Being a companion to someone like him, so rich and full of long, clever words, suddenly seemed very scary.

Rose sucked in her cheeks, and put on her poshest voice. "So…you know the mistress well?" She felt her face flush.

The boy hid a smile. "Yes, I do. I know Miss T very well, and through the power of observation I try to know a great number of other things too. Actually, I am in training as a detective. For the past five years, Miss T, your mistress, my old governess and dearest friend – well, my only friend, actually – has been sending me the Sherlock Holmes books. I am his greatest admirer," he gushed.

Who the heck is Sherlock Holmes? Rose nodded, smiling, pretending to know anyway. The boy continued.

"He is the greatest detective known to man and I have taken it upon myself, through his insights, to study the art of detection. If I may, let me tell you what I have deduced about you, to demonstrate."

Rose's smile exposed her clenched teeth.

"Four foot seven inches." He appraised her from tip to toe, before lingering on her face. "Large eyes, an unusual shade of grey, pretty," he said matter-of-factly. Rose could feel the glow rising in her cheeks. She turned away, but he grabbed for her hands, spinning her back round to face him.

He smoothed them in his and glanced up. "Your hands are work-worn and not from light work. Interesting." He searched her face. "You have a callus on your right hand, consistent with the type formed by some kind of hard labour. Yes?"

Rose tugged her hand free. She knew she had the blessed workhouse mangle in the laundry to thank for that.

"Also, you find yourself in a different job: elevated. Those boots are brand new; so new they hurt your feet, pinch your toes?"

Rose gawped but did not answer.

"Your dress is new too, it fits well enough, but due to its newness it hangs a little from your waist. A correctable detail, and one most ladies would see to, *if* they had the time." He waved his index finger in front of him. Rose opened her mouth to speak, but he cut in. "Your hair is neat but lacks finesse."

"Oi," she jutted out her chin, tapping her hair.

The boy shrugged. "Fact!" he added.

"Stop!" She drew a sharp breath. "Well, Master Rui, with your skills at knowing stuff, p'raps you'd be so kind as to explain a few things to me," Rose barked in a thick workhouse drawl – she was too cross to care.

He nodded. "Of course, Miss Rose, we must get to know each other well. I have been asked to take care of you, to protect you."

Rose's mouth clamped shut. "Take care of *me*?" she said, her hand on her chest. *What claptrap!*

"Yes!" He pulled a strip of crumpled paper from the pocket of his robes. "This secret note was delivered to me by stealth, to ensure I had the information herein, *before* I reached the house. A gypsy woman trailed me from the terminus at Hove Station to our waiting carriage and slipped it into my pocket."

Enna! Rose's mind was struggling to keep up.

"It reads as follows…" He coughed to clear his throat. "*Protect Rose Muddle. Danger.* And that's it, simple and concise."

Rose baulked. *Danger* – the word hung heavy in her mind like a thundercloud.

"Danger!" Rui scrunched up the paper. "Goodness knows I love that word." He discharged the crumpled ball into the air, allowing it to bounce off his forearm. He grabbed to catch it, but missed.

Lightning quick, Rose snatched it to her chest. "May I?" she smirked, already unravelling it. All she could see was a series of dots and dashes. "Hang on a minute, you're havin' me on." She waved the paper in the air between them. "There ain't no writing on this."

"On the contrary," Rui said, his dark lashes fluttering, "it is the first rule of detection to expect the unexpected." He brandished his index finger once more. "This note is in fact written using a form of Morse code known only by myself and one other. The "other" being the tremendous Miss Lucile Templeforth. An extraordinary woman. She used to tell me wild stories about England – and fantastical tales of her own adventures here in Hove. I promised myself that one day I would make the journey to have an adventure of my own. And here we are!" He met her eyes with a wide smile.

"Right," Rose snorted, "adventures here. In Hove!"

"Yes, Rose Muddle," he announced. "You and I are going to have the most fantastic adventure – I can just feel it!" And with that, he galloped up the stairs. Rose drew a deep breath.

Did he know anything about the pendant? Could she even trust him? "Oi, wait up. What danger am I in?" she stage-whispered after his retreating form.

He glanced back. "If you aren't already aware, then I suppose that's the first clue which requires deciphering. Which is to be my room?" he added, already at the top of the stairs.

"Second door on the right. Oi! Wait a minute." Rose stopped on the bottom step to wiggle her pinched toes inside her new boots. *How did he know all that stuff about me without being told?* She watched her new companion disappearing from view at the top of the stairs. *I haven't finished with you yet. In fact, I haven't even started,* she thought, as she ran up after him.

10

Faraway Places

Rose found Rui leaning back comfortably in one of two armchairs flanking a low table in his grand room on the first floor. Blue wallpaper interspersed with printed peacocks lined the walls, and the same design decorated the swags of fancy material adorning the windows.

Rui leaned forward and tapped the chair opposite him.

"Right, my turn," Rose said flinging herself into the seat, determined to get some answers of her own. "Who's that Mr Gupta you arrived with? Is he some kind of magician?"

Rui's eyebrows raised into high arcs. "No. Mr Gupta is a mystic, Miss Rose, and the curator at the Jaipur Museum. He locates artefacts for the museum's collection. He's undertaken many adventures – and even lost his hand during one such expedition! He was a true adventurer in his youth. He is something of a personal hero of mine."

"So you know him well then?" Rose asked.

"Well actually, I met him in person for the first time on board the ocean liner, *The Cape of Good Fortune*, shortly before our departure from Bombay. He volunteered to chaperone me on this trip and become my tutor as he has some scholarly studies to attend to whilst here in Hove. My uncle was delighted to accept his kind offer. We docked at Southampton last Tuesday week."

"Studies – like seeing that Amber Cup in the museum?"

"Yes, apparently so."

"So you *ain't* clapped eyes on him before, but he's now your tutor?" Rose searched his face.

"Yes, I was so thrilled to finally meet him. He's very well considered in Jaipur, though he's something of a recluse these days. But he's already taught me much about how to read ancient Sanskrit and even a little astrology. You know, during our stay here in Hove, there is supposed to be a planetary alignment, a very rare one. Truly fascinating. I concur that he is a little odd," Rui added, noticing her sceptical expression, "but who isn't?"

"And what about that monkey of his?" *That vicious hairball.*

"Oh Bahula!" Rui smiled, exposing his perfect white teeth. "He's a juvenile rhesus macaque. The shorter-tailed type indigenous to Jaipur. They can grow quite big as adults. Bahula is very loyal to his master; the two of them are inseparable. But he's very wary of strangers and particularly wary, it would seem, of you."

"Well, ain't that the truth!" Rose exclaimed.

"Monkeys are believed to sense things – invisible, otherworldly things. Perhaps he sensed something about you?"

"I doubt that!" Rose scratched her neck, her mind flashing back to the night before. "The creature's a menace. That's all."

"Ha! You know, back in Jaipur, monkeys are considered sacred, they are associated with Hanuman, the noble monkey god, and due to this connection they cannot be harmed. So the markets in Jaipur are overrun with packs of them stealing from the traders; they get up to all kinds of mischief. You must believe me when I say they are clever creatures, and our Bahula downstairs is not an exception."

Rose said nothing. Rui's words had conjured up strange and exotic pictures in her mind, like things from a book she'd seen once. She let her imagination burst into bright colours. How she would love to visit such faraway places, so full of sunshine, laughter, palaces and...monkeys.

She grimaced. *Well, p'raps I ain't so bothered about seeing any more monkeys.*

Rui clapped his hands. "Now," he began, "Rose Muddle, you still have not revealed to me where exactly *you* have come from? You intrigue me greatly. You are so... mysterious. And English!"

"Hmfff! Mysterious! You're having a laugh?"

"Well?" the boy pressed on.

"Oh!" Rose shrank back into her chair, not sure she wanted to tell him about herself yet. *What would he think if he knew where I'm really from?* "I-I thought you already knew everything about me," she said quickly.

"A-ha." He wafted his finger at her. "Very good. Yes, there is much to interpret from the outside. But, like a pocket watch, it is the inside, the hidden part, the mechanism that operates the hands that really interests me. Every English gentleman has a pocket watch, no? Tick, tick, tick." He tapped his head. "I should very much like to have a pocket watch. So?"

She smiled. He had a funny way about him that she couldn't help warming to. She longed to hear all about India and what it was like to live somewhere so different and so hot. Rose blinked. It suddenly struck her that this boy, even with all his fine clothes and fancy talk, might find her and Hove just as unusual as she found him and his world.

What does it matter where I'm from anyway? she reasoned. *Besides, who am I trying to fool? I am what I am, there's no changing that. He's bound to find out sooner or later.*

"Oh, all right, Rui, I'm from the workhouse. There!"

"Workhouse?" Rui peered at her, his chin resting on his knuckles.

"It's where they keep people who no one wants: invisible folk and nobodies. I ain't got no parents and all that." She didn't want to catch his gaze. Nor did she want to say much more about it.

"No parents?" Rui murmured, his head bowed.

Right, change the subject, Rose, and quickly. "What do you know about Miss Templeforth's pendant and about that cup?" The words shot out of her mouth before she'd a chance to think them through.

He craned forward. She thought she caught a spark of admiration.

"Do you believe in magic, Rose?" he asked, his eyes glittering.

Magic?

A sharp knock at the door interrupted them, and Mr Crank appeared at the frame. Rose wondered if he'd been eavesdropping on them – it wouldn't be the first time. "Miss Templeforth has requested your company shortly for luncheon, at one o'clock." His lips twisted down as his gaze met Rose. "Both of you." He strode away, his disdain hanging in the air.

"Come on," Rui said to Rose. Then leaning in to her, he whispered, "If you want to know about magic, there is but one person who is best placed to tell you...Miss T!"

And with that, he jumped up, and a second later Rose could hear him already hammering down the stairs. She took a moment to compose herself. Life outside the workhouse was certainly VERY strange. *And*, she thought with a quick smile, *very exciting!* To think a workhouse girl like her was to have lunch with the mistress of the house. Placing her hand on her chest she swayed a little. Maybe she'd find out more about being a guardian to Miss Templeforth's pendant and about the magic it contained! She couldn't wait.

Exhilarated, Rose rushed from the room, swerving just in time to miss Mr Gupta striding along the corridor.

"Sorry, Sir." Rose pinned herself against the wall, allowing him space to pass. Mr Gupta nodded as he swept by, while his monkey, perching on his shoulder, hissed at her. She watched Mr Gupta enter his room, and heard the key turning in the lock behind him.

Rose paused. *There's something very wrong about that pair. I don't trust 'em one inch.*

"Come on, Rose!" Rui shouted from the lobby below.

Old Friends

As Rose reached the library door, she could see the fire cheerfully burning in the grate, while Miss Templeforth laughed at something Rui had said. A table had been drawn up to Miss Templeforth's armchair, set with a tablecloth, cutlery and three steaming bowls. Rose breathed in the delicious aroma. Rui was sitting at the table with a space free next to him for Rose.

"Rui," Miss Templeforth gasped, wiping a tear of happiness away. "How I have missed your company."

"And I yours," Rui replied.

Rose coughed lightly from the entrance, but they were too engrossed to hear her, so she stood and watched a little longer. The pair seemed so happy alone together, it seemed a pity to interrupt.

"Now, tell me, before young Rose gets here, how are the two of you getting along?" Miss Templeforth asked.

"Well, I've little experience of spending time in the company of English people my own age. I've only encountered adult etiquette and formalities here. I do worry that I may be getting things wrong. I don't mean to, you understand. I've tried to make the right impression on her, but I'm not certain it's worked at all."

Rose stepped out of view behind the door frame. *Make the right impression on me!* She listened closely, though the stuffed animals goggled at her from the lobby walls and made her feel guilty.

"You haven't been Sherlock Holmesing her, have you?" Miss Templeforth enquired.

"Erm… A bit." He coughed.

"I see. No, I wouldn't say Rose would find that too agreeable."

"But tell me, Miss T," he whispered. "What danger is she in?"

Miss Templeforth choked a little. "All will be revealed." She cleared her throat. "Just be sure to take care of her during your stay. She has some important work to undertake. Now, where the devil is she?"

Rose pinned herself against the wall, uncertain what to do next. *I can't go in now,* she panicked. *They'll think I've been eavesdropping – which I have.*

The grandfather clock opposite her gonged once, and Rose jumped. She couldn't hold off any longer, so she stepped up and tapped lightly on the open door. Immediately the two faces turned towards her.

"Ah, Rose, there you are," Miss Templeforth said. "Rui tells me you have been getting acquainted? Do shut the door, my dear."

"Y-yes!" Rose stammered, pushing it to.

"Come, Rose." Rui patted the seat next to him, and then gestured to the lunch set out before them. "It's English soup, vegetables boiled with water, no spice or flavour. You will love it." Rui caught Miss Templeforth's stern look and shrugged. "It's the truth. The Englishman's taste in food is like his choice in clothes. Bland and sombre, but…assuredly practical."

"Manners, Rui," Miss Templeforth chided, with a wry smile.

Rose took her seat at the table.

"It's just an observation, no malice intended." He picked up the pepper pot, "and I will love this soup too, after a little tinkering." Pepper particles filled the air as he smothered the soup with grey powder. "Perfect," he grinned.

Cook's soup smelled delicious, and Rose's eyes settled hungrily on the bowl set before her. Then she spotted the tray of cream fingers piled high on a plate in the middle. Oozing with jam and clotted cream: *pudding!* Catching Rose's interest, Rui grabbed the plate and offered her one. She shook her head, knowing they were meant for afters. But Rui grabbed one and dunked it in his soup. "Umm." He pulled a quizzical face. "Interesting."

Rose wasn't sure if he'd just done it for a laugh – to impress her, or whether he genuinely didn't know.

Rose tried not to giggle, but caught Miss Templeforth's smile. "Do you remember nothing that I taught you?" She leaned to Rose and whispered, "You'll have to keep an eye on him, dear," adding a little louder, "he's *very* strong-willed."

Rose nodded with a grin.

"What?" Rui asked, dunking it in again.

Rose tried to eat her soup slowly as she imagined a companion would, rather than rushing it as she wanted to. She popped a bit of bread into her mouth.

"Now…" Miss Templeforth continued, picking her words carefully. "Tell me about your tutor, Rui. Mr Gupta… how do you…find his company?"

I knew it! She don't trust him much either. Rose's interest pricked as she remembered her mistress's reaction to him earlier. She stopped chewing her bread to listen.

"Quite enthralling, Miss T," Rui enthused.

"And you trust him?"

"Of course. With my life."

"Very good...he is...certainly a learned man." Miss Templeforth's voice trailed off as she stirred her soup.

Rui picked up his bowl and downed it. Smacking his lips together, he tapped his mouth with his napkin. "Magic, Miss T – is it time?" He grinned.

"Yes, now, Rui has chosen a story for me to tell you both, Rose. The story he has picked may interest you... It is about the legend of the Amber Cup, and about my pendant too."

Rose's neck stretched forward.

"Yes!" Rui began, clapping his knees with excitement. "In India Miss T always wore her pendant and it fascinated me, you see. She would tell me many stories, but the one about the cup was always my favourite and—"

"Why, you made me tell you it so often you must know it by heart. Perhaps you should tell it, Rui?" Miss Templeforth giggled, pushing her untouched soup away.

"No, no, absolutely not! Only you can make the stories come to life. You make everything sound mysterious and exciting." He rested his chin on his hands and stared across adoringly at the old woman.

A rustling noise outside the door drew Miss

Templeforth's attention. "That will be *all*, John," she called out, adding, "I am feeling quite well. At ease, man, at ease."

"Oh…er…yes, Ma'am," Mr Crank snivelled from behind the closed library door. His footsteps retreated down to the kitchen below.

"That man's devotion in his service to me is quite remarkable. But a little overbearing at times," Miss Templeforth cooed.

He's a blessed nosy parker, more like, Rose thought. *He'll get that lughole of his stuck fast to something he shouldn't, if he don't stop all that listening.*

"Well, let us begin." Wheezing, Miss Templeforth leaned over and supped some medicine before beginning to speak. "This pendant, just like the Amber Cup in the museum, is ancient. Both items have a connection to Hove. I believe that objects as well as people have spirits, you see. And this," she held up the luminous amber disc, "above all others, has a strong and wondrous one." Her eyes turned to Rose.

Rose's skin prickled as she took herself back to the feeling she'd had when she'd held the pendant. The way it had throbbed like it was a part of her body. Her fingers twitched, and she longed to reach out and touch it – *just… once…more…*

Miss Templeforth tucked it away inside her blouse again.

"But Miss T!" Rui urged, gripping his chair. "You need to start by telling Rose about the cup!"

"Shush now, Rui, I'm not as young as I once was. I need to concentrate." She patted her throat. "Now, as Enna said yesterday, they unearthed the Amber Cup in my lifetime, some fifty years ago, when I was just a girl of about your age, Rose. A stranger came to try to steal the cup, while it was being unearthed, but I overcame him, with the help of a boy – a dear friend – named Anthony Funnel." Miss Templeforth's eyes flicked briefly to the portrait of the woman with a fan. "But Anthony's story is another tale altogether, and he is unfortunately no longer with us." The old lady sighed and looked down, her eyes wet. "But I digress. Where was I? Oh yes, the Legend of the Amber Cup, and the evil trapped within." Miss Templeforth settled back into her large chair, and Rose forgot about her unfinished soup and the jam fingers for dessert. Instead she leaned forward, eager for the story to begin.

The Legend of the Amber Cup

"Many lifetimes ago," Miss Templeforth began, "in a time we know now as the Bronze Age, when the ways of magic were very strong…"

The words drew Rose closer; she balanced on the very edge of her seat.

"…the legend of the Amber Cup took shape. In Denmark at this time there was a man called Tor, who had sons by two different women. One son was born to an immortal forest spirit – and this child was named Verrulf," Miss Templeforth said.

Forest spirits? Rose blinked, wondering what exactly they were.

"The other son was born later to Tor's wife, and this human child was called Albion. Neither woman knew about the other."

"So, these two were half-brothers," Rui interjected. "One named Verrulf and one named Albion. Got it?" He looked at Rose.

"Got it." She nodded.

"Thank you, Rui, yes. Now, I should warn you, Rose," Miss Templeforth said, "this is a tale of terrible betrayal." She paused staring into the fire. Her watery eyes danced with the reflected flames. "Now, Verrulf's mother, the beautiful forest spirit, was known as Mags. She resided in the human world, in a forest in Denmark. She became besotted with the human man, Tor, who lived in a village on the forest's edge. She followed him everywhere secretly, until one day, when he'd become separated from his hunting party, she revealed herself to him. They spent one evening together. After this, Mags wrongly believed Tor loved her back. But he did not." Miss Templeforth's bony fingers teased the air. "Giddy with this misplaced devotion, Mags changed herself from a forest spirit into a mortal human and returned to surprise Tor at his home. She assumed they would marry." The old woman looked between Rose and Rui, her eyes glittering.

"Many months had passed by the time Mags returned

from the spirit world, and Tor had all but forgotten about her. Plans were under way for him to marry one chosen for him, with whom he *was* in love. He was horrified when he saw Mags again, and heard she had borne them a child Verrulf. Tor would have told her of his horror at her news too, had she not revealed her magic gifts to him."

"Magic gifts?" Rose asked Miss Templeforth.

"Yes. Mags had taken with her an amber cup and two pendants – which she'd stolen from the spirit world. With these three magical objects she promised that together she and Tor could have everlasting power over the people of the human world."

Wheezing a little, Miss Templeforth reached for another sip of her medicine.

"Tor had no interest in Mags or Verrulf, but he was *greedy* and wanted the powerful objects for himself. So he set a trap. He arranged to meet Mags on an island in the lake and told her they would marry secretly by moonlight." Miss Templeforth lurched forward, her eyes suddenly wild. "And there he betrayed her monstrously."

Rose gasped.

"Tor took the gifts from her – the cup and the two pendants – and with them he immediately became powerful. Mags pleaded for his mercy as she held Verrulf in her arms, but it was of no use. Tor used his new-found dark magic to banish them both inside the cup. He planned never to see them again." Miss Templeforth paused to catch her breath. "Tor's act was barbarously evil; he had no right to treat Mags and his own son so brutally. And from that moment everything went horribly, horribly wrong. You see, Mags managed to snatch back one pendant as she was sucked away, but it was too late to stop anything – the gateway was already open. She and Verrulf were banished into the cup."

"So where did she end up?" Rose asked, filling up with pity for the woman.

"In a gruesome shadow dimension, where violent creatures lurk beneath a black sun."

"A black sun?" Rose whispered to herself, suddenly remembering the tattoo she'd seen on that man's wrist, and the same curious image on the back of the departing carriage.

"This shadowy world has existed since creation. The wickedest and oldest creatures dwell here. It's energized by a black sun that hangs low in a mauve sky, but the black sun does not radiate energy like ours – it sucks it away, endlessly hungry. Its inhabitants, the Creeplings, are filled with greed and hate and crave destruction." Miss Templeforth looked out of one of the windows, her expression fierce. "Tor had activated the cup with both pendants, and it became like a tunnel to transport Mags and Verrulf to this sinister place, you see."

"Creeplings?" Rui asked, looking confused.

Rose nodded, her pulse quickening. She remembered the horrible creatures she'd seen in her mind. Could they have been Creeplings? Did they belong to this shadowy world?

"In the time that passed after Mags and her son were imprisoned, Tor married and had a human child, Albion, whom he adored. Tor grew to fear the cup, and kept it hidden. But he always wore the pendant, which helped him to become wealthy, and to make the right decisions in trade and barter. Tor never gave another thought to the suffering of his other secret family. Meanwhile, Verrulf, trapped in the world of the Creeplings, grew to despise his own human half. And within this terrible abyss, a deep hatred grew, both for his father and for the human race."

"And then he came back," Rui told Rose.

"He did?" Rose stared at Miss Templeforth, her mouth agape.

"Yes. Some years later, Verrulf used his mother's pendant to return through the cup. He murdered both Tor and his wife, and then he set about hunting down his half-brother. Albion had immediately fled from Denmark across the sea, and finally found himself in Hove with the remaining pendant and the Amber Cup."

"Here?" Rose said.

Miss Templeforth nodded. "Here."

"Albion – I should say," Rui interjected, "despite his father, was a good person. Right, Miss T?"

"Quite so, Rui, Albion was." She smiled at him. "Verrulf, by contrast, was driven by toxic hatred, and was enormously strong. He skulked in the shadows of this earth, planning to avenge his father's betrayal by finding the second pendant and the cup, and using them along with his own pendant to unleash his army of Creeplings. A reality that would see our sun replaced by his black one, and in that darkness Verrulf would rule supreme – no longer thrust aside for another. At last, the master of his own destiny, while his Creeplings could feed and multiply."

"Miss T, what the devil *are* the Creeplings? You never mentioned them before today."

"I spared you the details, Rui, till now." Miss Templeforth's eyes darkened. "They're wretched beings." The old lady squeezed her eyes shut. "They feed on human fear and greed. They are unspeakably…evil."

"How do they…f-feed?" Rose managed, not at all sure she really wanted to know.

"The more fear a victim exudes, the hungrier and stronger they become. They enter our soul through our shadows, and we…become one of them."

"Become a Creepling?" Rui asked, raking his hand through his black hair. "Miss T, why did you not tell me of these creatures before?"

"You were too young, Rui." Miss Templeforth trailed off and, reaching for her medicine, she took a greedy gulp.

"They're...horrible," Rose murmured, feeling sick.

"But enough of those unspeakable things for now. Back to our story. Where was I?"

"Well, Verrulf was after his half-brother, Albion, to get the pendant and the cup, and make him pay for what his father did." Forgetting herself, Rose urged Mrs T on. "Did he find him?"

"Yes, he did. Albion had fled by boat to our shores, here in Hove, taking the Amber Cup and his pendant with him. Despite being only a boy of your age, Rui, Albion overcame Verrulf after a fierce fight on the shore where the West Pier now stands. The beach was filled with the terrified local inhabitants watching as the brothers fought. Albion overcame his half-brother and pushed Verrulf back inside the enchanted amber of the cup, trapping him for all eternity in the shadowy dimension he'd sprung from. The local people of that time hailed Albion as a hero. His bravery became the stuff of legend." She peered at them both over the rim of her medicine tumbler as she took another sip.

"But Verrulf's pendant?" Rose murmured. "It is still 'ere?"

"Alas, Verrulf sired a child during his time on earth. His human heir – the pendant became theirs – and has been passed down generation to generation ever since. Shielded by dark magic."

"And, so what became of Albion?" Rose asked.

"Albion died some years later – of natural causes. His wife, along with the local people, erected a giant burial mound in his memory, here, overlooking the sea. Close to where Palmeira Square is in Hove today."

"Albion was buried in Hove?" Rose asked.

"Yes, even the place name, Hove, is derived from his monument – it comes from the Danish word, Hof, which means burial mound," Rui added with an assured nod.

Rose thought about everything she'd just been told and realized she believed it. If the pendant was magic – then couldn't other magical creatures and places be real too? Forest spirits, Creeplings, different worlds, even *Verrulf*... She tensed, as these possibilities spiralled in her mind.

"The Amber Cup was buried with Albion, for safekeeping, under a mountain of earth." Miss Templeforth leaned close. "The cup was never supposed to be removed. It's a dangerous object that connects our world to Verrulf's, where he still rules supreme."

"But the cup *was* dug up?" Rose asked.

"Yes, Rose, it was. Enna and I were there on the sorry morning they excavated it. From that moment, a dark energy started to grow again." She shook her head. "The cup now rests in the Brighton Museum – safely under lock and key. Thank goodness."

Miss Templeforth held her pendant aloft. Rose's gaze was drawn to it, the space between them filled with static charge.

"Each pendant follows the separate bloodline of the brothers, as both sired a child in this world. The two pendants hold a special magic all of their own, independent of the cup, a power that can be used for good or evil. The spirit of every guardian – a memory of them is preserved within the amber. This one once belonged to Albion."

The old lady gave Rose a pointed stare. *Albion?* Rose's skin tingled.

"The pendant chooses its own champion. You, Rose Muddle, are the next guardian to Albion's."

"Truly?" Rui's eyes shone. "Rose, you never said!"

Rose gulped and forced a nod.

"But how can I be related to you…to Albion?" she asked the old lady.

"Rose, I am sorry that I do not have all the answers to your questions – we will find these in due course, but you must stay vigilant, these are not safe times. Things have been quiet for many years. Verrulf has been silent. We were foolish to think that would last..."

"What? You mean he is back?" Rui gasped, drawing his seat closer.

"Yes, dear Rui. He *is* attempting to come back. Things started about six months ago, when I became ill with the tuberculosis." She sighed, looking up to the ceiling. "It was then the dark visitations started. The pendants share a connection, even after all this time. The guardian to Verrulf's pendant is strong; he's worked out a way to send Creeplings to torment my mind. He wants me dead."

"Miss T!" Rui exclaimed.

"Hush now, Rui." Miss Templeforth tapped his knee. "My time is almost up. And Verrulf's guardian knows it. They are after my pendant when I die and it will be vulnerable until it bonds with Rose properly – during this transition time it could be taken from you, Rose. You must protect it with your life." She choked a little. "You must discover who is the guardian of Verrulf's pendant and... stop...them." Her words trailed into panting breaths and she lurched forward upsetting her soup bowl; the broth dripped down the tablecloth.

"Miss T?" Rui rushed to her side, his eyes wild.

"Ma'am, are you all right?" Rose asked, grabbing for her medicine.

Miss Templeforth's eyes rolled upwards and her whole body shook. "A...visi...tation..." Miss Templeforth rasped, her hands beginning to tremble uncontrollably. The remaining bowls and the glasses on the table vibrated and chinked.

"They have come for me!" the old woman gasped. The flames in the grate roared and stilled, then roared again, as if being pumped by a set of bellows. "The...Creeplings!"

Rose picked up the bell and shook it furiously. "Help!" she shouted.

The library door flew open and Mr Crank dashed in. "Ma'am, I am here," the butler said, snatching the glass of medicine from Rose. "Get out of here," he sneered at her. "She needs *me*."

"Should I get the doctor? Or Miss Lee?" Rose asked, stepping closer, feeling helpless. Miss Templeforth's frail body shook over and over again.

"I am all she needs," Crank said, stroking Miss Templeforth's forehead. "I know what to do. Now leave!" he barked.

Speechless, Rose and Rui backed out of the room.

They turned to face each other. "Dark visitations," Rui muttered, his brow creased with worry. "Creeplings... Whatever is going on here?"

Rose stood in the lobby unable to speak.

"Master Rui." Mr Gupta suddenly appeared at the top of the staircase. "It's time for your tutorial. He will not be needing your company again today, Miss Rose."

"B-but," Rui managed. "Miss T is…ill."

"Then she must rest," Mr Gupta clipped, the monkey poking its head from behind his legs. "We have much we need to cover."

Reluctantly, Rui climbed the stairs, leaving Rose alone with her thoughts. She watched him disappear from view, her head swimming with images of a black sun, warring half-brothers, evil Creeplings and magic as Miss Templeforth's pitiful moans echoed around the big house. How was Rose ever to find the guardian to the dark pendant?

13

Gone

"Noooooooo!" Mr Crank's despairing cry reached Rose's attic bedroom the following morning.

She sat bolt upright in bed, waking from a terrible dream in which a black sun had eclipsed the earth's sun, and shadowy creatures had pulled at her sheets and body. She squinted at the October sunshine streaming in through her attic window as another pitiful scream rang out from below.

Rose flung off her covers and in a flash she was on her feet, tearing down the attic stairs and along the corridor, her new nightdress trailing behind her.

She heard Rui's door open as she passed. "What's happened?" he asked, rubbing the sleep from his eyes.

Rose leaned over the bannister. The heavy library door below swung back, smacking the wall. Mr Crank stumbled out and collapsed onto all fours. Rose ran down to him as fast as she could. She glanced at the grandfather clock in the lobby. It was already gone nine. "Sir," she kneeled by his side, "what's wrong?"

"A dark visitation took her." He pointed a quivering finger through the open library door. Miss Templeforth's arm hung limp by the side of her chair.

Rui sped past them both in his striped pyjamas. But when he reached Miss Templeforth, he staggered backwards.

"What is it, Rui?" Rose asked, her heart in her mouth.

"She's dead!" he whispered. "My dearest friend is dead."

Miss Templeforth lay slumped to one side, her head pushed back, with lips dry and parted. Her high-necked blouse was partly unbuttoned, revealing the bare white flesh beneath.

"And the pendant's gone!" Rose covered her mouth. She turned towards a chill breeze. The heavy curtain billowed into the room, away from the open window behind it.

"Her pendant's gone?" Mr Crank mumbled in a daze as he got to his feet.

Rose rushed to the window and leaned out. The narrow walkway running between the neighbouring houses was deserted. If someone had got in through the window they were long gone now.

Pale with shock, Rui ran his fingers along the frame of the sash window. "The window was opened from the inside. It has not been tampered with."

"I-I opened the window earlier," the butler said from behind them. "At Miss Templeforth's request. After she had breakfasted with Mr Gupta."

Rose flinched. *She had breakfast with Gupta?*

"I administered some medicine and left her to rest. I'm sure she was wearing the pendant then..." he managed through broken sobs. "A few minutes later I heard her moans. I rushed to her...but I was too late. I found her... like this. I don't understand!"

He only left her for a few minutes? Rose's mind ticked. *So whoever got in through the window would have had to be quick. Quick like a...monkey.* Rose's eyes darkened. "Where's Mr Gupta now?"

"Death is but the greatest adventure," Mr Gupta announced from the doorway, the monkey clinging to his neck like a grotesque scarf.

Rose twisted to face him. *How long has he been standing there?*

"She was a woman of tremendous spirit," Mr Gupta continued. "May her soul be liberated." He bowed his head.

"Yes, she was wonderful!" Rui sobbed. And then, as if

the realization had just registered in his brain, he shouted, "NO, no, no!"

Rose steadied him, but her gaze remained on Mr Gupta.

There was no surprise on Gupta's face – as if he already knew Miss Templeforth was dead. The monkey glared back at Rose. Every sinew of her body told her that nothing in this room was as it seemed. *He arrives from the East. The book travels with him – the cup awaits him at the museum.* The words of the man in the carriage rang in her mind. *Was they talking about Mr Gupta? And now Miss Templeforth is dead and the pendant's gone! The pendant!* Panic coursed through her. Miss Templeforth had warned them that Verrulf's guardian was after it. Her shoulders tensed. *I've got to get it back – I'm the guardian now. I'm the rightful keeper.* The enormity of Miss Templeforth's expectations felt crushing.

The scene before her played out in slow motion. Mr Crank leaned over Miss Templeforth. He lowered her eyelids and pulled up her blanket to cover her face. Rose threw aside her terrible memories of the workhouse and the despair that accompanied death in that horrible place. She had to be strong.

The butler took an unsteady breath as he stood back from the old lady's body. "Excuse me, please, I must compose myself." Sobbing, he squeezed past Mr Gupta in the doorway. "There is so much to do, so much to prepare.

I must send for the physician... Oh Lord, we are all doomed. Without the mistress, what will become of us?"

Rose felt certain Miss Templeforth would have sorted things for the staff – she knew she was dying. But had she had time to include Rose in her plans? What if she hadn't? Anxiety gathered in her chest. Crank would surely get rid of her, given the chance.

This all feels so final, so quick...too quick.

"The pendant – her pendant," Rui spluttered. "The police must be informed that Miss Templeforth's pendant has been taken!"

Rose nodded.

"I will see to it, Master Rui." Mr Gupta swept into the lobby. "Miss Rose, you must stay with Master Rui and comfort him," he shouted back. "Please, return to your quarters at once. Neither of you should leave the house."

Rose helped Rui out of the room.

Mr Gupta continued speaking as they reached him in the lobby. "I will inform your uncle, the maharajah, of this tragedy. Master Rui, we will be cutting short our stay and returning to London as soon as I have attended to some... private business at the museum."

"Leaving?" Rui protested.

What private business at the museum? Rose tensed.

In the lobby, Mr Crank was on his knees. Mr Gupta

helped him up and assisted him down into the kitchen below. The butler's sobs quietened as the two men disappeared from sight.

Rose gripped Rui's shoulders. "Rui, I must find the pendant. With Miss Templeforth gone, I'm the guardian now. And if I don't find it, terrible things will happen."

Rui's large eyes stared at her, bloodshot and weepy. "I vow I will not leave this place until we find it," he sniffed.

Rose tried to keep her thoughts still. "Enna Lee," she murmured to herself. "I need to find Enna Lee."

"Rose?"

"Rui, there's someone I gotta go see," she whispered, looking around to make sure no one was listening. "The gypsy lady who slipped you the note from Mrs Templeforth at the station. She's called Enna Lee. I must find her."

Rui drew a deep breath and straightened. "Then we will go together. We must leave the house undetected." He wiped away his tears. "To do this, I require a disguise. Even if Miss T's death looks to the outside world to be natural, we know the truth. The shock of the visitation killed her. Rose, she was murdered."

A steely resolve filled Rose's eyes. Whatever had happened here this morning, whoever had taken the pendant, she was determined to get to the bottom of it, to avenge Miss Templeforth's death and get her pendant back.

14

A Quick Escape

Rose held on to the canvas loop of the carriage they'd boarded outside the house. With Rui opposite her, they jolted back and forth. They were heading to the Pleasure Gardens to find Enna Lee.

Rui picked at the filthy coat and breeches he'd insisted on swapping with Jack Billings next-door. Rui said he didn't want to draw attention to himself in his fancy clothes, and Jack had been happy to oblige – for the right price. Rui's eyes looked sore from crying, but he'd been determined to come with her. And she was glad of his company.

Back at the house things had moved quickly. Crank had

already sent Cook and the day maids home – he'd seemed quite crazed after the shock of losing his mistress. Rose knew the only reason she remained there was because she was Rui's companion. And the thought niggled at the back of her mind, that once Rui went too, the butler would have her shipped back to the workhouse quicker than she could say Jack Robinson.

But the workhouse and Mrs Gritt seemed the least of her worries right now. Time was ticking away. They had to find Enna Lee and tell her that poor Miss Templeforth was dead, and that the pendant had been stolen. Rose hoped Enna would know what to do.

She knew they didn't have long outside the house. Rose and Rui had sneaked out, taking Cook's discarded house keys with them so they could slip back in. They had to wait until Mr Gupta had left for the museum and Mr Crank was accompanying Miss Templeforth's body in the mortuary carriage. It only gave them a couple of hours at best before they had to be back, and it was already gone three o'clock as it was.

Rose squinted through the carriage window at the whitewashed houses bobbing by outside. "Answers is what we need." She hadn't meant to say it aloud.

"Indeed we do." Rui looked up, his mouth set in a grim line. "You think your gypsy friend will help us?"

Rose nodded, straightening her bonnet. "I hope so."

"Good." His brow creased. "With the pendant missing we are in grave danger. We must discover who the evil guardian of Verrulf's pendant is and find yours, Rose, before it is too late. I owe it to Miss T."

"Yep." Rose's eyes flickered. She had her suspicions about who had taken it. Her mind switched to Mr Gupta. He'd had breakfast with Miss Templeforth and straight after that the pendant had been nicked. *Who else could it have been?* Plus, he hadn't stopped talking about the cup since his arrival at the house. She looked over at Rui. There seemed nothing to be gained from keeping quiet about it.

"Your Mr Gupta," she began. Rui shot her a sharp look, but she carried on. "No matter which way round I look at things, him and that monkey of his seem stuck in the middle of all this."

"You can't possibly suspect Mr Gupta!" Rui protested, sitting forward.

"I do. He never got the police this morning like he promised, did he?" She didn't give Rui a chance to reply. "And you heard the same as I did, him going on about the cup in the museum and how surprised Miss Templeforth seemed about it. I don't think she trusted him one bit neither. He was the last person to speak to her, and with the library window left open, his monkey could have easily sneaked in and taken the pendant. Plus, even with all what's gone on in the house, Mr Gupta still went for that meeting at the museum. And—"

"Coincidence does not equal guilt," Rui cut in. "I think you are very wrong about him."

"Hmfff." Rose folded her arms. "Well, if you're the detective, explain how I'm wrong."

"Mr Gupta is a scholar of antiquities and a good man. Given his specialist studies of mythical cups, his prior knowledge about Hove's Amber Cup is hardly remarkable. Nor is it remarkable that he would be arranging to see it during his stay here." Rui pulled at his jacket collar. "Having travelled halfway around the world to see it, I'm not in the least surprised that it's a priority for him to get to the museum. No." He shook his head. "With the window left open, anyone could have taken it. Fact."

"A'right then. If you say he didn't take it, who do you suppose did?"

"Well, who did Miss T fear?"

Rose thought about this for a moment. "Them dark visitations what haunted her?"

"Yes, Rose. And who did she suppose sent those… dreadful creatures?"

"The one who's got Verrulf'spendant."

"Do you think it is Mr Gupta who has the other pendant?

And that he is the one responsible for her death?"

Rose knew that the man inside the carriage had the other pendant; she'd seen it with her own eyes. "No," she admitted.

"Precisely. So we may deduce that it must be the other pendant holder who Miss T feared, and not Mr Gupta."

"I s'pose." Rose looked down, hoping that Enna Lee would hold the answers to these questions. "The way you say things, it makes it all sound right somehow, but how can all the stuff about evil cups be true? Do you really believe that story what Miss Templeforth told us?" Her eyes flashed at him. She just wanted his reassurance.

"Indeed I do. I believe everything that marvellous woman ever told me. Why would I not?"

"It's just…I've been thinking. How would she know about stuff that went on all them years ago? What if the cup was dug up in Hove, like what she said, and she made up the story to jolly you along? I mean, to believe it all really happened is just—"

"Extraordinary? In India, the ordinary is in constant flux with the extra-ordinary. The world of our gods exists in everything. It is everywhere."

"Well, it ain't like that in Hove." She doubted these words even as she spoke them. "Not usually." The memory of holding the pendant and all that happened flared in her mind. She knew she had to come clean and tell him everything. They were in this together now. "Or…at least it wasn't until about five o'clock the other night when I first held the pendant."

Rui's face lit up. "Tell me, Rose. Tell me exactly what happened."

The Pleasure Gardens

Bouncing up and down in the carriage, Rui listened intently as Rose recounted the events of that fateful evening in the library when she'd first held the pendant.

Rose explained how she'd seen the hand of Verrulf's pendant guardian, and the tattoo of the black sun on his ageing wrist. The way she'd been inside his head, listening to his conversation with the stranger – and how, when he'd realized she was inside his mind, he had set the Creeplings onto her too. She held Rui's attention and he didn't flinch once, just nodding his encouragement until she'd finished.

"Elephas Maximus! You saw through the eyes of the

other guardian?" he gasped at the end.

"I think so. It was strange."

"And you overheard them talk about a man from the East, travelling with a book to the museum."

"Yes, that's right."

"Umm." Rui stroked his chin. "Interesting – I can see now why you are suspicious of Mr Gupta. But we must not judge him as guilty yet, I beg of you. However, if we can solve these clues you overheard, it might lead us to your pendant. And Rose," he lifted his index finger, "together, I believe we can do it!"

Rose nodded. A welcome relief washed through her: sharing the burden of all that had happened felt good.

"So, the symbol of the black sun was on his wrist – the same design you'd spotted on a carriage leaving the house." Rui tapped his cheek.

"Yes." She grimaced. "But I never told no one that it were outside the house," she suddenly realized, wishing she had. "I didn't know all this was going to happen. I should've said something, shouldn't I? Maybe that could've made a difference."

"We cannot worry about that which is done. We must worry instead for that which remains undone... Moving on." Rose could almost hear the cogs turning in his complex mind, as he stared out of the window. "So, Miss Templeforth was amazed that you could see inside the other pendant-holder's head. That's what makes you special. And as the new guardian, you must have a direct blood link to Miss T, one that stretches all the way back to Albion, the half-brother of our nemesis, Verrulf."

"That's what they told me." But even as she said it, she felt uncertain.

"If the pendant chose you, then that much is fact."

Without warning the carriage swerved to take a sharp left. Rose and Rui slid sideways along their seats. The driver shouted something. Rui gripped the window ledge. Outside, a delivery boy brandished his fist at their retreating carriage. He sat in the roadway amongst a pile of loaves of bread that had spilled out of an upturned basket.

The carriage now sped eastwards, alongside the iron railings of the Pleasure Gardens. They were nearly there.

"Rui, it don't make no sense why the pendant picked me. I was told my ma died giving birth to me." Rose sank into her seat. "And my pa got lost at sea. So Ma had me in the workhouse. And that's where she died...my mum wasn't no Templeforth. That's all I know."

Rui's expression softened as he spoke. "Not having parents makes you feel lost, doesn't it? I know, you see, because...because I lost my parents too."

"You did?" Rose tilted her head. "You never said."

"I don't much like talking about it. They died on a hunting trip, just before Miss T was hired as my governess. That woman helped me through my grief, befriended me, gave me hope. She let me taste the potential of life's great adventure. I owe her everything. And now…well, now she's dead too." His voice cracked to a whisper as he wiped away a tear.

Rose recalled Miss Templeforth suggesting the two of them had a lot in common. It had sounded so silly back then. *But now…*

"So, you see," he composed himself, "I am determined to find out who sent those creatures to haunt her –"

"– and who stole her pendant," Rose cut in.

The carriage heaved to a sudden stop.

"First thing's first," Rose continued, with renewed optimism. "Let's find Enna Lee. She will help us, I'm sure of it."

Rui opened the carriage door and inhaled a lungful of the autumnal air.

"Good job I'm in disguise." His determined eyes shot back to her. "And ready to solve this terrible crime with you."

Rose couldn't help but smile as he jumped down from the carriage. Rui patted Jack Billings's shabby coat. Being a couple of sizes too small, the sleeves didn't even reach his wrists, and the breeches had patches on both knees. *No one would ever believe he's the nephew to some maharajah – Indian royalty no less! He's the oddest boy I've ever met.* But she liked him all the same.

Rose jumped down and paid the driver. The entrance to the Pleasure Gardens lay before them, and Enna Lee was in there somewhere. Rose hoped with all her might that she had the answers they needed.

A barrel-shaped man patrolled the gated entrance to the Pleasure Gardens at St Ann's Well. Whistling through his teeth he stopped when he spotted Rose and Rui and swung back onto his heels.

"Good day to yez," he said, hooking his thumbs into his canary-yellow waistcoat. "Threepence a piece so you can see all the wonders awaiting yez. The best pleasure park in the whole of Europe." His gaze fixed on the money-pouch dangling from Rose's finger.

Rose tightened the bow of her bonnet. She could hear music and drums, and she peered behind the man at the thrum of people gathering around stalls and exhibits. Colourful bunting flapped in the afternoon breeze.

"We've come to see Gypsy Lee. Where can we find her?" Rose fished out some change from the purse of coins Enna had left for her.

The man placed the back of his hand to his mouth.

"A mysterious woman to be sure, a confident seer of folk. Follow the path to the top of the furze, by the Chalybeate Spring, just past the hermit, you can't miss her caravan." His words fell with seasoned aplomb.

Taking the coins, he tipped his top hat as they entered. "I wonder what your future holds?" he shouted behind them.

Rose didn't want to even think about her future – she couldn't think beyond finding Enna Lee and the missing pendant. Her pace quickened. *It must be close to half past three by now.*

"Hove is just as Miss T described it – full of adventure," Rui hollered, as he dodged through the mass of well-to-do people milling about. Rose felt dizzy with the place. The sweet smell of toffee apples hung in the air, the colours and the sound of laughter. She had never been anywhere like this before.

"It ain't usually like this," Rose shook her head, "normally it's just hard work and grime. But since you've turned up everything's been spun on its head."

A brass band struck up, and Rui became swamped by a large crowd gathering around him.

A man stood on a plinth up front and shouted through a mouth trumpet. "In a feat of aviation magic, I will be travelling at the mercy of the winds to Europe," he bellowed over the crowd, holding his deerstalker hat in place with his free hand.

"What a hat!" Rui said.

Pushing her way through, Rose joined Rui, balancing on her tiptoes to see to the front. She peered between two ladies' hats, stacked with fruit and feathers, and saw the man pivot into a wicker basket anchored to the ground by a series of ropes. A huge expanse of silk, in stripes of red and yellow, inflated behind him.

"It is a death-defying act of bravery. Many have died," he boomed, amid the gulps and sighs of the watching ladies. "I am nearly ready to ascend."

"A flying balloon, of all things," Rose muttered, a smile creeping across her face. She turned to say something to Rui, but he had gone. *Gone?* She spun in a circle, her vision obscured by bearded men, top hats and children on shoulders. *I can't have just lost him!* She panicked.

She fought her way back to the path. A small boy darted in front of her, clanking a stick against a metal hoop. He weaved up the pathway, making his way in between a sea of prams, fancy hats and walking canes. She couldn't see Rui anywhere. Rose jumped from side to side to allow people to pass her. Worry spiralled inside her. *I've lost him in all of this madness, and now I'm lost in it all too.*

Then she caught sight of Rui peering around the side of

a large wheeled cage, one of the Pleasure Gardens' many exhibits. Her relief switched to irritation. Picking up the hem of her long coat she marched towards him.

"Oi!" she poked his arm and stepped back.

He spun around, lifting his finger to his mouth, gesturing with his other hand to stay low. She shuffled forward and peeked over his shoulder.

Eee eee eee oh oh oh!

Rose jumped at the shrill noise coming from the cage. She couldn't believe her eyes. Inside, amongst the exotic shrubbery, were a group of agitated monkeys – all tails, teeth, arms and fur. A sign creaked in the breeze overhead. "Monkey House," she read aloud. "I hate monkeys." She gritted her teeth.

"Shh," Rui pointed. "Look."

Scanning the area ahead, she spotted none other than Mr Gupta. He stood out like a sore thumb in his jewelled turban and cream coat. "What's he doing here?" she whispered. "He's supposed to be at the museum!"

"And who's that with him?" Rui added.

A man wearing a floor-length black coat stood opposite Mr Gupta. Rose strained to get a better look, but his upturned collar concealed his face.

"This doesn't look like no museum business to me."

"Ummm," Rui muttered.

Mr Gupta looked furious. He stabbed the air with his hook.

"What are they having a barny about?" Rose wondered aloud. *I bet it's about the pendant – I knew that thieving blighter nicked it.*

The stranger pinched a stubby cigarette between his fingers and withdrew something from his pocket that he thrust into Mr Gupta's outstretched hand. Mr Gupta turned, obscuring her view.

"What's he given him? It looks like he's getting paid for something!" Rose murmured.

Rui said nothing, but his face was like thunder.

Mr Gupta took a cursory glance across the crowd, and Rose and Rui ducked back behind the cage.

"Lor', Rui. What's he up to?" Rose whispered.

"Something unexpected," he answered, his eyes flashing.

16

Monkey Business

"Why's your Mr Gupta here, when he's s'posed to be at the museum?" Rose scowled.

"That, dear Rose, is what I intend to find out." Rui bent low and dashed from the cover of the cage. "This way," he urged.

Rose stepped forward to follow but something small zipped in front of her, blocking her path.

"What the—?"

Mr Gupta's monkey, Bahula, eyeballed her, his ears pinned back on either side of his fez. Standing on his hind legs he exposed his teeth.

"Shoo! Go on, get away with ya!" Rose kicked out with

her boots. With one agile leap, Bahula swung up on top of the cage. He jumped about, hooting, pointing down at her.

The caged monkeys beside her suddenly crashed against the bars, forming a wall of teeth and fangs.

Eeeoow EEEOOOW EE EE EE oo oo oo.

Rose fell to the ground in fright. The monkeys were rattling the bars, snarling and shrieking, their thin arms grabbing for her. Her boots ripped the hem of her new dress as they scraped deep indentations into the grass. "Bother!" she cursed. Her dress was ruined now, thanks to a bunch of miserable monkeys. Rose bared her teeth at them and growled.

But, undeterred, they continued. She realized they were reacting to Bahula's shrieks. "He's eggin' them on," she raged, sneering up at Bahula. "I'll make a hat out of ya!" she shouted, brandishing her fist at him.

A man with a straw boater turned to look and, one by one, other heads swung round towards the din.

"Mr Gupta is looking for Bahula," Rui said, dashing back towards her. "He will spot us if he comes any closer." Bahula remained concealed for now behind the swinging Monkey House sign, but not if Gupta came any closer.

"Well then *do* something," Rose yelled at him.

"I am assembling a distraction, using my sacred friends," Rui shouted as he ran past. A sharp twang of scraping metal drew Bahula's attention. "What this situation requires is a flavour of the markets of Jaipur."

Before Rose could make any sense of it, one of the caged monkeys bounded past – it wasn't in a cage any more! Rose fell back on her hands, her bonnet halfway down her face. Skidding on the grass, the monkey tore away into the crowd, its path punctuated by a succession of ladies' shrieks.

Rose got to her feet just as three more monkeys careered past.

The open cage door swung in the breeze behind them. "Rui, you didn't?"

He shrugged, an impish smile forming on his lips. "Welcome to India!" he announced, his hands raised high.

Ahead, the monkey-infested crowd surged and pulled in every direction. A woman dashed by with a monkey fastened to her wide-brimmed hat. A dark shadow fell over them and Rose looked up to see the hot-air balloon billowing just feet above, its basket jerking madly, with dangling ropes beating the air. A tweed-clad head peered over the rim.

"Abort! Abort! Monkey on board!" he squawked through his mouth trumpet. Rose slapped her hand to her mouth just as a gust of wind took the balloon away, sweeping the man and his stowaway high into the heavens.

"Rui. What've you done?"

A deerstalker hat fell from the sky and landed squarely on the ground between them. Rui picked it up. "A gift! Thank you, Sir! Godspeed," he shouted up to the disappearing balloon pilot.

Rui thumped the tweed hat back into shape before pulling it over his head. "Sherlock Holmes at your service, Ma'am," he said, executing a low bow.

He's as mad as a flea, Rose thought with a shake of her head. She turned to Rui. "I don't need no Sherlock," she huffed. "What I *need* is that blessed monkey gone!"

"*EEoo oo oo ooo!*" Bahula shrieked, still jumping up and down on the cage above them, enjoying the whole spectacle.

Rose chanced a look at Mr Gupta, who spun in a circle, confused by the monkey mayhem twisting through the crowds around him. He'd never find Bahula with all of this going on. His mysterious companion had turned away, sucking on his cigarette.

"Look, up there," a woman's voice called out. Bahula froze. "Get him." An ample lady waddled up, directing a man holding a noose on a long black rod. The man rushed forward, swiping at Bahula, trying to hoopla him, but missing.

In a trice, Bahula launched off the cage and belted through the crowd towards his master. The man took chase, his noose nodding in the air above him.

"Bahula!" Mr Gupta's voice broke over the havoc.

Speeding off, Bahula leaped safely into Mr Gupta's arms as he strode away, following the lead of his darkly clad companion. They disappeared into the crowds.

Rui dashed forward. "Quick, they're leaving!"

"Coming!" Rose stumbled behind him, gripping her bonnet, but by the time they got to where Mr Gupta and the man had been talking, it was clear they were too late. People swarmed around them like a shoal of netted mackerel, blocking their view in all directions. "Fiddlesticks!" Rui slapped his fist into his palm. "We've lost them."

He crouched down and retrieved a smouldering cigarette butt discarded in the grass, and examined it closely. "Unfiltered and strong," he muttered sniffing it. "Wild Woodbine," he deduced.

"How do you know all this stuff?" Rose asked in awe.

"Like Sherlock Holmes, I make it my business to know the business of other people." He tapped his nose. "This particular brand is known also as "gaspers", due to the heavy toll the cigarettes take on the user's lungs. I first read about them in *A Biased Judgement: The Sherlock Homes Diaries, 1887*. Plus, I had the misfortune of sitting next to a smoker of such cigarettes on the voyage over here. It's a filthy habit. But at least we have a clue about our stranger."

The Gypsy Caravan

They hurried up the network of paths, which criss-crossed up the tiered elevations of the gardens. They'd already passed the hermit cave, just like the man at the gate had told them, so Rose knew they were heading the right way. *Mr Gupta would have to wait. Once they'd found Enna Lee, everything would be all right.* Rose bit her lip.

Overhead, elm boughs shaded the walkway, scattering multicoloured leaves in the breeze. The mood felt different up here – quiet but for the crunch of leaf-litter beneath their feet, and the gentle rush of autumn wind. The main park spread out a little way below them, but the whole place looked deserted now. As it turned out, Rui's trick with the caged monkeys had not only stopped Mr Gupta from spotting them both, but also unintentionally cleared the park of visitors.

Rui dashed ahead in his ill-fitting disguise, the flaps of his new hat swinging up and down over his ears. *He's barmy all right, but plucky too*, Rose thought with a wry smile.

"So now d'you think it was Gupta what nicked it?" Rose panted, chasing up behind Rui, pulling her thick coat tightly around her against the afternoon chill.

Rui suddenly jumped into the undergrowth to their left, and pulled Rose with him. Branches clawed at her coat. "Oi, what you doing?"

He leaned out and inspected the pathway behind them. "Good, we're not being followed." Satisfied, he leaped back out. "Come along then," he called back to her, "the coast is clear, as you English say."

"Don't you 'come along' me," she said. "It was you who stopped me. I was coming on just fine till then." Rose unhooked her coat from a bramble, tugging herself free.

Rui strode away mumbling to himself. "It is a capital mistake to theorize before one has accurate data. Insensibly one begins to twist facts to suit theories, instead of theories to suit facts. Which will never do." Rui's fist rested on his lips, deep in thought.

"God's teeth!" Rose exclaimed, chasing up behind him. "Whatever are you bleating on about?"

"Oh, it's a quote from Sherlock Holmes in *A Scandal in Bohemia*." He marched on. "This situation throws up more questions than it answers. What we need are cold, hard facts."

I'll give him cold, hard facts. Rose poked him on the shoulder. "What you after? A signed confession? Now I ain't no Sherlock Wotsit. I ain't full of fancy words and long ideas. But even I can see it looks like Mr Gupta pinched the pendant. And if you want facts, I'll give you facts. He wasn't at the museum, like where he had said he was going. He was here, with some stranger. It even looked like he got paid for something. Come on!" She threw her hands in the air. "We should have grabbed him whilst we had the chance."

"My tutor, Rose," Rui pressed on, "would not steal anything. It simply doesn't feel right. I know what we just saw. But...he's considered so honourable back in Jaipur."

"Phhf." Rose pulled up the damaged corner of her dress hanging down from under her coat, to stop herself tripping on it. "You've barely known him five minutes, you said you only met him on the boat over here, so how can you be so sure? Anyway, *honourable* or not, there's no denying what we just seen."

It was as plain as chalk to Rose, and she just couldn't

understand why Rui was being so difficult.

"Mr Gupta is a brave and honourable man. You know, he lost his hand on a mission for the Jaipur Museum. He was returning from Bombay by train, with some scriptures thought to be cursed, when a fire broke out on board. Despite his injuries he selflessly took charge of the rescue operation. His quick thinking saved a great number of stricken passengers. A hero, you see. The kind of valour he demonstrated is rare, Rose. He is no petty thief."

"Look here," Rose said, struggling to keep level with him, "all I know is, sometimes people do bad things what don't make no sense." Rose thought about the devilish Miss Gritt back at the workhouse. "But one thing I'm sure of, we need to find Enna and quick. She'll know what to do." *I'm counting on it.*

The pathway curved around a copse of trees, where the track stopped abruptly. Ahead, was a large horseshoe-shaped clearing, surrounded by mature trees and clumps of furze covered in yellow flowers.

And there, beneath a bough of weeping willow, stood the gypsy caravan, its large red cartwheels locked in place by bricks. It had an arched roof and green panelled sides adorned with a mixture of golden scrolls and colourful flower motifs. A broad wooden ladder led up to the closed doors. It looked deserted.

"I don't think she's 'ere." Rose suddenly felt so deflated and tired.

Rui inspected the remains of a small fire in the middle of the clearing. Bunches of scorched herbs filled the air with a heady sweetness. He rubbed some of the ash between his fingers. "It's wet; someone tried to put this out, and recently." He stood up and looked around, but noticing something he bent back down. He ran his hands across some prints left in the mud. Rose leaned over him. "Animal prints," Rui said.

"Monkey prints more like!" Rose pointed at the unusual shoe prints that ran alongside the monkey paws. "They're pointed slippers of the Mr Gupta variety, I would say, Sherlock," she dusted her hands together. "Them shifty travelling companions of yours have been up here already."

"But why?" Rui examined the evidence, deep in thought.

Rose left him and followed the sound of running water to behind the caravan, discovering a strange red-coloured pool with mist clinging to its surface. Roughly circular, it extended to about ten feet across and brimmed over at the far end to fall as a brook that trickled down the hill.

Birdsong filled the surrounding trees. Rui stepped up behind her.

"This looks like the water Enna gave to Miss Templeforth!" Rose said.

Rui peered over the bank. "Red waters," he whispered, dipping his hand into the water. "This must be where the spring starts – its source." He dipped his hands in and closed his eyes. "In India, red waters such as these are sacred. Known as Amrita – the nectar of immortality fallen to earth as a result of heavenly conflict. This place is special. It feels magical. Can you feel it too?" Standing, he backed away.

"Nah," she lied, feeling goose pimples on her skin. Nervously, she dipped her hand into the metallic swell. *It's warm! Even on a cold October afternoon.*

In that very moment, a curious emotion swept over Rose. She shivered. An ancient but familiar sensation of deep belonging stirred inside her, something she recognized, something she craved – the pendant.

"Rose?" Rui asked, pulling her arm.

"Hang on." She shook him off, trying to still her mind. Several faint voices called to her at the same time. She couldn't quite work out their words, but she knew instinctively that the spirit of the pendant was calling her to find it... The voices faded away. "Wait!" Rose called out, her eyes wide. But it was too late, the feeling had gone. She slumped forward.

"What is it?" Rui whispered from beside her.

"It's the oddest thing," Rose began. "I think the missing

pendant tried to speak to me, but I couldn't hear what it was trying to say. But, Rui, it wants me to find it. It ain't too far away. I can feel it in here." She tapped her heart. "It's like it's scared too – like it needs me."

"Extraordinary!" Rui said.

The trees above them shook suddenly, and hundreds of birds took flight from the overhanging canopy. Rose shielded her face with her arm. The air thickened with beating wings. "S-starlings," she stammered. The birds gyrated in the sky above her, like a living thing of one mind. She scrambled to her feet and turned to Rui, but he'd gone. She spotted him running to the caravan.

"Hang on!" she shouted, rushing towards him, pulling her bonnet down with both hands. "Wait for me."

Fabric of Time

Rose jumped up the steps leading to the closed caravan doors, and joined Rui as the swirling mass of starlings overhead flew out towards the sea.

The two doors to Enna's caravan creaked apart without being pushed. At nearly four o'clock, the late afternoon light outside cast Rose and Rui's silhouettes across the floor of the windowless interior. The fragrance of lavender drifted out.

"It's bigger than it looks." Rose examined the sparsely furnished room, a brown tapestry pinned all around the walls.

"Shall we go in?" Rui offered, already stepping inside.

"We can wait for her here."

Dried bunches of lavender hung at intervals from a high shelf of knick-knacks.

"Do you s'pose this is where Enna lives?" Rose noticed the raised area at the back. "There's a bed up there."

Moving forward, she ran her fingers across a central table, its top crafted from a slice of polished tree trunk. On it sat a solitary candle, a box of matches and a strange bowl carved from a lump of black rock. "She don't own much, does she?"

"No." Rui spun in a circle, taking it all in.

"Well, if we are going to wait here for a bit we may as well make ourselves comfy," Rose suggested, reaching for the matches.

The candle sparked into a lively flame as Rui shut the doors, extinguishing the afternoon light. As he swung back around his mouth fell open. "R-Rose," he stammered, looking about.

Rose blew out the match and followed his gaze, holding the candle in front of her.

"Well I never!"

The dull tapestry now shone in the light, awash with deep reds, greens and blues and flecks of golden thread, as a multitude of previously hidden details sprang to life as if responding to the candle's flame.

"Look, Rui, the cup!" She ran her fingers over a small stitched red cup set in the tapestry. Hovering next to it, on either side, shone the two pendants. One she recognized as hers – golden amber with the central darker dot. And the other as Verrulf's, a dark disc but with a centre of orange. The cup looked quite simple, small, with a round base and a handle, it sat upon a rock.

"It looks like an ordinary teacup, dunnit?" Rose watched spellbound as the gilded threads glowed and throbbed in the light. "But it looks alive!" *Just like the pendant did when I held it.*

Rui hovered by her shoulder, his brown eyes glittering in the flame of Rose's candle. "Yes, it must be the Amber Cup. And look, it reappears all the way along."

He was right. Its image peppered the tapestry. Rose moved the light of the candle along the strange landscape, noticing a girl with black curly hair who kept reappearing beside a blond boy who held the cup.

"It's the story of the cup, Rose. Just as Miss Templeforth told it. Look over here – the trees look dead." He studied a blackened copse, with trunks all willowy and broken.

"Those." Rose pointed, the image took her back to her vision. "Those ain't trees, Rui. They look like dead trees, but they're things like what came at me in my mind when I held the pendant." Their elongated black bodies lurched skyward and their shadows dripped beneath them, in what seemed to be blood.

"Creeplings, Rose! And who is that?"

A giant figure hovered in the night sky, with stag antlers branching from his head. Ape-like arms dangled by his sides, and he was totally shadow-black apart from his eyes, which glowed red like the cup.

"I dunno, but I don't like the look of him," Rose muttered.

Rui went to touch the image, but changed his mind. "It must be Albion's half-brother. This must be Verrulf."

Rose moved along and studied a hillock set back from the sea.

"Ah, the burial mound," Rui said joining her.

Rose nodded, tracing her fingers over the people who stood linking hands around it. She stopped as she reached the girl with black hair. Except, she wasn't a girl any more, she was a young woman. Her blue eyes matched the sea behind her. She stared out at Rose, as if she had been waiting to be recognized.

"This woman looks exactly like your gypsy friend, Enna Lee!" Rui's words cut into Rose's thoughts. "The same lady who delivered Miss Templeforth's note to me at the station. The likeness is uncanny! Extraordinary."

"I—" Rose couldn't form a sentence. "P'raps...I don't

know. It can't be?" No number of excuses could hide what Rose knew deep inside. "But how could the same person be alive today that was alive then?" Rose recalled how Enna had described knowing Miss Templeforth since she was a child, even though she looked a quarter of the old lady's age.

"That's how Miss Templeforth could recount the detail of the story with such authority, Rose. She'd been told it by someone who was there."

"Yes, I mean, I don't know, I—" Rose looked to the end of the tapestry, which she realized told the ongoing story of the cup. Her uneasiness grew. Would it tell them more about the pendant holder – or provide more clues about where the pendant might be, and about Mr Gupta?

Other images flashed out at her as she looked. A giant pile of broken metal. A young boy standing with a top-hatted man dressed in black. Further along still, the mound being removed by workmen. The cup again. Then other people she did not recognize. Rose stumbled around the wooden trunk, impatient to see the last part of the embroidery. It showed the half-completed face of a girl. Rose gasped.

"Rose," Rui stammered from behind her. "That face looks exactly like yours!"

Skrying

Rose swayed as she focused on the image in front of her. Her unfinished, unwritten future stretched down one side of the caravan to the door where the tapestry was blank.

"Just one half of your face, Rose? Do you think that's significant?" Rui said, inspecting the tapestry. "And where am I? I feel rather cheated."

"I need a seat." Rose slumped onto the stool and placed the candle on the table in front of her. She stared back at her face in the tapestry, wishing it could tell her more. She felt trapped, like a pea sealed in a drum that rattled and bounced about to the beat of someone else's tune.

Suddenly, the caravan doors burst open and a flurry of leaves blew in from outside. Rose jumped up. A pale face peered through a tangle of black curls.

"Enna!" they both said together.

Enna rushed forward, and the caravan shook a little as she pulled Rose into a warm embrace. "I have been so worried. I left for the house but found it empty, and—" Enna glanced at Rui. "You weren't followed, were you?"

Rui shook his head. "I kept constant vigilance. If I had spotted anyone I would have shaken their trail. No self-respecting detective would fall foul to such a trifle, Ma'am." He executed a bow.

Rose didn't want Enna Lee to stop holding her. In her arms she felt cocooned from everything, but she knew Enna had to be told the terrible news. "M-miss Templeforth is d-dead." The thought of that kind old lady's body stuck in the cold morgue filled Rose with sadness.

"I know." Enna shut her eyes and drew a deep breath. Gently releasing Rose, she turned away for a moment to compose herself. "Lucile Templeforth was my faithful friend and a strong guardian."

"A-and the pendant's gone as well. And everything's messed up and I didn't know what to do. So we came here to find you and—" Rose's words ran dry.

"Things are happening quickly –" Enna sat at the small

table and Rose joined her – "time is running away from us. We *must* find the pendant. Do you know where it might be?" Enna placed her hand softly over Rose's.

"Well, the pendant called to Rose," Rui interrupted, waving his arms about, encouraging her to speak.

"Rose?"

"Well, yes. I think it did. When I sat by them waters outside. I heard it, from far away – it was like it wanted me to find it. Like it was – scared." Which is how she felt now. She stared up to the ceiling of the caravan to stop her tears from falling.

"Rose, if it wants you to find it, it will show you the way." Enna's broad smile didn't reach her eyes, which remained etched with worry.

Rose suddenly remembered Mr Gupta with a start. "Has a man with a monkey been to see you up here?"

"No." Enna shook her head. "Why?"

Rose's mouth opened and closed, but she didn't know where to begin.

"There are some prints outside your caravan," Rui cut in, "consistent with theirs. It would seem that perhaps they tried to pay you a visit?"

"No? Do you suspect he may be involved in the pendant's disappearance?" Enna leaned over the table.

"Yes!" "No!" Rose and Rui cried together.

"We don't know." They shrugged in unison.

In truth, Rose didn't feel she knew anything about anything. She rested her elbows on the table and gripped her head, trying to hold her thoughts still. She glanced at the image of Enna by the burial mound on the tapestry. Enna followed her gaze.

"Who are you?" Rose murmured, wiping away a tear. "I mean, who are you *really*?"

"Were you truly with Albion all those years ago?" Rui asked creeping forward, his eyes hungry.

"Yes." She paused. "I have been around for a very long time, and have a deep connection with Hove. I watch over it." Enna sighed and pulled her shawl more tightly around her.

"I knew it! So you *are* immortal?" Rui's eyes ignited as he dragged his stool next to her.

"But how?" Rose whispered, trying to straighten out her impossible thoughts.

"A long time ago, back when magic existed in everything, I was a human like you, and the High Priestess to the red waters here."

"Them waters outside?" Rose managed.

Enna nodded. "I offered up my own mortality to protect this place from Verrulf. I used dangerous magic to ensure I remain here until the threat of his world passes." Enna exhaled and watched the dancing candlelight, her thoughts seemingly far away.

"My body tires so of this world. To live for ever, to watch the people you love and care for die, is a heavy burden. The pain of loss is not something that lessens with the passing years – the passing millennia. But I stay to guide the guardians to Albion's pendant."

"And how do you know who the pendant chooses?" Rui asked.

"The waters guide me." Enna gestured to the strange black bowl set before them on the table. Rose stared at it, puzzled.

"Hang on!" Rose gripped the table's edge. "Why can't *you* be the pendant's guardian then? You'd be better than me, better than anyone?"

"No." Enna shook her head. "Albion and I—" Enna cleared her throat "We had a daughter. Our daughter's ancestral line carries forward the guardianship of his pendant. I cannot handle it, only one chosen from his bloodline can. You, Rose."

"So, you and Rose are…" Rui began.

"Related?" Rose blinked.

"Very distantly," Enna smiled. "Over a great number of generations."

Rose stroked the back of her neck, trying to calm the self-doubt needling her.

As if sensing Rose's uncertainty, Enna reached over and cradled her hand, and the metal of her many rings felt cold. "These are dark times. Verrulf is trying to come back; he has people helping him who must be stopped. The black sun – the symbol you saw tattooed on that man's wrist. It is connected to Verrulf. The symbol his followers use in this world. It is a symbol of their loyalty to him."

"The black sun?" Rui interjected, looking at Rose.

"Enna," Rose began, "that last girl that came to be interviewed in the library. The one with the blonde ringlets."

"Yes, Rose, I remember her." Enna frowned.

"Well, I watched her leave in a carriage. And that sun sign, just like the tattoo, was on the luggage hold."

"You're certain of that?" Enna gasped. "The pendant had the most violent reaction to her in the library. I sensed a darkness in her, of the sort I have rarely before encountered."

"I'm sorry I never said anything about it earlier," Rose added.

Enna's eyes widened. "We always thought Verrulf's guardian would be unable to resist sending someone. And it seems the plan worked. They believe we've not found our champion. You, Rose, remain undetected."

Relief flooded through Rose. Not just because Enna

thought she was safe for now, but because she hadn't messed up by not telling anyone sooner.

"But someone has taken your pendant, Rose, and it must be found," Enna said, her eyes fierce.

Rose nodded. Enna was right, but who had it? Was it Mr Gupta? Was he really something to do with the black sun?

Rui's fingers tapped his lips. "When did you last encounter this black sun symbol, Miss Lee?"

"My last meeting with them was when the Amber Cup was removed from the burial mound. A clever boy helped me and Lucile Templeforth overcome Verrulf's guardian when he attempted to take possession of the cup." Enna walked over to the tapestry, and the caravan shook a little. She pointed to the image of a top-hatted figure, standing next to a young boy. "Verrulf's guardian back then used the insignia of a black sun, just as they do now. Verrulf's pendant simply vanished after that. It is an object with great cunning... But now it has resurfaced, and with its new host, they are growing strong."

"Who is the boy who helped you?" Rose asked. "Might he help us now?"

"No. His name was Anthony Funnel, but he died abroad in a terrible accident some forty years ago. A great tragedy. Such a lovely boy." Enna shook her head.

Rose recalled Miss Templeforth mentioning Anthony Funnel's name before. *But he's no good to us dead,* she thought.

"So how can we find who has the other pendant, and do you think they already have Miss Templeforth's?" Rui asked.

"Come, let us see what we can discover from the skrying waters." Enna gestured to the strange black bowl.

Skrying waters? Rose stared at the curious basin set before them.

"This flask contains the chalybeate waters from outside," Enna said, withdrawing it from her pocket. "The waters have been considered health-giving for hundreds of years. They contain salts and iron which make them red. But they can be magical too, in the right hands." The candlelight danced across her multicoloured rings. "The waters talk to me through my skrying bowl."

"They do?" Rose said in awe.

"This is how you read your clients' futures!" Rui marvelled. "With this kind of magic on our side, how can we possibly fail? Sherlock Holmes – this case will shortly be solved."

"If only it were so straightforward." Enna smiled at him. "The ways of the cup and the pendants are not easy to interpret. The magic that accompanies them is very old and well shielded. But we can try."

Rose studied the curious bowl set in the middle of the table. It was carved from a lump of black rock, its centre polished into a deep curve.

"It was the waters that showed you to me, Rose – in tho workhouse. I came to find you at once. I had been watching closely for news, knowing that Lucile's time was drawing near."

Popping the crystal stopper from her flask, Enna poured some of the contents into the bowl. The red water gathered in the black basin forming a cloudy pool which shifted beneath the still surface. The candle flame grew long and Rose suddenly felt very cold.

Enna stared into the bowl, holding her curls back. The waters within eddied and stirred. Enna looked up sharply, her blue eyes wild and searching.

"The waters speak…"

Rose's skin tingled, her curiosity and anticipation cartwheeling. She stared into the bowl, but couldn't see or hear anything.

"They tell me that your two halves are what make you special, Rose. They have said this to me before, when you were first revealed to me."

Rose swallowed as she glanced at her half-completed face in the tapestry. "What halves?"

"You must discover what that means for yourself.

The pendant could help you. We *must* find it." Enna drew back her black curls once more as she leaned back over the bowl. "The pendant is no longer in Sackville Road, but it is not too far away. It…yearns for you, Rose."

Rose nodded. "Ask 'em where I can find it?" she begged, her grey eyes wide and glittering.

"The image has gone. Wait, now it is showing me a man clutching a thick silver book of some kind, with an eye on its cover?" Enna looked up. "The book is somehow important. And I recognize this man – I've seen him before, I saw him with you –" she turned to Rui – "when I delivered Miss Templeforth's note to you, outside the train station at Hove. Who is he?"

"Mr Gupta!" The name flew from Rose's mouth. "The one whose footprints we saw outside here."

"Wait!" Enna's voice sounded urgent. "The waters are showing me something else."

"What is it, Enna? What have you seen?" Rose squinted into the bowl. The waters swirled in the basin, thick with white particles, but she couldn't see anything in them at all. The candle flame grew fierce and sparks flew from it.

"The museum is not safe, the cup is in peril. They seek the other pendant…your pendant."

"So they ain't got it?" Rose rallied.

"And…the waters say someone is in mortal danger,

someone is going to be…murdered."

"WHO?" they both shouted together.

"I see the symbol of the black sun. It's blocked me!"

The candle puffed out, plunging them into darkness. Rose shrieked, and Rui grabbed her arm. "Elephas Maximus!" he exclaimed.

Enna flung open the caravan doors. The weak evening light entered, cold and unwelcoming.

"You must leave at once. It is not safe for you both here." Enna pulled her shawl up over her head. "I am going to the museum. I saw Verrulf's followers were there: twelve men who hold power and influence in the local area. If they plan to remove the cup, I will uncover who they are and stop them."

"We will come with you," Rui said with gusto.

"NO…no." Enna drew a deep breath. "You must not be seen. It is vital that Rose stays undetected. Protect her, Rui."

Rui nodded.

Enna picked up her skrying bowl and, standing on the top of the caravan's ladder, she emptied the water onto the grass outside.

"Go back to the house –" Enna instructed, placing the empty skrying bowl back on the table – "and wait for me there. I will return to you by six o'clock. If I don't…"

Her eyes trailed to the ceiling. "Do what you can without me." She grabbed her flask of water and tucked it in her dress pocket. "Hurry," Enna said, ushering them to leave.

Outside, dusk had painted everything grey, and dead leaves floated around them on smoke-scented breeze.

"B-but—" Rose began, from the bottom of the wooden steps.

Enna turned and held her shoulders, shaking her gently. "See if the pendant calls to you again, Rose. Believe in yourself. But stay vigilant; both of you." She shot a fierce look between the two of them. "There is a great danger hanging over us. Be careful. When I return we will set about locating your pendant. We must find it before Verrulf's followers can use it. Rose, with your power over it, I believe we can find all the answers we seek. Trust no one."

20

Murder Most Horrid

Shortly after five o'clock, the pair charged up Sackville Road towards the house. Dusk threw long shadows from the smart townhouses into the street. All was silent.

"Let's get back in the house, I don't feel safe out here," Rose said. Her thoughts switched to Mr Crank and Mr Gupta, who surely would have returned by now, and the trouble she was going to be in for leaving. Should she tell the butler? Would he even believe her if she did? *Can we trust him anyway? No.* She shivered, remembering Enna's words. *We can't trust no one.*

"Murder, Rose?" Rui said as he hurried along by her side. "Whatever are we involved in?"

Rose felt the same fear that she saw on Rui's face. "Enna won't let no one get murdered." She wiped beads of perspiration from her brow.

Ching Ching Ching Ching!

A bell rang out behind them, and Rui instinctively pushed Rose against the railings next to them.

"Coming through!" A boy of about their age swooped towards them on a bicycle, holding a long pole like a knight's lance.

"What on earth!" Rui exclaimed, trying to protect Rose's body with his own. Rose squeezed out from behind him.

"It's only the lampy." Rose exhaled. The boy took aim at the street lamp a little way ahead and with one swift twist of his pole, lit the wick. Without dismounting he sped off to the next.

The welcome light flooded the pavement around them as they hovered between the two lions at the entrance to the house. Rose looked up at the unlit windows of number thirteen Sackville Road.

"That's odd. It looks like no one's in? Mr Crank and Mr Gupta should be back by now." *And we should be in the doghouse for leaving.*

"Oi! Rose and Master Rui. Is that you? Where've ya been?" Jack Billings's voice carried from the laundry basement next door. "Something terrible has happened."

"Wait up." Rose unlocked the metal gate to the kitchen yard, her mind going back over the events of the day. *What more awful things could have happened?* Rui followed behind her down the steps before she climbed onto the upturned pail and peered over the wall. "Where is everyone?"

Jack Billings scurried towards her, his feet slipping in Rui's brocade slippers, the golden gown sweeping up the dirt behind him.

"What d'you look like?" Rose giggled, suddenly feeling reassured at the sight of someone she knew. Rui scrambled up next to her, supporting his weight on his arms.

"Why, Your Highness," Rui added, bobbing his head.

Jack lifted his heavy fringe, revealing the panicked eyes beneath. "It's all been going on at your place," he gulped. "The house is empty now. Nanna Potts said John the butler's gone to see his ma. In a right old state...and... something awful's happened. I've been looking out for you coming back and—"

"Hurry up and spit it out, Jack Billings, this is taking too long."

"Rose, listen up. This is serious," Jack panted. "The police, Rose. They was 'ere."

"Why, what you done?"

"No, it ain't me." He shook his head. "Not this time." He glanced at Rui. "They said they'd found the body of a one-handed man wearing a ruby turban down by the footings of the West Pier." His wide eyes met Rui's. "They said he'd been…murdered."

Lock and Key

Rui slumped over the kitchen table and sobbed into his arms, his crumpled deerstalker hat discarded next to him. The shock of Mr Gupta's murder had stolen all his clever words and Rose thought he looked broken.

She placed her arm around him. "I'm so sorry," she whispered.

Rose couldn't work out who'd do away with Mr Gupta or why. Did they kill him to get the missing pendant he'd stolen? And if so, what might they do to her and Rui if they were discovered meddling?

She'd told Jack Billings to stay away so Rui could grieve in peace. But really she didn't want him sniffing out information on what was going on. It was safer for him that way.

Rui picked at the sleeves of his grubby disguise. "It's just…it's just, I feel so alone in this strange place. Both the people I knew here are now dead. First Miss T and now Mr Gupta. And I can't make sense of any of it. In truth, I'm…I'm scared, Rose."

Rose nodded. "Me too, Rui," she spoke softly. "I thought coming here to work in this big house was gonna be the start of something new for me – away from the workhouse, away from Mrs Gritt, the mean governess there – I thought this was somewhere I would be…safe. Things haven't turned out like I'd hoped. And I know how it feels to be lonely too." She remembered the penance cupboard with a chill. "It can be frightening. But…the thing is, you ain't alone, Rui, and nor am I." She wiped away his tears with her thumbs. "We got each other now. And remember –" she kneeled beside him – "we've got a mystery to solve."

"Indeed we have." Rui gripped her hand. "Thank you, Rose." He drew in a long breath.

"And Enna should be here soon," Rose rallied, "and she can get hold of your uncle if you want, and—"

"No, no, no, my uncle would insist I return immediately. I'm not leaving here. I'm not leaving you! I made a promise to Miss T to help and protect you. To keep you safe.

I'm not about to break that promise."

Keep me safe. Rose shivered. *Two people are already dead,* she grimaced, *and I've only known about the pendant for three days.* The grand house suddenly felt very big, empty and cold. She didn't feel safe at all. Standing, she pulled away the black shroud from the kitchen clock – all the timepieces and mirrors in the house were covered, following Miss Templeforth's death that morning.

"It's not far off six now." Rose tried to hide the quiver in her voice. "Enna shouldn't be long. Hopefully she's found out more at the museum." But a horrible feeling gnawed at her. What if she bumped into whoever murdered Mr Gupta? Might they do something to her too? And what if they already had the cup and both pendants?

Rui's chair scraped the floor as he stood. "We are no good to anyone just sitting about moping We should continue our investigation. The book!" he announced, his eyes fierce.

"Yes!" Rose looked up; she had forgotten all about it. "Mr Gupta's journal. Enna said it was important. D'you reckon they took it, you know…when they…" She thought of the picture Mr Gupta had shown them in the library, with the sketch of the Amber Cup. "Do you s'pose it might have something important in it? About the cup…? About my pendant?" Rose's eyes blazed.

"Maybe! We should check his room." Rui pulled his detective hat back on.

They set off up into the dark house. Rose turned on the lobby lights as they passed. The stuffed animals glared down at them as they climbed the grand staircase two steps at a time. Finally, they reached Mr Gupta's room.

"It's open!" Rui gasped. "He would never leave it unlocked. He always kept his belongings under lock and key on the boat. This is most unusual."

Rui was right. Rose remembered she'd seen Mr Gupta locking his bedroom door as soon as he arrived at the house.

They peered in. Loose feathers from ruined bed pillows covered everything, ripped-up books and pulled-out drawers were scattered around the room. Mr Gupta's coloured tunics spilled out of an upturned wooden trunk.

"It's been done over!" Rose said, marching inside.

A sharp breeze sent some loose pages of paper up into the air. Rose hurried towards the window ledge where the lace curtains blew in. Sweeping them aside, she leaned out. A flat roof jutted from the back of the house, just a short distance below. "They must have broke in through this window."

Rui slumped onto the messed-up bed and Rose joined him.

"What now?" Rose asked, staring at the mess. "None of this is making any sense." Rose leafed through some of the debris, but it was obvious whoever had done this had made a thorough job of it.

"Enna's skrying waters were trying to warn us of Mr Gupta's murder, not of his involvement." Rui swung around to face her.

Rose wasn't so sure about Mr Gupta not being involved. She still felt certain he had taken the pendant, but she didn't want to upset Rui any more than he already was, so she kept quiet.

"Mr Gupta is an innocent man. I owe it to him to solve this mystery and prove his innocence. He has paid the highest price," Rui began. "And we may well have been the last people to see Mr Gupta – when he was with that stranger in the Pleasure Gardens."

"The one who smoked them Wild Woodbines," Rose added. "And they exchanged something." *Like a stolen pendant*, she thought to herself.

"Correct! So, the questions remain: where did they go next, and what were they discussing?" Rui pondered. "We know they discovered Mr Gupta's body under the West Pier, and—"

Just then something shot through the open window, ripping the curtain from its hooks. A furry ball of thrashing limbs thumped onto the floor ahead of them, writhing about, all entangled in lace.

"Bahula!" Rui cried.

Mr Gupta's monkey emerged, dishevelled. He pulled away the ripped material. Jumping free he stood on the ruined curtain and shrieked.

Bahula's red hat had gone and his waistcoat had a nasty rip under the arm. "He looks in a dreadful state. Shh, Bahula," Rui hushed, offering his hand for Bahula to sniff. "Whatever happened to you?" Rui straightened. "He's terrified."

"Or angry," Rose said, keeping her distance.

Bahula pointed at the window. "*Ah ah ah oo oo OO!*" he screeched, his hair on end.

"It's like he is trying to speak." Rui kneeled down and rubbed the creature's head. Bahula calmed, his tiny shoulders still trembling. He lifted a thin arm onto Rui's shoulder. Rui pulled him into a cuddle.

"Rose, do you think he saw what happened to Mr Gupta?"

"*EE ee ee OO oo oo!*" Bahula bounded across to the furthest corner of the room and began flinging Mr Gupta's colourful belongings in every direction.

"I think he's lost his marbles. Gone crackers," Rose muttered. "Should we trap him in the cupboard and call someone to get rid of him?"

"Absolutely not, Rose!" Rui chided. "It's like he is trying to show us something."

Bahula clawed at the floorboards he'd exposed and looked back at them, his short tail a-twitch.

Rui kneeled by his side and ran his hand over the cleared space, stopping as one of the boards wobbled.

"This floorboard is loose!" Rui said.

"Well I never!" Rose watched him lever it up.

Bahula dashed backwards and forwards, chattering. Rui removed the board and, placing it to one side, peered into the darkness beneath. Rolling up his sleeve he reached in up to his shoulder.

"Well?" Rose asked.

His green eyes glittered. "I have something!" Grinning, he withdrew a thick silver book.

"Is that Mr Gupta's?" Rose crouched beside him.

"I believe so. Clever creatures, monkeys, and our Bahula is no exception. The gods are on our side, Rose." Rui beamed.

He held the book aloft, and the enamel eye on the cover glimmered in the lamplight. "I think we have found our first clue, or maybe even the advantage." He leaned over and patted Bahula's head. "And you, my hairy friend, you are…"

"Proper clever!" Rose finished off, and she meant it. Bahula tilted his head and grinned at her. *Perhaps,* Rose thought, *this monkey isn't such a rotter after all.*

A Strange Keepsake

Rose and Rui lay on the floor of Mr Gupta's room, the book opened flat in front of them. Rui flicked through the singed pages.

"What's that writing, Rui? It looks like more code," Rose asked.

Rui sat up rolling his shoulders. "It is a very rare form of an ancient scripture called Sanskrit. Not understood by many."

"Can you read it?" she asked.

"Yes, Rose." His eyes widened with disbelief. "It's the strangest thing. On the voyage over here I told you Mr Gupta had taught me to translate some ancient scripture.

Well this is the same type! It's as though he knew I may have need of it."

"And what's that?" She pointed at the loose piece of paper poking from the front.

Rui flipped the book to the beginning. "It's a newspaper cutting," he remarked, studying it, "which Mr Gupta has carefully attached inside."

"What's it about?" Rose strained to see it.

"It's an article from *The Times of India* dated June, 1863."

"That's over forty years ago."

Rui nodded. "The headline reads: 'The Cursed Scriptures Strike Again.' Rose." He glanced up. "It's about the accident – the one in which Mr Gupta lost his hand."

"That's a strange keepsake," Rose said.

"And look here, this photograph shows him meeting the British expedition leader who returned the cursed scrolls. It's taken at the docks in Bombay." Rose looked over his shoulder.

The black and white picture showed a younger-looking Mr Gupta exchanging a scrolled parchment with a stony-faced army man, whose head had been circled in black. On Mr Gupta's left-hand side stood a beautiful lady wearing a sari, whose long dark hair reached her waist.

"Why has he ringed that man like that?" Rose asked. "And who is the lady?"

"It's intriguing, isn't it?" Rui traced his fingers along the caption beneath. "It says this is Mr Gupta from the Jaipur Museum, accompanied by his wife, accepting the return of ancient Indian scrolls from British expedition leader, Sergeant Anthony Funnel."

They both stared at each other.

"Anthony Funnel!" Rose's eyes narrowed. "That's who Enna mentioned in her caravan earlier."

"Yes, the boy Miss T once knew. Enna said Anthony Funnel helped overcome the guardian of Verrulf's pendant many years ago." He ran his hand through his black hair. "Surely this is more than just coincidence, Rose." He passed the cutting to her.

"So that's Anthony Funnel." Rose examined the photograph. He looked like a very sad young man, Rose thought. His thin lips were cast at a lopsided angle across his narrow face. Then Rose caught sight of something else. "It can't be!" She scrutinized the strange disc-shaped pendant hanging around his neck. "Rui – I think he's wearing Verrulf's pendant. Look!"

"Elephas Maximus, he is! But how did he come to have it? Didn't Enna tell us that the pendant had disappeared after its old guardian had been defeated?"

"That Anthony Funnel must have taken it after all. We must let Enna know." Rose's mind started ticking like a speeding clock. "So what happened next? I mean after this picture were taken for the newspaper? You said Mr Gupta lost his hand in an accident, or something?"

"Indeed…" Rui returned his attention to the article. "Yes, the train crash," Rui mumbled to himself as he hurriedly read. Rose tingled with anticipation and tried to crane over Rui's shoulder.

"This says that Mr Gupta travelled to Bombay to greet the arriving expedition – that must be why Funnel was there," said Rui, looking up. "The scriptures he was returning were extremely valuable. They contained ancient spells – some of the oldest known to exist. His bringing them back to India caused quite a stir –" He paused to read further. "It mentions that the maharajah had planned a grand ceremony to celebrate the scriptures' return. They were to be exhibited in the newly appointed museum in Jaipur."

"Where Mr Gupta worked," Rose added. "Right?"

Rui nodded. "But a terrible fire broke out. The train derailed and there were many fatalities, including Mr Gupta's own wife!" Rui looked up. "Gracious, I had no idea."

"Poor Mr Gupta," Rose said, and she meant it.

Rui carried on. "It then describes Mr Gupta's heroic behaviour – you know, running the rescue operation despite having lost his own hand."

"And his wife," Rose interjected.

"The scriptures themselves perished in the flames," Rui continued. He stared at Rose. "Even today people talk about those scriptures being cursed, you know. That the spells they contained were evil – some even say it was their curse started the fire."

"What about that Anthony Funnel? Did he survive too?"

"Ah, let me see." Rui ran his finger along the article. "Here is his name. No." He looked at her. "It says he too perished in the flames and was buried on Indian soil close by."

"So Enna was right. He did die abroad."

"It would appear so. But—"

Rap! Rap! Rap!

A series of urgent knocks came from the front door below.

They stood as one.

RAP! RAP! RAP!

The same sequence, but louder.

"Enna!" Rose said.

"We can't be sure," Rui cautioned. He concealed the book in the waistband of his scruffy breeches, covering it with his jacket. Rose replaced the floorboard and as an afterthought pushed some of the clothes over it.

Outside the front door, a shadowy figure swung up and down on his heels, smoking a cigarette.

The Police

Rose and Rui rushed down to the lobby. Rose hoped with all her heart to see Enna Lee at the door – they had so much to tell her. Not only had they found Mr Gupta's book, but they'd also discovered that Anthony Funnel had deceived both Enna and Miss T, and taken Verrulf's pendant all those years ago. She opened the front door a crack and peered outside.

But instead of Enna, a policeman wearing a floor-length coat and domed helmet stood with his back to them.

"H-hello?" Rose stuttered.

Swinging around, the policeman flicked his cigarette into the basement yard below.

"Good evening, I'm Jonathan Banks, Detective in Chief of the Hove Constabulary." He slipped into the lobby. "I wasn't certain anyone was in." He pushed the door shut with his back. His auburn moustache twitched as he removed his helmet, revealing neat hair of the same colour that was greased back on either side of a centre parting.

"Detective!" Rui stepped forward, eyebrows raised. "Welcome, Sir," he announced with a bow. "I myself am adept in the art of detection and subterfuge. What's more—"

A real Sherlock Holmes to help us. About time, Rose thought with relief as Rui continued talking.

"I have read every Sherlock Holmes novel to date, and—" Rui grappled with the band of his trousers, searching for Mr Gupta's book.

"I see," Banks interrupted and placed his helmet on the dresser. "Now, who is in charge here?"

"Well I s'pose that'll be me." Rose shrugged. "The house is in mourning following our mistress's death. The other staff have been sent home and the butler is away visiting his mother, so it's just us two what's left here."

Banks coughed into his leathered fist. "Well, I regret to inform you there's been a murder. Down on the seafront, this very afternoon," his deep voice geared up, "and we have reason to believe the gentleman concerned – the deceased – was staying at this address. A man wearing a turban with a missing hand." As he peeled off his gloves, a tattoo on his wrist flashed momentarily into view, an inky black sun with a human face.

Rose backed away. *The peelers are in on it too!* She glanced at Rui, whose hand shot to his mouth.

Banks leaned forward. "You know this individual I speak of?" His pupils dilated.

"Yes," Rui said, stepping between them, purposefully drawing the detective's attention away from Rose, who he was keen to protect. The waistband of his breeches now sat very high concealing the book that was wedged there. "Mr Gupta was my tutor for my trip to England and a renowned scholar back in my home town of Jaipur. My uncle, the maharajah, will be expecting a thorough investigation, Sir. How did he die?"

"Strangulation," Banks grunted. "You say you are nephew to a maharajah?" He appraised Rui's moth-eaten outfit, his chin pressing against his neck.

Before Rui could respond, Bahula hurtled down the staircase and into the lobby.

"THAT monkey!" Banks declared through clenched teeth, as he loosened his collar and stroked a scratch mark on his neck.

Bahula hissed at the detective and arched his back.

With his tail curled beneath him the monkey sidestepped away.

"Have you met Bahula before, Sir?" Rui asked, one brow raised.

"No, no, no, I said that IS a monkey…an unusual house guest in these parts. I suffer from a revulsion of ALL primates…" His words ended in a hiss, revealing teeth blackened at the gum line.

Bahula scuttled across the tiled floor and sheltered beneath a chair.

"Anyway," Banks clicked his heels together, "back to my official business. A witness came forward claiming to have overheard a heated discussion between the deceased and a stranger. A discussion about a book…of some kind."

They're after Mr Gupta's book! Rose realized with a gulp.

Banks rocked backwards and forwards on the balls of his feet. "We believe this item may be pertinent to the investigation. Have you seen it?" He searched their faces.

Rose shook her head, her mind running in rings. Could he be the same bloke they'd seen with Mr Gupta in the Pleasure Gardens? He'd worn a similar coat and he was smoking… *But he's a policeman!* Rose thought, alarmed.

Whoever he was, she wanted him gone.

"No, we ain't seen a book. Shocking about poor Mr Gupta and thank you kindly for letting us know. Now, you must be awful busy – we won't keep you." Rose gestured towards the door.

"In that case, I wish to inspect his room here. Show me to it." Banks strode across the lobby, his stale odour trailing behind him.

"It's upstairs." Rose followed, glancing back at Rui.

On the landing, Rose led the way to Mr Gupta's room. "In there, Sir." Rose switched on the light.

Banks gripped the door frame. The veins in his beetroot neck bulged.

"Someone's already been here. Did you not hear anything?" The words twisted from his mouth.

"No, Sir!" Rose said with feigned shock. "We was out. Not been back long since you came."

"Very well." He stomped off down the stairs with Rose and Rui following behind.

In the lobby he turned to them. "Should you think of anything, FIND anything, see ANYTHING, you come to the police station and you ask for me, Jonathan Banks." Banks pulled on his gloves, his fingers splayed. "I'm leading this investigation. Have I made myself clear?" They nodded. "Good." He pulled up his high collar and walked to the front door, grabbing his helmet on the way.

"The funeral, Sir!" Rui's voice sounded reedy. "Mr Gupta must be cremated as soon as possible – it is our faith.

There is much to prepare, his family must be informed, and it is important that his body is—"

"I will see to it after the post-mortem," Banks scoffed with disinterest as he headed for the entrance.

They both jumped as the front door slammed shut.

Rose rushed to Rui. "Do you think it was him with Mr Gupta in the Pleasure Gardens? You saw his tattoo? He smoked too."

"Yes, the image of the black sun." Rui's lips pinched. "Do you believe he is the man you saw in the vision?"

"No." Rose shook her head. "The man I saw had much older-looking hands, and he sounded different." The memory made her shudder. "He might be the companion who travelled with him. But I never saw his face so I can't be sure."

"Just how many of them can there be in this group?" Rui muttered. "Enna suspected a dozen. Twelve men of power and influence." Rui tutted to himself.

"Enna!" Rose realized with a start, looking at the clock. "She ain't here and it's already half six." The knot of anxiety in her tummy tightened. "Whatever is going on? Now even the police are in on it, Rui! What are we to do?" She threw her hands in the air. "There's a bunch of crazies with black sun tattoos going around killing people, and some dark spirit, a few thousand years old, is collywobbling around in some old cup. And somehow *I'm* meant to be involved?" She drew a quick breath. "If someone had sat me down last week and told me all this would happen I would've thought them half-baked and—" She turned to Rui, who was pacing about with his finger pressed to his lips.

"Rui, you ain't listened to a word I just said, have you?"

He spun to face her. "This journal." Rui produced Mr Gupta's life's work and smoothed the embossed cover. "Enna told us it's important, but she didn't know how." Rui looked at Rose, deadly serious. "I believe it could help us to discover who these black sun criminals are...and stop them. It could help us find your pendant, Rose. I believe this journal holds the secrets we need to solve this mystery."

24

Mr Gupta's Journal

I n the library, Rui sat cross-legged in the large armchair studying Mr Gupta's unusual journal. Bahula had nestled behind him, his fingers busy as he inspected Rui's hair.

"Wild Woodbine!" Rose said as she rushed in holding a tray that rattled with crockery. Rui and Bahula looked up. "I checked the cigarette end that the detective flicked into the basement and it's filterless and strong – a Wild Woodbine all right."

On seeing Rose's tray of food Bahula jumped down to greet her.

Rose settled the tray down on the footstool next to Rui. "Cocoa, biscuits and some cheese sandwiches. It's all I could find." She wiped her hands on her green velvet dress and sat down.

A thin, hairy arm reached up from behind the footstool and snatched a handful of biscuits.

"As we expected," Rui muttered, grabbing a sandwich absent-mindedly, "it is looking more likely that Banks was with Mr Gupta in the Pleasure Gardens, but what we must discover is how is he involved and why he would meet with Mr Gupta." He stuffed the sandwich into his mouth.

"And now it's nearly eight o'clock and Enna still isn't here. She said she'd be here by six, didn't she? Do you think," Rose swallowed, "that something's...happened to her?" Rose didn't want to say it. She worried her words might make it true.

"We have to trust that she can look after herself. She's immortal after all. And she said that we must do what we can without her. What's the English delicacy in these sandwiches?" Rui asked grabbing another. "I detect some actual flavour."

"Cheddar cheese," Rose answered with a frown. Something deep in her belly told her all wasn't fine with Enna. "That police detective must be one of them twelve powerful local men Enna was talking about, and if they got the likes of him on their side who else might be on their books?"

Her mind recalled the newspaper article attached inside Mr Gupta's journal and she turned to Rui. "But I still don't understand what happened to Verrulf's pendant. How did it get back here from India if that Funnel character died in that train crash? It can't be chance that Funnel was with them scriptures, given that he'd already taken Verrulf's pendant for himself. What were he after? Something very fishy is going on there."

"I don't know, Rose, but as I expected, Mr Gupta was figuring something out."

"Or he was up to his neck in all this."

"Rose!" Rui protested.

"I'm just saying. Seeing Mr Gupta in that photograph with Funnel don't make him look any more innocent to me, and that's the truth of it."

She walked away and poked the embers in the grate until they licked back into flames. Bahula jumped down and stood next to her.

The clock in the lobby dinged eight times – and still there'd not been a whisper from Enna. Rose squeezed her eyes shut, willing her to be safe. She felt sick with worry. Someone had killed Mr Gupta and at least one policeman was siding with whoever did it, and her pendant hadn't called to her again. Did that mean Verrulf's guardian already had it? And that they had Enna too?

"This journal contains so much information – about places and objects all over the world. Unbelievable. It would take me a year just to read it all," Rui said, busily flicking through the pages.

Rose warmed her hands against the gentle heat of the fire and noticed Bahula copying her. She smiled at him, and he looked pleased. *Poor little mite has barely left our side since that horrid Banks went.*

"Aha, Rose! I've found something." Rui interrupted her thoughts. "You need to see this."

Rose dragged a stool close.

"Firstly, look at how all the pages of Mr Gupta's book have been scorched." He flicked through a few pages, showing the blackened corners.

"Yes, I noticed that before," said Rose, remembering Mr Gupta showing his drawing of the Amber Cup in the library when they'd first arrived. "Like they'd been burned."

"Precisely!"

"The train fire!" Rose picked up on his thread. She snatched up the newspaper article from the side table. "In the picture Mr Gupta had two hands. She looked closer, poking out of his pocket was...*his book*. "Rui, he's got his blessed book with him in the picture!" She showed him.

"Bravo!" He nodded. "Now bear with me. You see, it would appear that Mr Gupta, on that fated train journey from Bombay, managed to copy a spell from those scriptures before the flames took hold. It's recorded right here – and dated 1863."

Rose cocked her head. "The year of the train crash? Right?"

"Correct. Mr Gupta had kept this spell a secret for all these years. I've certainly never heard word of it back in India. Which means I may have in my hand the only spell surviving from those cursed scriptures – the rest having been lost to the fire."

"What does it say?" Rose whispered excitedly.

"The spell he transcribed is about a magic cup." His eyes shot to Rose.

"The Amber Cup!" they said together.

Drawing a deep breath Rui concentrated. "This spell concerns the murkiest and most dangerous form of black magic." He shifted uncomfortably in his seat. "The spell is called 'udayath shyaamala nakshatra'."

With his words, the wall lights flickered. Bahula hid his face in his hands, and peered out through his long fingers. Sparks shot from the grate.

Rose turned to face Rui. "What does that mean?" she murmured, her eyes jumping about the room.

"Its translation from Sanskrit is 'Rising a Dark Star'. The words say a vessel of spiritual purity is needed to carry

the risen soul," Rui whispered. "It's dangerous magic…
No one is sure it can even work." Rui suddenly looked
very pale. "It's…necromancy, Rose."

"Necro – what?" Rose breathed.

"Necromancy…" Rui paused, his hand trembling on
the page. "It means to communicate with the dead. But this
spell speaks about…bringing a dark soul back to life."

Necromancy

Rose clapped her hand over her mouth. A deep chill had filled the library, despite the flames dancing in the hearth. *Necro-something-or-other?* Rose thought with a shudder.

"So that's why they're after Mr Gupta's journal. For the magic spell that uses the cup to bring someone dead back to life?" Rui peered back into its pages. "Umm. Mr Gupta took great care in copying the illustrations that accompany the text. You need to see this." Rui offered the book to Rose.

A swirling image of black smoke trailed from a glowing red cup. "It's the same picture of the Amber Cup Mr Gupta showed us when you first got here," Rose said, studying it closely. By holding the page at different angles she noticed strange creatures hidden in the smoke trails. All of them were distorted and mixed up together· thin arms with crooked fingers, elongated bodies and mean shiny eyes and mouths stretching into unnatural chasms, all broken and twisting within the tendrils of the smoke.

"I think they're C-creeplings – or bits of them." Rose gulped, passing the book back to Rui. She couldn't bear to look at them.

"And beneath," Rui continued, "it says that this spell must be performed when the planets align. Elephas Maximus!" Rui shot up.

"What?"

"It's just that Mr Gupta told me something else on our voyage to England." His hands made a steeple by his mouth as he marched backwards and forwards in front of the fire. "He told me that a mystical alignment was to occur during our stay in England, in which five of the planets would form a rare astronomical arc in the sky. At this time, the supernatural forces will be strengthened... He said that it was going to happen on the thirty-first of October... That's tomorrow night!"

"It's called All Hallows' Eve here," Rose said with a swallow.

"Is that good?"

"Nah, I wouldn't say so."

A memory of the workhouse came to Rose unbidden. Miss Gritt would always say: "All Hallows' Eve is when the devil takes to horseback to steal all the naughty children." And the housemistress always insisted the window to the dormitory be left open that night – just in case the devil wanted to stop by. Rose shivered.

"Mr Gupta said it will mark a time when the space between this world and other worlds will be at its thinnest. This particular astronomical event is extremely rare."

Rose noticed that Mr Gupta's book had fallen open on a page marked by a ribbon. It was the very last entry Mr Gupta had written.

Rose picked it up. "Look, Rui, some of these letters are English." She traced her fingers across the initials *JB*. "What does the rest of it say?" She offered him the book.

Rui hastily buried his head in the text. Clearing his throat, he read directly from the book with gusto. "'JB took Miss Templeforth's pendant.' There!" He prodded the page.

"JB? Well, that copper said his name was Jonathan Banks; it must be him!" Rose offered, trying to keep up. "And, if we're right about Banks being the stranger with Mr Gupta at the Pleasure Gardens, that makes sense, don't it?"

"Mr Gupta also writes: 'the Brotherhood of the Black Sun mean great harm'."

"The Brotherhood of the Black Sun?" Rose repeated, her eyes widening. "So that's what they call themselves."

Rui pressed on. "'They intend to use the cup to raise a dead spirit'," he read. "'They must be stopped from getting the second pendant'." He looked up, eyebrows arched. "I knew Mr Gupta's intentions were honourable. He'd been carrying out his own investigation, trying to stop them!"

Something fluttered from the pages of the open book and fell to the floor.

"What's that?" Rui leaned over it.

Rose picked up a small rectangular card about the size of a matchbox. Spidery letters were scrawled across it in a rushed hand.

BBS meet at headquarters 30th October. Nine o'clock.

"BBS?" Rose read the initials aloud. She turned the card over. The other side was matt black, with fancy gilt lettering.

*Stitchworthy & Co, Tobacconist
47 Church Road, Hove.*

Rose caught sight of something glimmering beneath the

gold lettering. "Hang on a minute, there's something else here." She walked to the fire and angled the card to try to get a clear look at it. An image lurked behind the writing which could only be seen if the light caught it at the right angle: a sullen face framed by the blazing spokes of a black sun.

"It's them all right. The rotters."

Rui craned behind her. "BBS is the abbreviation of the Brotherhood of the Black Sun! This must be their calling card."

"Rui, it's not far off nine now," she said, glancing through to the clock in the lobby. "That road isn't more than half a mile away. But –" her shoulders slumped – "Enna, we said we'd wait for her here. What should we do?"

"We must go!" Excitement flooded Rui's face. He grabbed the last sandwich and stuffed it in his pocket. "Rose, this is our chance to uncover the identity of this secret group and get your pendant back. Enna would want us to go. If we don't get word from her tonight, we will search for her, I promise." He pulled on his deerstalker hat and ran from the room, clutching the journal. "I'm going to hide this somewhere safe. The Brotherhood of the Black Sun must not get their hands on it. I intend to finish the job that Mr Gupta started." He disappeared through the door. "By the way, we need matches, rope and –" he stuck his head back around the door frame – "Rose, do you have a revolver?"

"God's teeth, Rui. No, I do not!" Rose threw her hands in the air.

"No, no. Very well. So, rope, matches –" he counted the list off on his fingers and disappeared from view once more – "and, now let me see – a hatpin. Yes, a hatpin would do us very well."

Rose could hear him climbing the staircase. "I don't have none of those things you're after, except the matches maybe," she shouted after him.

"In that case we shall rely on our wits!" he called from the top of the stairs.

Rose pulled on her frayed gloves. *I'm the guardian,* she told herself. She knew Enna would want her to go, to be brave and to do everything she could to stop this horrible Brotherhood of the Black Sun and stop Verrulf. If not, she knew all merry hell was going to break loose from the cup. She gritted her teeth. *No matter what, I'm gonna get my pendant back.*

26

Stitchworthy's Tobacconist's

It was a dark and starless night, whipped by a biting wind. Rose linked arms with Rui. "It's freezing." She shivered. Leaves and rubbish flew along the pavement as they hurried towards Stitchworthy's Tobacconist's. Bahula clung to Rui's warmth inside his coat.

With a sharp rush of laughter and shouting, the door to the Albion Public House suddenly crashed open in front of them, and a man stumbled out backwards. Rose and Rui jumped to the side as he staggered past, slurring a sea shanty. Rose breathed a sigh of relief. "Stay close, you hear," she said to Rui. "Being out at this time is no place for the likes of us. Come on." She pulled him along with her.

Ahead of them, the grand Town Hall loomed into the night sky like a cathedral. Its large clock face glowed moonlike from the impressive tower.

"It's already gone nine o'clock. It must be one of those," Rose said, counting down the shop numbers.

"Here it is!" Rui stopped ahead.

The shop sign hung above them: *Stitchworthy & Co, Tobacconist, est. 1907*. The gold letters glinted against the black board.

"Look!" Rose pointed to the barely visible insignia beneath the lettering – a face set within a black sun. Only noticeable from an angle, Rose observed, and if you moved a pace either side it vanished – a trick of the light. *Just like that business card.*

Rui had noticed it too. "Strange, don't you think? How you'd completely miss that, unless you *knew* to look for it."

Rose blew through her gloves onto her numb fingers.

"The hornets' nest," Rui muttered. Bahula's head protruded from Rui's coat, and he gnashed his teeth.

"Rui, someone's in there." A velvet curtain hung behind the window display, blocking the view into the shop. But above its rail, an internal light flickered.

Rose edged along the shopfront, peering at the items exhibited in the window. She wasn't really sure what was sold in a tobacconist's beyond tobacco, but she could see silver drinking flasks, gentlemen's pipes and snuff boxes, all arranged on a swathe of black velvet.

"Over here, Rose. I can see in." Rui signalled from the doorway.

The "closed" sign was sandwiched flat behind a black roller blind that was pulled all the way down. Rui's face pressed against the curve of the bay window in front of the display. It offered them a narrow but elevated view into the sunken interior of the shop. "They're down there." His breath fogged the glass.

Men in tailored suits were gathered inside the candlelit shop.

"They all look well-to-do, don't they?" Rose grimaced.

"We have the Brotherhood of the Black Sun in our sights, Rose. But we can't hear anything from up here. We need to get closer."

"Closer, right." Rose stepped a few paces backwards and peered into the shadowy alley at the side of the shop. "Oi, down 'ere," she said, tiptoeing into the darkness of the passage. "P'raps this leads around the back."

Rose felt her way along the damp brickwork, which formed a crumbling archway above. Foul water dripped overhead and the place stank.

On the other side of the passage, a wide cobbled path

stretched unevenly around a tall brick wall which concealed the backyards to the shops. They followed it until Rose stopped at a black gate fixed into the wall. "This is it." She pointed to the notice nailed there.

TRESSPASSERS BEWARE

THIS GATE REMAINS LOCKED AT ALL TIMES; TOBACCO DELIVERIES SHOULD REQUEST SUPERVISED ENTRY FROM THE SHOPKEEPER.

Rose turned the handle and forced her weight as quietly as she could against the door, but it wouldn't budge. "What now?" she whispered. Stepping back she pulled her coat closer against the wind whistling up behind them.

In a flash, Bahula leaped on top of the wall.

"Bahula!" Rui murmured, swiping his arms to try to catch him. *"Ee ee ee,"* Bahula cackled. With his short tail swinging wildly he disappeared over the other side. Almost immediately, there was a scraping noise, as the bolt was drawn back. The doorway to the yard creaked open to reveal Bahula dangling by one arm inside the open frame, grinning.

"You clever boy, Bahula," Rose said under her breath.

Bahula let go of the frame and jumped onto Rui's

shoulder as he passed through the open gate. Rose gently pushed it to behind them.

The stone yard of the tobacconist's was strewn with wooden crates of various sizes, most of which had been prised open. One had "CHERRY TOBACCO" printed in block letters, with "GUATEMALA" emblazoned underneath.

Rose stared up at the unwelcoming facade of the back of the shop: brown-bricked with unlit windows and cold stone steps leading to the back door. She stepped over a dead rat and shivered – the place felt evil. She poked about looking for a clue or some way of sneaking in, when a curious silhouette in the shadows caught her attention. She crept forward.

Something narrow and tall stood shrouded beneath a thick oilcloth, just next to the backdoor steps. Rose lifted the cloth. It hid a full-length standing mirror, on a swivel frame of dark wood. She stroked the polished surface. It felt expensive – not something that would normally just be left outside.

"Rose, down here," Rui whispered, crouching in the shadows of the building. The cold flagstones stung her knees as she rested beside him. Rui examined a large trapdoor fixed flat into the yard floor.

"This must lead to a cellar," Rose said.

"Umm." Rui tugged the chain attached to the handles. "Bolted and padlocked."

"Now what? That creepy lot of no-gooders are in there with my pendant, and we're stuck out here, with all the rats and empty boxes."

"Why, we break in of course." Rui disappeared amongst the crates, lifting the discarded lids and peering inside the open boxes.

"Break in? Using what?" She hugged her coat around her, her eyes hopping about. This whole place gave her the collywobbles.

"Well," Rui's head popped up at the same time as Bahula's, "these crates have all been forced open. One may therefore deduce that some kind of tool has been used to leverage the lids. Find that tool, and we have our key to opening those trapdoors."

Leaving Rui to it, Rose tiptoed up the steps to the back door and pressed her ear against it. It was silent. She squinted up at the windows to see if any were open, but they were all shut tight against the wind.

"It is quite elementary, you know," Rui continued, "that the majority of break-ins occur not by tools taken to the victim's dwelling by a thief, but by items found readily available outside. Something like…THIS!" Rui reappeared holding aloft a wrench.

Just then, a key twisted in the lock of the tobacconist's back door. *Someone's coming.* A cold fear shot through Rose. Rui and Bahula spun to face her.

"Hide!" Rose mouthed. Rui and Bahula ducked down amongst the crates. The doorknob turned and then clicked.

Rose jumped to the side, and hid in a narrow shadow. The door swung open. Rose's insides clenched as someone's shoes tip-tapped down the stone steps next to her. A man mumbled to himself.

Rose could just see his feet, buttoned into spats and trousers, unfashionably short, exposing socks pulled high over spindly ankles.

"Snodgrass do this, Snodgrass do that," the man whined. "Hand out the drinks, take the coats. Get the mirror," he huffed.

The man threw back the cloth covering the mirror, and Rose could see through his reflection that he had a moustache so thin he might have drawn it on himself with a ruler. She leaned back into the shadows.

Snodgrass heaved the heavy mirror onto his back with a groan as it squashed him low to the ground. He climbed back up to the shop, grunting with each step.

"Hurry along, Snodgrass," someone called from inside. "We haven't got all night, man."

The mirror banged into the door frame. "I'm coming –"

Snodgrass puffed – "Sir." He stumbled inside, leaving the door wide open behind him.

This is our chance. Rose tiptoed up the steps, and in a flash Rui and Bahula were by her side. They peered in. The sweet smell of tobacco oozed out along the thin corridor.

Ahead, Snodgrass disappeared inside the room at the very end. The hum of gentlemen's voices carried from the same direction. It led to the shop floor.

"Wait here, Bahula," Rui instructed. The monkey's ears pricked up crossly.

"Keep a lookout?" Rose suggested instead. "And stay out of sight." Bahula leaped back into the yard and hid amongst the tobacco crates.

Rui grinned. "We're in," he mouthed stepping across the threshold.

Rose nodded, her heart drumming, as they crept into the headquarters of the Brotherhood of the Black Sun.

Inside the Dragon's Lair

A ripple of applause carried from the open doorway in front of Rose and Rui, followed by muffled chatter and cheers.

Rose still couldn't quite believe what they were doing. With their backs against the corridor wall, she and Rui sidled towards the sunken shop. They knew the entire Brotherhood of the Black Sun were gathered there. *We must be off our rockers*, she thought, her pulse racing.

"Make room for the mirror," a voice boomed. "Put it in the middle, Snodgrass. And careful, don't break it, man!"

Rose and Rui crept up to a thick crimson curtain bunched up on one side of the internal doorway at the end of the corridor. Rose felt an icy rush of danger.

Before they could plan their next move, a gust of wind rattled down the corridor from the open back door and the curtain concealing them billowed.

"Snodgrass, where's that breeze coming from?" someone barked. "You've left the back door open, you fool. Close it at once."

He's going to find us! Rose's heart jumped into her mouth.

Her eyes darted every which way. Knowing they didn't have time to escape, Rui pulled Rose behind the heavy curtain just in time. They pinned themselves against the wall inside the shop, hidden by the drape. Snodgrass scurried by.

"That was close," Rose mouthed, trying to steady herself. The back door slammed shut and Snodgrass's footsteps returned. He paused in front of the curtain and Rose held her breath, squeezing Rui's hand.

Without a hint of suspicion, Snodgrass whipped the curtain across the rail, blocking their view into the shop. Rose stumbled into Rui as they tiptoed behind it.

Muttering to himself, Snodgrass picked his way back down the steps that led to the shop floor.

"Tremendous!" Rui mouthed back to Rose.

The thick curtain smelled musty, and pinpricks of light shone through its moth holes. Rui inched open a slit at one end and peered through. Satisfied it was safe, he shuffled over to make enough room for Rose to see too.

A dim central light hung over the strange mirror; the only other light came from the candles flickering in the dark corners. Shadows danced across the faces of the men, who chattered nervously to one another.

Whoever these men were, it was clear they weren't born with money. They had acquired it, and recently. *New money,* Rose thought, judging by the oversized cashmere coats, gaudy high-collared shirts and the whiff of spiced cologne that hung in the air.

No light penetrated behind the curtain and Rose felt certain they could not be seen, although in truth, she would have felt safer dangling on a threadbare rope with a bunch of hungry lions snapping at her heels.

"Look, by the door," Rui whispered.

She shuffled closer to him and nudged the curtain open a little further. A tall, imposing man stood near the shop entrance. He had neat auburn hair and a moustache of the same colour.

"Banks," she hissed to Rui. The detective stood apart from the others and puffed on a cigarette.

A slow hollow clap drew Banks's attention.

"Who is that?" Rui murmured. The crowd parted just enough for them to see.

An old man stood behind the glass sales counter opposite, his head bowed. He was clapping slowly.

Looking up, his thin lips cut a lopsided smile. His hollow cheeks sprouted wild sideburns.

Rose's hands shot to her face. She recognized him at once, the thin face, the lopsided smile – "That's... that's—"

"An aged Anthony Funnel," Rui whispered. "But how can it be? The newspaper said he had died in India some forty years ago?"

One half of Funnel's face was shiny with scarred skin and a nasty black hole beneath his eyelid where his eye should have been. *It looks like the train fire got him, though.* Rose swallowed.

Funnel's good eye stared eagle-like at the twelve smartly dressed men before him.

Then Rose spotted it with a gasp – a large circular amber pendant dangling around his neck. Dark, but for the dot of orange in the middle. The opposite design to Miss Templeforth's: *It's Verrulf's pendant,* Rose realized with a start.

"He's got the other pendant, Rui!" Rose studied the man's hands with growing horror. They perched on the counter like two spiders embalmed in skin. *You can't forget hands like them.* "It's him, the old fella I saw before in

~ 185 ~

the carriage. And that's the other pendant for sure," she breathed. "But where's mine?"

"Welcome, my brothers." The old man's rasp sent a chill through Rose, his voice thick and shifty, like smoke.

"Let us begin," Funnel continued, a wicked smile creeping sideways between his sideburns.

The old man tugged a gold-tassled cord and the red curtains behind him parted, revealing a gilt-framed portrait of himself. The painting mirrored him exactly; the same wonky smile, the same fierce sideburns brushed upwards, the same missing eye, but…in the portrait he wore red robes and a thick ornamental chain of latticed gold.

"Me," he said, pointing at the large brass plate inscribed beneath. "Captain Cuthbert Stitchworthy, Mayor of Hove, October, 1907." Funnel twisted his sideburns and gave a long-toothed smile.

The brotherhood tittered and applauded.

"Stitchworthy?" Rui breathed.

"We've found the guardian of Verrulf's pendant, and it's…Funnel," Rose breathed.

"Except," Rui cut in, "he's somehow changed his identity and now—"

"He's the bloomin' mayor!" Rose panted.

The clapping petered out and Funnel continued. "Yes, as of today, I am officially Mayor of Hove. Each of us has been elevated thanks to the guidance of our masterful Lord Verrulf. Ormerod is the newly appointed curator at the museum, replacing that interfering Mr Thomas."

Rose's heart missed a beat. *The museum – where the cup is…?* What did this all mean for Enna? She squeezed her eyes shut, worry pulsing through her. Rose knew Enna had trusted Funnel, liked him even. Would he hurt her now? He'd tricked her after all, and taken Verrulf's pendant.

Funnel continued. "And our faithful brother, Banks, is now detective in chief of the local constabulary."

Banks tipped his ash.

"Snodgrass – well, your time will come."

"Thank you, Sir," Snodgrass snivelled.

"I could go on –" Funnel paused to tickle his spindly fingers through the air – "Our Shadow Lord, Verrulf, has granted each of us our every material wish."

"Verrulf has got them all into positions of authority and power," Rui murmured. Rose's lips pursed as she listened to Funnel's words.

"Verrulf has advised us…guided us, and been our oracle into the affairs of men. He is a gifted seer, who speaks to me through this." Funnel gripped his pendant and held it aloft.

Seeing Funnel's pendant gave Rose a sudden pang.

Why had hers not called to her again? Had it forgotten about her? Was it in this shop somewhere?

Murmurs of agreement rumbled through the brotherhood. Taking a moment, Funnel produced a jar from beneath the sales desk. He unscrewed the lid and popped a striped humbug into his mouth.

Rose remembered the scent of peppermint she'd smelled on him and her lips pinched shut. She felt sick.

"And now, my brothers." The humbug clicked against Funnel's teeth and balled in his scrawny cheek. "The time has come to repay his kindness. Lord Verrulf wishes to walk the majesty of this earth in his human form once more, with us by his side."

The brotherhood cheered. Buoyed by the heightening mood, Snodgrass stuck two fingers in his mouth and made a shrill whistle. But the others scowled at him, and he shrank back.

"As you all know, Lord Verrulf is my powerful ancestor. He was betrayed by the people of this earth – betrayed by his own wretched brother – many thousands of years ago. If he hadn't been imprisoned –" Funnel's words burned, and spittle flew from his mouth – "I would by now – being of his royal blood – be in a position of great worldly power. It is my BIRTHRIGHT." His good eye glistened with anger as he slammed his fist on the glass service counter.

Rose jumped and tried not to gasp out loud. *So Funnel were after the pendant all along. He weren't helping Miss Templeforth all them years ago, he was trying to help himself.*

"Now, clear the circle and take up your positions," Funnel spat. The brotherhood slowly backed away, revealing a black sun motif painted on the floorboards. The mirror stood in the middle.

"What's the mirror for?" Rose breathed, a dreadful worry threading through her.

Funnel hobbled around the sales bench, using a black cane for support before entering the circle. He stopped in front of the mirror, turned and drew a deep breath. "Ormerod, bring it forth."

Rose felt Rui stiffen by her side.

A man with a monocle perched over one eye presented Funnel with a black satin cushion; nestled on top was a small reddish-brown cup. "The Amber Cup, Sir," Ormerod announced proudly.

Rose gripped Rui's arm. Panic scurried up her spine. "They've got it," she whispered. Matching the image sewn onto Enna's tapestry, the Amber Cup looked just like a chunky teacup.

"Funnel said that Ormerod has become the curator at the museum," Rui whispered into her ear. "He must have taken it. This is very bad, Rose," Rui said, fear glazing his eyes.

Funnel laced his horrid fingers together and bent them until they clicked. "This mirror is backed with amber resin. It will reveal Lord Verrulf's image briefly, and... he will speak to us."

An audible shiver of anticipation travelled around the brotherhood. "Bravo!" a deep voice called out. The others cheered and clapped.

Funnel waved down their adulation. "Our Shadow Lord Verrulf has important news to share about the missing pendant we seek."

"What? So, they ain't got it?" Rose listened, confused. Rui edged forward.

"Let us begin! Fill the cup of souls with the waters."

Snodgrass appeared with a silver flask that glistened against the light.

"That's Enna's flask!" Rose gasped. It was the same one Enna had taken with her to the museum. "What are they doing with that? What have they done with her?"

Snodgrass popped off the stopper, and his thin moustache twitched as he poured the water into the Amber Cup.

The ceiling light flickered on and off.

"Thank you, Snodgrass." Funnel elbowed him away.

"These waters were kindly altered, magically, by our heathen friend, who alas, could not be with us tonight."

Banks sniggered.

Rose's tummy hollowed. Rui's cold hand gripped hers.

Kneeling, Ormerod offered up the Amber Cup. Funnel's spidery fingers twitched for a moment, then he seized it.

"Now I will show you what is possible with one pendant and the cup." Funnel swirled the liquid around inside the cup and in one fluid movement, gripping his pendant in one hand, he thrust the cup above him, balancing it on his outstretched palm. It began to glow, a beacon of red, exposing dark fissures and cracks within the body of the amber.

The brotherhood began chanting words Rose didn't understand. The whole room filled with a nasty energy that snaked into every crevice.

Rose couldn't take her eyes off the cup. "It looks alive, don't it?" she spluttered, watching it pulse and flash in a rhythmic sequence.

"Rose, it looks like a human organ. A heart."

BOOM – BOOM – boom – boom – boom.

Dark shapes materialized in the bowl of the cup, dancing, sending shadowy projections around the room, like a magic lantern.

The brotherhood intensified their chants, which grew

louder and louder, until in unison, they pulled up their sleeves, each revealing the hideous sun tattoo on their wrists. Their mouths moved faster, their voices boomed, building to a crescendo. The towering glass jars behind the counter wobbled and chinked together, and as one they shouted, "SOL-NI-GRA!"

BOOM.

Now the cup shone bright and constant, blasting a ray of light through the gap in the curtain. Rose and Rui shielded their eyes, and the men stumbled backwards, covering their faces. The candles suddenly blew out. The lamp above Funnel shattered, showering him in fragments of glass. A new mauve light broke through the darkness, emanating from the mirror.

Funnel's mirrored reflection revealed the demonic grin cut sideways across his face. The crooked bodies of the brotherhood surrounded him, bent away in fear, pinning themselves against the display cabinets.

"I don't like this, Rui."

The air thickened with something invisible, but heavy.

Inside, a black mist fogged the mirror, concealing Funnel's reflection. When it finally lifted a new shadowy figure filled the mirror, one with broad shoulders and long muscular arms that hung low. Stag antlers branched from its huge head.

"What the—?" Rui murmured.

Two eyes sprang open on the creature's face. Veined, pulsing, red eyes. The eyes of the creature that was stitched into Enna's tapestry. The same antlers.

"It's him...V-verrulf," Rose murmured, her hands hovering over her mouth.

Verrulf blinked. Rose felt an icy breath blow through her as the creature in the mirror spoke.

"They have a new guarrrdian." The room shook as Verrulf's ancient, guttural voice vibrated through the air. "A girrrl who shares the blood." Rose's chest heaved. "She is strrrong. The pendant calls to her, but she does not possess it. My Crrreeplings see it somewhere darrrk, held by someone weak. GET THE PENDANT AND THE GIRRRL. Or, she will destrrroy us alllllllll."

Verrulf vanished, plunging the room into total darkness.

28

Uncovered Plans

Back on the pavement outside the tobacco shop, Rose bent over trying to catch her breath. Verrulf's words still echoed in her mind. *Get the girl...*

Bahula circled her, his fur standing on end.

"Rose." Rui gripped her arm. "They don't have your pendant."

"But they must have got Enna? They had her flask," she panted. A cold wind blew the hair hanging loose from her bonnet.

CRRRr-pringgg!

The coiled bell of Stitchworthy's Tobacconist's cried out as the shop door swung into the street next to them.

"Let us make haste!" Funnel's booming voice travelled through the doorway. "Our sun will indeed run black after our lord and master is raised. It's time for us to make our preparations."

"The brotherhood are coming," Rose squeaked. She cast her eyes in every direction. "Back this way, into the alley."

Rui scooped up Bahula, and huddled behind Rose in the shadowy alleyway next to the tobacconist's.

"Hide Bahula," she spluttered. Rui tucked him inside his coat. Bahula yelped.

"Shh!" she whispered to the monkey. He quietened down.

Out of view she could hear footsteps, coughs and muffled voices as the brotherhood piled onto the pavement. Snodgrass hurried past with several other men, their faces pale and drawn, their coat-tails flapping behind them in the wind.

"What have we got ourselves involved in?" a portly man stammered, wringing his gloved hands. "What was that thing? It's not natural." The men bustled by.

The shop door creaked shut and a key ground in the lock. "Banks, a word," a gravelly voice hissed.

Rose recognized it as Funnel's rasp. She leaned further into the shadows, her palms touching the cold brick wall behind her. Dank water dripped slowly from the archway above. She could feel Rui's body next to her own and prayed Bahula would keep quiet. Holding her breath, she listened.

"You've somewhat scared our brothers, Sir," Banks chuckled.

"They'll soon change their tune when they see what I can do with both pendants. The gypsy is…not going to be troubling us further, I take it?"

Rose's brow furrowed as she strained to hear over the wind.

"No, Sir. She is silent," Banks laughed.

Silent! What does that mean…that they've killed her? NO! Rui squeezed her arm.

"And Gupta?"

"I didn't log the murder so there's no paper trail back at the station. And by the day after tomorrow, the world will be a very different place," Banks sniggered. "The arrangements have been carried out just as we planned. It's regretful that neither the book nor the pendant were on his person. But, rest assured, I *will* find them."

Rui glanced at Rose.

"You must! Now, you heard our Shadow Lord, Verrulf," Funnel continued, "he warned us about the new guardian, and that the pendant calls to her. Time is running out.

You must find the pendant, and dispose of the child."

Rose flinched. *Dispose of me!*

"But which girl? We made sure that Missy was the last girl interviewed. No guardian had been discovered before her. Missy was certain of that," Banks protested.

Rose remembered the girl with ringlets getting into the carriage on that fateful afternoon.

"Well, she's wrong. They tricked you. Someone was in my head that evening, someone uninvited. Whoever she is, she is strong – too strong, and they have hidden her identity from us. She must be found."

"Everything will be in place by tomorrow night, Sir."

"It has to be. You hear me, Banks?"

"I will see to it."

"Hmfff." Funnel's ebony cane clicked the pavement as he walked past, filling the air with his strong scent of peppermint. He headed down Church Road following the others towards the Tamplins Brewery.

A figure suddenly lurched in front of the alley and stopped. Rose held her breath. Banks, framed by the brickwork arch, pulled a tin of Woodbines from his pocket and tapped one loose. A top-hatted man stopped alongside him: Ormerod, the museum's new curator. Shorter than Banks, he had a monocle wedged in his eye socket and an oversized pipe dangled from his lips.

"That was hideous. I would not have believed it had I not seen it with my own eyes," Ormerod said, his pipe trembling. "Our small group of brothers, we've only dabbled in the occult – nothing serious like this. But since Stitchworthy has joined, things have taken a much more sinister turn. And I'm not sure that—"

"Ormerod, calm yourself, man. Tonight, Stitchworthy has proved his power over the cup. If that's what he can do with one pendant and the cup, then we must believe what he claims to be able to achieve with both," Banks grunted.

"I'm not sure I want to know," the other man stammered.

"You're in too deep to back out now." Banks leaned over his associate. "Stitchworthy is a powerful man. Remember what he's already done for us – we are rich! He's proved to us he speaks with this Lord Verrulf. By Jove, we just saw him! We've made a pact, remember. A pact that can't be broken." Banks pulled up his sleeve to reveal his tattoo. "Unless you—"

"No, no, quite so. It's just…in there, things seemed so… dark."

"Control your nerves, man. By releasing Lord Verrulf, we ensure that in future we will serve beneath him as his human rulers. Stitchworthy has promised us great riches, power beyond our wildest imaginings. Don't lose sight of that. Besides, we need you to translate the spell tomorrow night. Once I get the book."

Rui stiffened.

Banks took a drag on his cigarette; he exhaled and the wind took the smoke away up the street.

"No, no, no. Fear not, I shall be there. It is for the greater good, we are as one on that point." Shakily, Ormerod struck a match and cradled the flame, but a gust of wind extinguished it. "Chfff," he exclaimed. He looked around for some shelter, the pipe hanging ladle-like from his mouth, and on spotting their archway he moved forward.

Rose heard Rui's sharp intake of breath. Her eyes shot around. *We're trapped.*

Street Scum

Ormerod leaned into the archway where Rose and Rui hid. He struck his match and sucked on the pipe. Embers glowed bright in the bowl. This new light inflated Rose and Rui's shadows against the damp brickwork. Ormerod squinted at them through his monocle.

"Spare any change, Sir?" Rose spat, covering her face with her coat collar. With a disinterested snort the man backed away, blowing out the match. Rui squeezed Rose's arm with relief, but it made him let go of Bahula.

The monkey leaned forward, his face highlighted in the street lamp. Rui snatched him back, but it was too late.

Ormerod recoiled at the sight of him. "Good Lord!" he said withdrawing his pipe.

Rose's heart pumped in her throat.

"I swear the street scum are getting more and more wretched-looking by the day," Ormerod blustered.

Banks swaggered behind him. *If he recognizes us we're done for.* Rose scrunched up her fists at the ready. Banks sniffed and stepped back, taking a deep drag on his Woodbine.

"Well, I wager the vagrants and the workhouse scum will be the first to be cleansed from this town once the shadows are walking," Banks chuckled through a plume of smoke as he strolled away.

"And it will be a kindness, I say," Ormerod added, trying to curry favour as he beetled alongside the detective. "Let's first collect the vessel of spiritual purity we need for the spell."

As their voices faded to silence, Rose let out the breath trapped in her throat.

"Rose, I can't believe we got away with that, but what are they collecting? It's something to do with the spell. They plan to raise Verrulf!"

Rose stepped onto the pavement. "We got to stop 'em."

"But, Rose, they're after *you*."

"Then we have to be careful. I believe it all, Rui.

Everything. That Verrulf, he's real. And I am somehow related to his half-brother, Albion. This is bigger than my life, bigger than anything. If they've done something to poor Enna then it's just down to us. And if they think I'm a danger to them, then we need to find out why – and fast. That pendant, my pendant, it tells me stuff. Enna said it would help me, didn't she? We've got to find it so we can figure this out. Got to get to it before that lot do."

"We *will* find it first, because we have you, and the pendant calls to you, Rose. This situation is extraordinarily dangerous!" Rui raised his eyebrow, then grinned. "But it feels good, too. You agree?"

"Yep." She closed her eyes and breathed in, her adrenaline bubbling. "Right!" Rose looked down the road as the men began to disappear from sight. "Let's see where this bunch of toffs are going. And then we'll find out who has my pendant and get it back."

Neither noticed the pale face of a girl watching them from behind the curtains of the shop display, her white face framed by a shock of perfect blonde ringlets. Her mouth curled into a tight-lipped smile.

Body Snatchers

Staying within the shadowed half of the pavement Rose and Rui followed the direction the brotherhood had taken, quickening their pace under the glare of each street lamp.

"When we get back to the house we'll see if you can make contact with the missing pendant," Rui said, running along beside Rose. "And then tomorrow we will get word to my uncle and formulate a plan."

"I can see them. They've stopped," Rose said, jumping to the side. She and Rui pressed themselves against Slater's Ironmonger's. Eventually Rose crept forward, signalling for Rui to stay behind.

She returned a moment later. "They've gone into St Andrew's churchyard. Quick, follow me, and stay low."

She lifted her skirt and coat to her knees and took off at a run. "I tell you what, you're right about my new boots not being comfy. I can't do anything in these heels, it's like I've got a turnip nailed to each sole." Her feet pounded the pavement at crazy angles. Rui chased behind.

Rose flung herself below the churchyard's flint wall and pulled her knees into the margin of its shadow. Rui copied, with Bahula crawling free by his side.

Still catching her breath, she peered over the wall and squatted back down.

"Can you see them, Rose?" Rui asked.

"Yep, all of them by the looks of it, standing around a grave. We need to get closer; close enough to hear 'em."

A carriage clattered out from the road opposite. They waited for it to pass by, but instead it drew to a noisy halt about thirty feet along from them, by the pathway leading to the church.

"Wait." Rui leaned forward. "It's theirs," he said, pointing at the emblem of the black sun on the back.

"Yep, the same one I saw at the house." Rose nodded.

The horses whinnied, their hooves scraping the cold road. Rose chanced another look over the waist-high wall. The men were chattering amongst themselves against the yellow light of a lantern, all of them looking in the direction of the newly arrived carriage.

"Rui, this is our chance to get into the graveyard," Rose whispered.

Rui leaped up and grabbed Bahula. "Tally-ho," he mouthed as he hopped over the wall. Rose followed, and they quickly moved behind the low branches of a yew tree. The canopy above cracked and shifted in the wind.

Peering through the branches, they could see the men huddled together by the church now, the large graveyard spread out before them, unkempt and moody, with long grasses waving in the wind between the broken statues and fallen gravestones.

"Good, they ain't spotted us." Rose flexed her icy fingers.

"What are they up to?" Rui asked, straining to see. "Do you think we can risk getting any closer?"

Rose nodded, and together they scampered from one tombstone to another, edging ever closer. Cloaked by darkness, they stopped behind a large stone angel covered in ivy, only a few yards from the men.

Rui gave a satisfied nod.

The brotherhood stood around a deep grave-pit with a high pile of soil stacked next to it. Snodgrass's lantern swung in the wind, casting its light at different angles.

A man dressed in a greasy coat leaned on the handle of a spade. He doffed his flat cap at Funnel. "I've dug the grave, nice 'n' deep, Sir, just like the policeman said. And I kept a good watch over it 'n' all. And no one's said boo to a goose anywhere near."

Funnel dug deep in his pocket and flicked two shillings to the ground. The man fell to his knees. "Gord bless ya, Mr Stitchworthy," he mumbled, stuffing the coins in his pocket.

Rose and Rui looked at each other. Anthony Funnel had faked his own death and become Cuthbert Stitchworthy, and no one but she and Rui seemed to know.

"That will be Mayor Stitchworthy, to you," Funnel spat. "And mark my words, if I ever get an inkling you have opened your trap to anyone about this, I'll feed your guts to the gulls. Have I made myself clear?"

Terrified, the man nodded.

Funnel leaned in close. "Now SHOO!" Jumping back, the man scooted off. "And take that stench with you."

How could Enna ever have liked Funnel? He's so nasty, Rose thought, with a frown.

Laughter echoed around the brotherhood as the poor man slipped in his haste to take the corner. He disappeared into the night.

"Where's Banks?" Rui whispered.

Rose looked about. "He's not here?"

"So, let us begin!" Funnel spun round, his wonky smile slapped across his face.

Several men took hold of the ropes coming from either side of the grave. To the whispered count of three they heaved, until a plain wooden coffin came into view. They dragged it out onto the damp grass.

Funnel forced his cane under the coffin lid. "The cold ground," he huffed, levering it open, "should have kept the body…fresh. Banks arranged for him to be kept here, ready for us to collect tonight. What better place to hide a body than in a graveyard, hey." The coffin's lid creaked open. He smirked and peered under the lid. Others clambered to look behind him.

With a gasp, Ormerod backed away, his monocle dangling loose on its chain.

"It's perfect!" Funnel boomed. "Banks has done well and he will be rewarded. Get the body out, bag it, and take it to the carriage," Funnel growled. "Where he – our vessel of spiritual purity – can be prepared in the shop cellar tonight, for his starring role at midnight tomorrow." He rubbed his hands together greedily.

Rui looked at Rose.

"Prepared ready for the spell," Rose asserted, peering back around the statue.

"Now, we just need to find the blessed spell and the other pendant." He stabbed his cane into the cold earth. "Tomorrow night is All Hallows, when the planets align and the supernatural energies will be at their zenith. There is no margin for error." Funnel clapped his hands together. "Hurry along!" he barked at his men.

Three of them tipped up the coffin and a body covered in cream silk thudded onto the ground. The head landed last, swinging to face them, a turban toppling loose from its head.

Rose's hand snapped to her mouth.

Mr Gupta's bulging eyes seemed to cast a look of surprise in their direction. His hooked arm stretched towards them.

"*Ahhhhwoooohhh.*"

Bahula's gut-wrenching wail filled the graveyard.

Spirits of the Undead

Rui pulled Bahula back towards him, his eyes jammed open with terror.

The men standing around the grave looked about at each other.

"It's him!" Snodgrass whined, pointing at the corpse. "His tortured soul has returned to punish us." Backing away, he misplaced his footing and teetered on the edge of the grave-pit. He cried out, his arms flailing, only just managing to find his balance in time.

"Quiet, Snodgrass." Funnel's good eye scrutinized the graveyard. Rose and Rui pinned themselves against the cold statue as his shoes squelched towards them. He leaned over, sniffing the air. Rose could hear his laboured breath above them.

Just then, a freezing gust of wind whipped through the graveyard, bending the trees and tall grasses.

Rui's eyes squeezed shut, his lips moving as if in silent prayer. Bahula clung onto him, shivering. Rose dared not breathe as fear anchored her to the spot.

Branches snapped in the yew tree behind them, drawing Funnel's attention. "What the—?" Funnel turned. A large white owl broke free and swooped just inches above the men's heads. It let rip an ear-piercing screech. The men lunged to the ground. Only Funnel remained upright.

"An owl. See?" he confronted his men.

Rui placed his palms together, looked up to the sky and bobbed his head in thanks.

"Now, enough of this claptrap." Funnel teased his sideburns. "This is no time for indecisiveness, Brothers." He smiled.

Their cheers and mumbles of agreement were cut short. *CRW-aCK!*

Rose stiffened and slowly peered back round. Funnel's cane had struck the side of the empty coffin. Grunting, he swung the cane high, and thwacked it again. Each strike shook Rose, until the empty coffin clattered back into the grave. Funnel wedged his cane under his arm and wrung his hands. "Bag him, Grobbs."

Funnel sauntered away with Ormerod and seven others, leaving Grobbs, Snodgrass and a man swamped in a cashmere coat by the graveside.

Grobbs, an ox-sized man with a tiny head, stooped over the body and, with the help of the man in the big coat, shunted Mr Gupta's corpse into a hessian tobacco sack.

"Rose, how could they treat his body like this?" Rui sniffed, turning away to shield Bahula.

Rose placed an arm around him, anger coursing through her. "Coz they're monsters," she hissed.

Snodgrass grabbed the loose turban and readied himself to stuff it in the sack too, but then he paused and examined it. His thin moustache twitched.

"He's spotted the ruby, the greedy toad," Rose murmured.

The jewel glinted in his lamplight. Turning away from the others, Snodgrass prised it off. An oily smirk turned up the ends of his moustache as he stashed the gem in his pocket. Turning back, he shoved the turban into the sack with the body.

"Let's get out of here," the man in the coat muttered. "I feel like we're being watched."

"Yes, I feel it too, it's the spirits of the undead," Grobbs grunted.

With the scraping and shuffling of booted feet, the three men dragged the sack along the path.

Funnel's carriage rattled away and the remaining figures departed into the windswept night. They were alone.

"Where is that wretched detective now? He weren't here with the others, was he?" Rose pressed her back against the angel statue and rubbed her temples, her teeth chattering against the cold.

"This is deeper and darker than I could possibly have imagined," Rui said as he stood up and gazed far away into the distance. "Banks murdered Mr Gupta, and now they plan to humiliate him further by using his body for this wicked spell. We must stop them."

"And Enna – they've done something with her 'n' all." Rose clenched her fists; she couldn't bear to think about what might have happened. "Who can we trust?" She frowned as they sneaked past the tombstones and through the graveyard exit.

"No one," Rui said, his eyes fierce. "And who would believe us if we tried?"

Rose knew he was right. Verrulf wanted to return to the earth, and only they could stop him. "Then it's just down to us."

Rui nodded.

The buildings of the Tamplins Brewery cut into the

roadway ahead creating a dark bottleneck on the otherwise wide thoroughfare. They slipped down the narrow passageway separating the brewery from the shop opposite. Smoke still blew inland from the brewery's simmering chimneys.

Rose's mind raced. *So, Banks doesn't have my pendant. Could Mr Gupta have been wrong about "JB" having it? But if he don't have it, who does?* Rose felt exhausted.

The giant barrel of the gasometer came into view, signalling the junction of Sackville Road.

"We've got to stop them – no matter what – from doing that necro-thingy, tomorrow night, when the planets line up," Rose said, breaking through the silence again.

Rui glanced back the way they had come. The road remained deserted right back to the brewery, but beyond that he couldn't see. Satisfied no one had followed them, he nodded. "What we need now is a brilliant plan."

Rose agreed, her loose hair blowing wildly around her face.

"We must hope the pendant tries to contact you again," Rui said over the wind.

Rose nodded. It was their only hope. With the pendant they could find the answers to everything. Of that she was certain. "And if the brotherhood don't have it, we're still in with a chance."

They both failed to notice the trail of Woodbine smoke carrying on the wind as they walked back past the shadowed alcove just a few houses before thirteen Sackville Road. Banks chuckled to himself as his shoe squished his cigarette butt into the pavement, obliterating it.

A Most Brilliant Plan

There'd been no trace of Enna Lee at her caravan when they'd visited early the next day, and no clues left as to what might have happened to her. The man on the gate to the Pleasure Gardens said he'd not seen sight or sound of her since she'd left for the museum the day before. *Which means the Brotherhood of the Black Sun must have…* Rose couldn't bear to think about it. Besides, Enna had told them to do what they could without her, and they had done just that. And now they'd formulated a plan: a brilliant one.

"Any contact from the pendant?" Rui asked for about the twentieth time that day. It was seven o'clock in the evening as Rose changed into her disguise in the pantry cupboard.

"Not a whisper," she said, placing the last golden threaded scarf over her shoulder, just as Rui had instructed.

"Fear not, it will happen. We must be patient a little longer," Rui said. Rose hoped he was right. They were depending on it. But in the meantime, they'd spent the day doing everything they could without it.

Rose sniffed the material, which smelled of faraway places. Places where people laughed and monkeys roamed freely. She touched the jewel hanging from her hairline and smiled to herself.

"So," Rui broke into her thoughts from the kitchen, "we have seen the Brotherhood of the Black Sun and we now know that our missing, and presumed dead, Anthony Funnel has changed his identity and become the Mayor of Hove, and goes by the name of Stitchworthy. We also know that the police are involved."

She could hear Rui pacing backwards and forwards on the tiled floor. "But, the spell they require will already be halfway to London town by now."

"Yep." Rose grinned.

That morning, they had carefully wrapped Mr Gupta's journal and taken it to the post office addressed to his uncle, the maharajah, who was staying at the Savoy Hotel in London.

"Meanwhile," Rui continued, "our urgent telegram should already be with my uncle." Rui recounted its message with gusto:

"GRAVE DANGER (STOP) WILL BE ABOARD LAST TRAIN TO LONDON VICTORIA (STOP) BRINGING FIRST CLASS COMPANION (STOP) IN DISGUISE (STOP) TRUST NO ONE (STOP) THIS IS REAL NOT HOLMESING (STOP)."

And he'll help us find Enna Lee, Rose thought, biting her lip. "But, do you think your uncle will believe you? You know, with all your 'Holmesing' and what have you."

Rui ignored her. "Plus, I have managed to compile some notes in our decoy book."

Rose tapped down her disguise. She loved it. No silly stockings and heavy dresses – this was the sort of outfit you could run in, and from Rui had told her, *probably ride elephants too,* she imagined with a quick smile.

Rui didn't even notice her when she stepped out of the pantry. Standing with his back to her, he held the decoy booklet aloft – now carefully covered in a piece of embroidered silver Indian silk. They'd purchased the booklet together at Hanningtons department store in Brighton Town earlier that day. "It's not an exact replica, but at a glance it looks the same size as Mr Gupta's," Rui said to himself. He stroked the eye that had been made using a mussel shell from the beach, and painted by Rose, and which now sat stuck fast to the front cover.

He paced backward and forward, still not noticing Rose. "I have filled it with nonsense. But, importantly, nonsense written in Sanskrit, with diagrams of the Amber Cup and a few astrological red herrings. It should be enough to intrigue, and buy us some time, should we get caught – which we won't."

"Brilliant," Rose beamed. "Really brilliant!"

"Quite." Realizing she was there, Rui spun around. "R-rose!" he managed. His jaw dropped and Bahula's head popped up from the pile of fabric heaped up on the kitchen table.

"You look so beautiful," Rui said in awe. "Every inch an Indian princess!"

Rose's smile lit up her face. She did feel beautiful in these clothes.

"Now hobble," Rui instructed.

Rose's smile fell. "You what?"

"Remember, you are disguised as my Great-Aunt Uma, who is sixty-three and sadly riddled with arthritis. So support your back with your hand."

"Right. Like this?" Rose did as he instructed.

"That's it, now stoop...and drag your foot a little. Perfect!" Rui gave her a toothy grin. "We will need to add some more jewels. I find the more jewels one wears the fewer questions people ask." He began sifting through the bundle of colourful fabrics and necklaces piled up on the kitchen table. Bahula joined in too.

"So, are our cases packed?" Rui asked as multicoloured scarves flew through the air.

Rose nodded. "By the front door."

"Cheddar cheese sandwiches?"

"Packed," she replied.

Rui stopped, holding up a sparkling necklace that Rose thought couldn't possibly be made with real gems.

"Pepper pot?"

"Packed, obviously." She smiled.

"Good. My wardrobe and Mr Gupta's have come in most handy for your disguise. You will fool all but the most observant. And, best of all, your face will be concealed by a veil."

"Oi!" Rose protested.

Ignoring her, Rui continued, "I will do all the talking on your behalf – as you will not speak or understand English. We have a private compartment on the ten o'clock, the last train from Brighton to London Victoria. So we will not be overheard or queried. I will be travelling as your servant and translator."

Rose grinned. She started to speak, but something

familiar tugged her insides. An ancient something that belonged to her... She wobbled for a moment, as a breeze ran through her middle, then she stumbled over to the kitchen table and slumped across it.

"Rose?"

She could hear voices calling to her from far away. *The pendant!* She rallied, trying to keep hold of the connection.

Bahula squeaked and picked his way across the table to her. Rose held her head. In her mind's eye she could see someone clutching the pendant in their fist. The space around it was dark – and she could hear a squeaking noise and pitiful moaning. She recognized the moans, but she just couldn't...quite...place them. She tried to keep hold of this picture, but the image rushed away like a train disappearing into a tunnel. Gone. Rose opened her eyes wide.

Rui placed his arm around her. "Are you all right?"

"The pendant," she panted. "I heard it again. It called to me. But this time I seen it too – in a dark place, and the person holding it sounds in awful pain or something. But Rui, I nearly had who it was. I recognized the sound of their sobbing."

"Try to think, Rose," Rui said.

"I dunno." She threw her hands in the air.

Rui paced behind her. "Well, Mr Gupta in his journal

seemed certain 'JB' had the pendant. I thought it had to be Jonathan Banks."

"Me too. But it ain't him." Rose shook her head. "Something don't add up. Banks was rattled that Mr Gupta's room had been done over, right? P'raps that's the bit we're missing. Who broke in and why? If it weren't them from the Black Sun, who was it?"

"You're right! Someone else with the same initials? Hmm. JB." Rui's fingers tapped his lip. "Jack Billings!" He held aloft his index finger. "JB!"

Rose shook her head again. "Nah, Jack Billings ain't smart enough. And even if he was, his mouth's been oiled at the hinges, he can't keep nothing to himself. It's gotta be someone else. Think. Think. Think. JB…" Rose banged her fist against her forehead. She'd felt that the pendant knew she'd recognize whoever had it. Rose squeezed her eyes shut, if she could just think…hard enough. "Wait…" she clenched her fist.

"Yes, Rose. What?"

She paused to organize the thoughts in her mind, and then she grinned. "We have to think of this like we're Mr Gupta. What if it ain't Jonathan Banks or Jack Billings…? What if the letters aren't a name but a title?"

Rui blinked. "Explain?"

"I knew I recognized that sobbing. JB…John the Butler!

It was him. He was with Miss Templeforth just before the pendant went. And we ain't barely seen hide nor hair of him since." She clicked her fingers. "And he had the run of this place, he's got keys to all the rooms in the house! How come we found Mr Gupta's door unlocked? You said yourself it was odd. P'raps he left the window open to make it seem like a break-in but forgot to lock the door? Plus, the two of them, your tutor and him, were the last ones to see Miss Templeforth alive."

"Yes, but if he already had the pendant why did he need to stage the break-in; what was he looking for?" Rui leaned on the kitchen table.

"I honestly don't know. Mr Gupta's journal maybe?" She stood up, still deep in thought. "He knows everything that goes on in the house. Always listening in at doors. Why didn't we think of him sooner?"

"Elephas Maximus! Nothing is more deceptive than an obvious fact." Rui pounded his fist. "He's been hiding in plain sight all along. But you worked it out, Rose!" He patted her back.

She looked up and saw his pride in her and threw her shoulders back.

"Now, transform back into Rose Muddle. We have a pendant to find before we set off for London, Watson."

"Watson?" Rose asked standing.

"Sherlock's left-hand man. Do you know something? You actually make a jolly good sidekick! Ouch!" Rose kicked him as she passed. "What was that?"

"A sidekick." She pretended to frown, but then grinned, shutting herself back inside the pantry cupboard to get changed.

"But where do you think John is now?" he called out.

Rose stepped out of her comfortable disguise, and pulled on her itchy green dress. "Jack said he went to his ma's, and I bet he knows where that is," she smirked. "Jack Billings knows everything."

"Tremendous," she heard Rui whisper excitedly, and she smiled.

The Missing Pendant

Heavy clouds gathered in the sky above as the wind pushed Rose and Rui along the rabbit warren of narrow streets. They still had time to get the pendant before the last train to London, but they had to be quick. It was already gone eight and very dark. But they both knew that without the second pendant or the spell inside Mr Gupta's journal, the brotherhood wouldn't be able to raise Verrulf from the cup.

There's a big storm brewing, Rose thought, noticing the seagulls circling in the sky above – they'd never come so far inland otherwise.

Bahula tugged at the corner of Rui's jacket, so he picked him up.

There was something bothering Rose. "The one thing I don't get is how did the brotherhood know about needing a body? Coz they don't have Mr Gupta's journal –" she looked at Rui walking level with her – "so how would they know what the spell says?"

"Hmm," Rui tapped his cheek. "Mr Gupta had been in communication with someone at the museum even before he commenced his journey here to England."

"Ormerod?" Rose remembered the man with the monocle and pipe.

"Quite possibly. And maybe Mr Gupta told them things – things that he later regretted. Thinking his contact at the museum was a confidant." He opened his palms.

"Or, p'raps he and that Funnel talked about it on the train all them years ago in India, before the fire," she suggested. "Oh, hang on. Down here," she said noticing the big building ahead.

Rose took a sharp right just before Maynard's Sweet Factory as Jack Billings had instructed. They'd got to Jack just before he'd left for his Aunt Ivy's up Ditchling village way. He and Nanna Potts would be away for the rest of the weekend – they were lucky not to have missed him. Rose grinned. Things were finally going their way, she could just feel it.

A couple of mean-faced women eyed them from a

doorway. Puffing on pipes, their conversation dried up as the pair sped by.

"Don't look at no one, you hear?" Rose whispered. "Right, number four, this is it." Rui clutched Bahula under his arms as Rose rattled the knocker.

A light appeared on the other side, visible through the tricoloured panes of glass above the door. Rose heard a lady's muffled voice. "Who is it?"

"Ma'am, my name's Rose Muddle. I have come with my friend to find the Templeforth butler, John Crank. I worked under him at the big house. We bring urgent news."

The door cracked open, revealing an elderly woman bent over an oil lamp. Dressed in black, her gossamer-thin hair was scraped into a bun on top of her head.

There could be no mistaking the likeness. *This is his ma all right.* Bleary-eyed, the woman squinted, brandishing the lamp in front of her.

"Mrs Crank? Is your son here? We've been worried about him. He ain't been in the house since the mistress died and he was awful upset the last time I saw him."

"I see you have a cat." The old lady peered at Bahula, who scrunched up his face. "Well, you better keep tight hold of him because I've a dog inside."

Rui nodded, and stepped across the threshold.

"Come, follow me. I am relieved you're here. I am at a

loss to know what to do with John, he just isn't right. You worked with him, you say? Maybe visitors will knock his memory. He's in the room at the back. Please, this way."

She speaks posh for round 'ere, Rose thought.

The old woman's lamp lit the otherwise dark corridor. The place smelled damp, like it had never been heated, with a whiff of mothballs.

A low growl came from the stairwell as they passed, and a white terrier stuck its head through the bannister and bared its teeth.

Bahula craned his neck and Rui gripped him tighter.

The old lady hobbled on, keeping her spare arm against the wall for support. At the end of the hallway she stopped outside a closed door and turned to them.

"Keep your distance from him. I fear he's lost his mind. The shock of losing his mistress weighed heavier on him than I could have imagined." She frowned, shaking her head. She pulled free a long iron key and, trembling, placed it in the lock. Rui and Rose exchanged a glance. *Why's he locked in there?*

The open door revealed darkness.

"John, dear, you have visitors," she called before turning to Rose. "Take this." She thrust forward her lamp and added in a whisper, "Remember, don't get too close. I can't understand what's come over him."

A whistling sound came from the dimly lit scullery at the end of the hallway. The woman went towards it. "I have to see to the kettle. Call if he turns on you."

"Turns on you?" Rui mouthed.

They inched forward. Rose picked up on a mumbling and squeaking sound. The mood inside the room made Rose's neck hair stand on end. Whatever she was going to find, she knew it wasn't going to be pretty.

Possessed

The lamplight revealed a sparsely furnished room with plastered walls broken away in patches, showing the raw brickwork beneath. A fringe of material was pinned above the unlit hearth and, in pride of place on the mantel, perched a framed picture of King Edward VIII on his coronation.

In the middle of the room, the light exposed a high-backed rocking chair in constant squeaking motion, and a hand, white with tension, gripping the side. The occupant's fevered mumbling echoed around them.

Rose edged closer. *Blimey, he looks old.* The butler's cheeks were drawn into hollow cups and his eyes jumped from one place to another.

"Stay away!" he whimpered, covering his face with a bent arm, staring at the empty ceiling. "The sh-shadows," he stammered, twisting from side to side.

"Look, in his hand, Rose," Rui whispered urgently.

A thin gold chain hung from it. Albion's pendant – her pendant – was clenched in his fist.

Rose rushed to the butler's side, filled with relief. The pendant was here and safe. She rested the lamp on the floor. "Sir, Sir, it's me, Rose Muddle. We come to find you, we was worried about you. You ain't yourself, Sir."

Crank's raw eyes stared into the middle distance but Rose pressed on.

"You ain't ill, Sir, it's the pendant what's doing this to you. It's making you sick. Let me help you, let me take it from you." She rested her hand on his clenched fist, the pendant just inches from her grasp. She felt a static charge from it, like it wanted her as badly as she wanted it.

Crank spun towards her, his mouth twisted, his eyes wild. "It is the only thing protecting me from them. You evil thief, I should kill you first."

His empty hand gripped her throat. "No!" she croaked, clawing at his fingers. Rose gasped for air but he just squeezed harder.

"Stop!" Rui shouted, dropping Bahula and rushing forward.

In a flash, Bahula launched himself onto the butler's lap. He placed his miniature hands on the man's shoulders and extended his jaw to expose his oversized canines.

"They have come for me!" the butler shrieked, slamming back into his chair. He released Rose and the pendant fell to the floor.

With her throat still burning, Rose grabbed the pendant and pressed it to her chest as she rolled onto her back. *I've got it!*

Her mind calmed instantly, like a missing part of her had been returned. She could feel the pendant pulsing in her hand. Slow and steady. *It's mine.* A sense of complete belonging blanketed her. Her pain numbed as the pendant synced to her heart's rhythm. The room dissolved, raced away to nothingness. Her senses drifted.

Time melted and she found herself spinning, over and over, like a sycamore seed. A white mist, like the particles from Enna's skrying bowl, surrounded her in clouds and she sank beneath them. She found herself face to face with the woman from the portrait in the library, who stared at Rose from behind her fan, not mockingly as before, but with playful affection. She's summin' to do with this – with me. *Rose knew it to be the truth.* She's my blood link. But who is she? *Curiosity bubbled inside her.*

Then everything went pitch black.

Her skin crawled as she made out the smell of peppermint. A room formed, hazy and uncertain.

A giddy, greedy laugh sent a rush of cold through her bones. I'm in his head again. No! *Funnel's laugh cut off. He wobbled and slumped in his seat.*

"She's here with us again," he spat. She could see his lap, feel his hands grabbing his head. "I know she's here. And she has the pendant. FIND AND ELIMINATE HER!"

Funnel's words faded into a deep blackness, punctuated only by the gnashing of hidden teeth.

Rose took sharp fast breaths as black willowy shapes snaked around her, barely visible amid the darkness.

Creeplings! she breathed, her heart hammering. "Go AWAY!" she ordered, just as she had before in the library.

But this time they did not go. Low voices hissed and jeered in a foreign tongue. Something lunged forward, black against black, its features concealed – its breath blew her hair. A choking stench swamped her. She had nowhere to hide, no one to help her.

Pulsing eyes sprang open. Covered in veins, they blazed through the powdery blackness. A mouth cracked apart and grew huge, extending into a tunnel. A sucking wind pulled her towards it. "NO!" she screamed, but the word had no sound. The mouth surged towards her…and swallowed her whole.

Grim Reality

Blurry images and faraway voices drifted away as Rose slowly came round.

"Rose!" Rui cried out.

She could see Rui, hundreds of him, circling like a kaleidoscope above her. "Stop moving, I can only handle one of you," she muttered as she sat up, rubbing the back of her aching head.

"Where am I? What was that?" Her words gained strength as the many Ruis settled into one person.

"Should you wear that thing, is it safe?" He was looking at the pendant.

"I got to wear it, Rui," she panted. The pendant's

warmth filled the empty, hollow space inside her, making her feel whole again. It needed her and she needed it. Rose was its guardian, and she knew that, given time, once she'd got to understand its powers, she could control it better too.

"What happened to you? You fainted as soon as you touched the pendant." Rui's voice trembled.

"What's going on?" the butler demanded from his hunched position in the rocking chair. He seemed as angry as ever, though calmer without the pendant, his face less gaunt.

Rose crouched on the floor, trying to catch her breath, clasping her pendant. "V-verrulf," she spluttered. "I saw him! It was terrible... And what's worse –" she was suddenly aware of Mr Crank and pulled Rui close – "they know I have it."

"They know who you are?" he whispered back.

"I dunno, Rui. But they're so strong. The cup...with the cup they're..." Fragments of the vision flashed through her mind. "I-I'm related to the woman," she said a little louder now. "The painting in the library. That woman with the fan," she looked at Crank, "who is she?"

"Emily Templeforth?" the butler scoffed. "She was our mistress's sister and she died many, many years ago. It was a tragedy and she had no children, so, to think you are related to her is just...well, preposterous."

"Enough!" Rui's lip curled as he confronted the old man. "Don't speak to Rose like that. You've got some explaining to do. You stole the pendant and look what happened. Its powers consumed you!"

"The pendant! Yes, I took it." He squirmed. "But only because your tutor, your Mr Gupta, told me to."

"He did?" Rui countered with surprise. "Right. Start from the beginning – tell us all you know," he said, lifting the lamp from the floor and brandishing it to illuminate Crank's face.

The butler rubbed his temples, his breath still short. "At first I knew very little. The dark visitations were killing my mistress – I suppose I knew that much. She had become dangerously weak from the tuberculosis. I knew too that her pendant was special in some way. But other than that I had not been privy to the danger Miss Templeforth was in. She had not, as it turned out, trusted me enough. Me –" he thumped his chest – "the servant who had devoted his life to her." Slumping back, he shook his head.

"Continue," Rui barked, lifting the lamp closer to the butler's face.

The butler blinked and shielded his eyes. "It was Mr Gupta who explained the full details to me after she had passed." His lips pinched. "A stranger to the house, left to reveal the truth to *me*! He told me that the search for an heir had been set up as a diversion to protect you." He squinted at Rose. "*You*, it turns out, who had been taken from the workhouse and introduced as a maid so you could be close by. I had no idea. I thought your promotion to companion was absurd, but I never imagined that –" he began rocking frantically in the chair – "I couldn't believe that *you* could be so important, but I knew I should keep Miss Templeforth's pendant safe. I owed her that much."

Rui grabbed hold of the chair and held it still. "How was Mr Gupta involved?"

"Over their breakfast together, Miss Templeforth had asked him about his contact at the museum, the new curator, a Mr Ormerod."

"Ormerod!" Rui interjected, facing Rose. He placed the lamp on the floor, next to the rocking chair. The lamplight sent crooked shadows up the walls to the ceiling.

"The man with the monocle and the pipe." Rose nodded. She spun back to the butler as he started up once more.

"This Ormerod had invited Mr Gupta to travel to Hove to see an ancient cup. Knowing this to be Mr Gupta's specialism." Crank placed his fingers to his lips, organizing everything in his mind before continuing.

"This explains why he stepped forward to chaperone me here!" Rui said.

Rose nodded, though she couldn't help wondering how

much Mr Gupta had actually *told* the butler, and how much Crank had eavesdropped.

"Then Mr Gupta talked about an Englishman he met many years ago," the butler continued, "who perished in a fire of some kind. He said his wife had also died in the accident. That the matter was very personal to him."

Rose and Rui leaned closer.

"This dead man was the only person who ever knew about some ancient spell he had translated and recorded in his journal. A spell that involved the Amber Cup. When Ormerod started asking about it, Mr Gupta became gravely alarmed."

"It's exactly as we thought, Rose," Rui said, rubbing his hands together.

"As their communications continued, he became suspicious of this Ormerod and the brotherhood he claimed to be involved with – especially when they promised to allow him to participate in a ritual they planned, involving the cup, should he travel to Hove with his journal. He knew then that they had to be stopped."

Rui stepped forward. "Yes, of course! He knew only too well of the cup's power and the danger it posed if used with the wrong intentions. And they certainly *did* want him involved in the ritual." Rui glanced at Rose.

They wanted his dead body. Rose held the back of her

hand to her mouth. It was horrible to think that they had tricked Mr Gupta to come here, not only to steal his journal, but to use his body in the spell too. "And then what happened?" she asked.

The butler continued. "Mr Gupta had explained to the mistress that he had met a man who owned a pendant like hers many years before."

"Yes!" Rose said, remembering the newspaper article showing both men together.

"And this Ormerod had charged Mr Gupta with removing Miss Templeforth's pendant on her death. Mr Gupta said he had gone along with it all in the hope of exposing them – letting them think he was their man, but he had brought with him all the evidence in his journal."

"Yes!" Rui punched his palm.

"After hearing all this, the mistress confided in Mr Gupta of the great evil at work. She was worried about the safety of the cup and she worried for your safety too." He glanced sideways at Rose, then looked away. "She told him you were to be the new guardian after her demise. YOU!" Again Crank began to rock back and forth. "I have devoted my entire working life to her service, and then it turns out that some wretch from the workhouse is to be lorded up as her favourite!"

"I didn't ask for none of this," Rose protested.

"What happened to Miss Templeforth?" Rui pushed on, the dusty room flickering in the lamplight.

"It was shortly after this conversation that she died. A visitation from the forces of darkness consumed her. I got there as soon as I could, but it was too late." Resting his hand on his brow, he shook his head. "The tuberculosis had weakened her so. Her last words were 'protect the pendant and protect Rose Muddle' and then she passed. God rest her soul."

"But how did you end up with the pendant?" Rui's eyes glared at him accusingly.

"I felt distraught with grief at her passing. It was Mr Gupta who hurriedly devised a plan. He'd arranged to meet with a member of the group later that day."

"The Brotherhood of the Black Sun." Rui scowled. Pacing over to the mantelpiece he lifted up the picture of the king, seemingly deep in thought, as he listened to the butler.

"Yes, but he changed his plans, intending to speak with Gypsy Lee at the Pleasure Gardens first. Miss Templeforth had identified her as an ally and confidant."

Rose remembered the slipper and monkey prints up near Enna's caravan. *So, he'd gone there to warn her – but she wasn't there.* Had Banks followed Mr Gupta, planning to take the pendant and the journal and then kill him?

Whatever had happened, she knew clever old Mr Gupta

messed things up by keeping the pendant and the journal out of reach.

"Mr Gupta wanted to discover the identity of the leader of the brotherhood," Mr Crank continued. "It had been suggested by Ormerod that, whoever this leader was, he held great power and influence. But his identity remained shrouded in secrecy. Mr Gupta had his own suspicions and he set off to prove them."

"I knew it, Rose!" Rui grinned. "Mr Gupta was an honourable man! He was carrying out his own investigation all along."

Rose gave a sad smile. "Yep, you was right. Poor Mr Gupta."

The butler scratched his neck. "He said he would hide his journal and asked me to make it look as though it had been stolen."

"So it was you what turned over Mr Gupta's room?" Rose said, as the pieces of the jigsaw puzzle slotted into place.

"I did. To lead them on a false trail. He instructed me to take the pendant and leave the house. Go into hiding. Keep it safe. He remained concerned for the safety of you both and wanted to divert attention away from you and from the house. He said he would return to me here at my mother's – but he never did."

Rui closed his eyes. "Mr Gupta was murdered yesterday afternoon."

"MURDERED?" The butler slumped back into the chair. "What do you mean? By whom?"

"The Brotherhood of the Black Sun finished him off," Rose said, placing an arm around Rui.

"Murdered... I'm a failure," Mr Crank began. "Before he left, he warned me not to touch the pendant with my bare hands. If I had been in possession of my own mind, I could have..." The butler choked.

"But you did touch it. You were holding it when we found you," Rui said.

"I know!" Mr Crank looked wretched, and Rose couldn't help but feel sorry for him. He gripped his head. "Forgive me. I saw how it affected those girls and I knew it was different when you picked it up... The mistress was impressed by you because of it. I wanted to know if I possessed the same qualities she admired in you. I was foolish, I couldn't resist the urge to see if it would control me. I thought I was...stronger."

"Stronger than some wretch from the workhouse you mean?" Rui muttered.

"She chose Rose over me. I felt confused," he said, lowering his eyes. "I was jealous." His shoulders trembled.

An unexpected wave of pity came over Rose. Crank

suddenly looked like a tired old man, as though his sixty years had marched up behind him and told him to give up, told him he was finished. "You were proper loyal to the mistress, and I know she thought the world of you, Sir."

"Do you really think so?" He wiped his eyes. "What would she think of me now though?" he sniffed.

Rose kneeled before him and took his hands in hers. "Don't go blaming yourself. None of us is perfect. Least of all me. You stopped some bad people from getting this pendant and that's a very good thing. The mercy is, we got to you before that black sun lot did."

John placed his hand over hers. "Can you ever forgive me?"

"I already have," she smiled. "There's much bigger fish swimming in all of this. And they need catching. And I think, thanks to you and Mr Gupta, we got everything we need to get 'em."

Outside the rain fell in sheets, filling the cold narrow streets which bled into one another. Rose was soaked through to her stockings, but she couldn't care less. She held the pendant with its chain around her neck. *I've got it back.* She could feel it humming next to her skin and happiness and relief filled her. They now had everything they needed to stop Funnel and his gang. Every member of that group would pay for murdering Mr Gupta she promised herself, gritting her teeth. And whatever they had done to Enna Lee.

Back at the house Rose and Rui's disguises and suitcases were waiting for them. With a quick change of clothes, they planned to escape with the pendant, bound for London town, before the brotherhood could work out what was going on. Rose would be Great-Aunt Uma and Rui her footboy.

"Once we are safely in London we'll ask my uncle to speak to his friend the King. He will send his own guards to apprehend these villains. We have the newspaper clipping of Anthony Funnel, proving Mayor Stitchworthy is a fraud."

"And they will find out what happened to Enna," Rose added.

"Absolutely." Rui nodded.

Thirteen Sackville Road loomed in front of them once more. Rose fished out the cook's heavy front-door key. A crack of thunder, followed immediately by a bolt of lightning, made her jump. They ran between the stone lions and up the steps to the main door.

Rose placed the key in the lock.

"You have Albion's pendant, Rose. We got it back and

outwitted the Brotherhood of the Black Sun," Rui exclaimed, peering beneath the rim of his dripping tweed hat. Bahula's face protruded from Rui's coat offering a gummy grin.

Rose twisted the key until it clicked. She was pleased to have got the pendant, and the journal was safe too. *Maybe I've turned out to be a good guardian after all?* Rose smiled to herself. The pendant vibrated against her skin suddenly, and a very dark feeling took hold of her. She pushed open the front door.

"Rui, something ain't right." Rose shut the door and turned, staring across the lobby to the library door, which slowly swung open. Rui gasped, and was suddenly rigid by her side.

Inside a roaring fire lit up the big room. Its flames silhouetted the figure of a man, with a familiar bushy moustache, sitting in the winged armchair staring at them unwaveringly, and next to him the smaller figure of a young girl with hair curled into perfect ringlets.

36

The Brotherhood of the Black Sun

"Come, come, I have been waiting for you." Banks's voice cut across to them as he slowly rose from the chair. "Snodgrass, block their exit, would you?"

"Boo!" Snodgrass appeared behind them. Pulling a face, he drew the internal bolt across.

Rose's eyes swelled with horror. *The pendant tried to warn me. That's why it vibrated.* She pursed her lips, hating herself for not realizing what it was trying to tell her soon enough.

"Detective Banks?" Rui dropped Bahula to the floor; the monkey whipped around and cowered at his heels. "W-what is it you want – and who let you in?"

"I've been letting you carry on your merry dance, hoping it would lead to the treasure. And sure enough it did. Now," he turned to Rose, "you have something that doesn't belong to you and I have come for it." Banks strode towards them, pulling on his black gloves.

Rose discreetly covered the pendant with her collar.

Yes!" Rui stepped forward and produced the decoy book he'd made earlier. "Erm, now, yes. The book you were after – that of Mr Gupta's, I found it quite unexpectedly. We planned to deliver it to the police station tomorrow and—"

"I don't need that. Because, you see…I have this." Banks retrieved something from his coat pocket.

"How did—?" Rui's shoulders slumped.

Banks waved Mr Gupta's real journal in the air. He gave a greedy smile. "Oh, and your urgent (STOP) Telegram (STOP) Didn't get sent either (STOP) Which means you're both mincemeat (STOP)."

Snodgrass burst into laughter behind them. "Witty, Sir. So very witty."

"Don't interrupt, Snodgrass," Banks barked, glaring directly at Rose. "You know very well what I want; I want the pendant." He wiped his nose on the back of his gloved hand. "You really thought you two dim-witted underlings and your bumbling monkey could outwit me –

an officer of the law!" He bent low, his teeth clenched. "I have had you under surveillance since I spotted you outside the shop. Watching and waiting. Stopped off at the post office straight after you. We knew you'd be after the pendant next – that it calls to you. We've been awaiting your return. Now HAND IT OVER." His spittle flew at Rose's face.

Rose stepped back, clutching the pendant to her chest. "It's mine –" *I ain't parting with it, not now, not after all this* – "and in the eyes of the law it…"

"SILENCE!" Banks lunged towards her. Bahula leaped from behind Rose, and made a grab for Banks.

"Now!" the detective ordered, quickly sidestepping the monkey.

A weighted net flew through the air, ensnaring Bahula mid-leap. He fell heavily to the floor, whimpering, his little arms waving about and entangling him further in the net with every movement.

"BAHULA!" Rui shouted. "You shall not harm my monkey and you shall not take Rose's pendant." Rui dashed forward, his fists flying at Banks. "I know it was you who murdered Mr Gupta." Rui pulled at the detective's coat as he tried to reach the journal, but Banks held it high above his head, laughing, before shoving Rui to the floor. Rui fell heavily backwards. Rose gasped as she saw Rui stuff something in his pocket, but before she could work anything out—

"Lights please, Missy!" Banks announced with a hollow clap. The lobby lit up.

Rose blinked, adjusting to the brightness as Rui scrambled back to her side. The girl with blonde ringlets stood balanced on a chair by the wall-lamp switch. She grinned at Rose.

"R-Rose," Rui stammered under his breath as he stared across the lobby. She followed his line of vision to the staircase, where all the members of the Brotherhood of the Black Sun were standing.

"The kitchen. Rui. Run," Rose whispered, not moving her lips, thinking they could escape from the backyard over the wall into Potts's Laundry Emporium.

"Well, well, well. How very entertaining," Funnel's wicked voice spoke from behind them. Rose spun around, grabbing Rui's arm. Funnel sat in the chair in the recess next to the door, his hands resting on his walking stick.

Rose's eyes found his pendant – the other pendant – which throbbed from red, to black, to red again. She whimpered. Standing up, Funnel rolled a mint humbug in his mouth. His cane clipped the tiles as he walked towards them, kicking Bahula as he passed by.

Bahula yelped and Rose wanted to comfort him, but a huge arm hooked around her neck dragging her to the floor. Iron handcuffs clicked onto her wrists, weighing her arms down. She tried desperately to struggle free but other hands gripped her.

"Gehr off!" she shouted, kicking out. A thin hand stinking of onions clamped over her mouth, but she managed to bite it hard.

"Yee-oooww!" Snodgrass shouted, gripping his hand to his chest. "The vicious scab just bit me!"

"Quiet, Snodgrass." Banks turned to the others. "Tie and gag them and take them through to the library."

"We know who you really are!" Rose spluttered at Funnel, determined to expose him, but someone thrust her head backwards. She tried to beat him off but another pinned her down and pushed a ball of muslin into her mouth. She retched as a length of cloth tied it in place.

Without a backward glance, Funnel strode away into the library. "Bring them through to me once they're secured," he ordered.

"I'm the nephew to the Maharajah of— Arrgghh..." Rose listened as Rui's words were smothered.

"And I'm the Queen of Sheba," a gravelly voice grunted back.

Foul laughter trickled around the room. The biggest of

them, Grobbs, hauled Rose onto his back, and the library lurched up and down as he carried her through on his shoulders, the heavy handcuffs biting into her wrists and the muslin drying her mouth.

He threw her onto the floorboards sending pain shooting down her leg. Seconds later Rui landed alongside her, handcuffed and gagged too, with a gash on his eyebrow and blood trickling down the side of his face.

Yelping inside the tangle of net, Bahula thudded down next to them. The brotherhood stood in front of tall bookshelves, next to where the shadows of the animal skulls danced in the firelight.

Rose glanced around the room in panic. The girl with the ringlets sat in Miss Templeforth's armchair swinging her legs beneath her and twisting a lock of hair around her finger. When their eyes met, she waved.

Next to her, Funnel stood warming his hands by the fire, staring at the grand portrait above it. "Emily Templeforth," he sighed. "A heavenly creature, by far the fairer of the Templeforth sisters."

He knew Emily Templeforth? Her thoughts gathered. *If Enna knew Funnel back then – as Miss Templeforth did – then of course her sister Emily may well have done too.* Rose watched him intently as he continued.

"Things could have been different for us, for you and

me, Emily. But now that seems like a lifetime ago. I have changed..."

Things could have been different for him and Emily Templeforth? What's he on about?

Funnel's soft smile contorted into a grimace as he turned to Banks. "You're certain the gypsy woman, Lee, is not going to be bothering us?"

"She's securely bound and incarcerated in the shop's cellar. Nobody could escape from there. Nobody. Not even that slippery charlatan," Banks clipped.

Enna is alive! A spark of hope ignited inside Rose.

"Nothing can stop us now." Banks rubbed his gloved hands together.

"Good," Funnel grinned, clenching his fists. "Verrulf wishes to end her himself. Tricky business, killing someone of her ilk."

"I bound her like an Egyptian mummy!" Snodgrass giggled.

Rose's heart sank. *Enna had been in the tobacco shop the whole time. We could have rescued her.* She sniffed.

"Well, let's get on with it then." Funnel turned to face Rose, striding towards her across the library. "I have waited a long time for this."

The clock in the lobby let out ten slow chimes. In two hours, the planetary alignment would be in place; there was nothing they could do to stop the brotherhood's evil plan. Funnel had everything he needed. She watched him approach, his pendant pulsating red and black, singing to the tune of hatred and greed that swam inside of him. Rose felt sick to her middle.

Banks dragged Rose up, holding her in a vice-like grip. Rose mumbled curses through the gag. "The pendant is yours to take, Sir," Banks smirked.

The pendant around Rose's neck started vibrating. She could feel its panic; it matched hers.

"Thank you, Banks. I intend to savour this moment. It has been forty years in the making." Funnel lifted Rose's chin and forced her to look up at him. She hoped he could see her hatred.

Close up, the scarred side of his face looked tight and shiny; the other half hung in gathered wrinkles.

In the moment of silence that moved between them he stared deep into her eyes – her soul. Her nostrils filled with the stench from his mouth – his mint humbug failing to mask the more repugnant smell of his breath. Vomit hovered at the back of her throat. She tried to struggle free but Banks held her even tighter.

Banks spoke. "This is the rat delivered here from the workhouse last Tuesday week, and employed as a maid. We had no reason to suspect she would become so pertinent to the operation," he growled. "They introduced her into the household by stealth, but, I, of course, figured it out –" he bent over, moving his lips close to her ear and she could feel the tickling whiskers of his moustache, the heat of his breath – "and trapped the vermin." Rose bashed him away with the side of her head.

"Ouch!" Banks winced. He dug his nails deep into her coat, stinging the flesh of her arm. Rose yelped, squeezed her eyes shut and tried to swallow the pain. He laughed.

"Well, well, well. You can take the girl out of the workhouse but you can't take the workhouse out of the girl. Heh." Funnel raised an eyebrow.

I'd rather come from the workhouse than be anything like you! She wanted to scream at him, but the gag prevented her so she scowled instead.

"So, the pendant chose you? I wonder *why?*" He tilted his head, his expression momentarily softened. "You have a look of the Templeforths about you. Your eyes, they remind me of…" He trailed off and his expression darkened. "It matters not; you have done your job of bringing the pendant to us." His words trickled with menace.

Funnel's gaze dropped to her pendant and the pupil of his only eye dilated.

A burst of panic rushed through Rose. The pendant pumped in rhythm with her heart.

"At last I have it," he hissed, lifting it with reverence from her neck by the chain. Rose whimpered. She felt all her fight leave as the pendant passed over her head, replaced by a hollow sense of total loss.

Suddenly, Funnel's mint humbug dropped from his mouth and skittered across the floor. Then his lips snapped shut like a mousetrap. He swayed off-kilter and stumbled, Rose's pendant gripped in his hand. Funnel crashed to his knees; his head dropped to his chest.

No one knew what to do. There were gasps of astonishment and fear. Grobbs crept closer, his eyes wide.

Funnel fell forward onto all fours. Convulsions shot along his body and his bowed head lashed about like that of a rabid dog.

Rose's heart clattered in her chest. *What's happening to him?*

She caught Snodgrass's panicked look as he backed away and huddled by the door, open-mouthed. Only Ormerod broke free from them. Pushing past Grobbs, he rushed to offer his assistance. "Sir!"

Banks released his grip on Rose and pulled Ormerod back. "Leave him!" the detective ordered. Free from his grasp, Rose slumped to her knees.

Funnel's body stilled and everyone silenced. Rose could hear her own heart thumping. The air filled with an invisible energy – a dark, clawing hollowness which seeped from Funnel and swam silently around the room. Everyone squirmed, feeling it too. Even Banks's eyes trailed around at the ceiling suspiciously Grobbs backed into the table in the far corner, his thick hands just managing to stop it from falling.

Funnel drew an enormous breath.

Rasping, he crawled towards the large armchair by the fireplace, where the girl sat, and heaved himself up. Missy bent away from him.

Funnel straightened with his back to them. He looked at least half a foot taller than he had been before and new hair grew on his scalp, thick and brown. The deep mesmerized silence was broken by a dark vibrating chuckle; Funnel's broadening shoulders shook.

"S-sir?" Banks stammered.

Funnel swivelled around and faced the room. His skin glowed, softer and younger. His good eye twinkled. He rolled his neck until it clicked. A guilty fear sheeted over Rose. *I've failed.* She couldn't bear to watch. A wicked smile drew up half of Funnel's mouth as he raked his hands through his new glossy hair. The scarred side of his face pulsated and then gradually filled and smoothed out, healing completely. Only the hole where his missing eye should have been remained.

Rejuvenated

The gathered group stared at Funnel, unable to believe their eyes.

"Master...you look half your age. So...powerful," Snodgrass snivelled, tiptoeing towards him. The others nudged each other in awe.

Missy sat forward in the armchair, her gaze, like everyone else's, transfixed on Funnel.

"What are you all staring at? I FEEL FANTASTIC!" Funnel bellowed in a tone much deeper than before.

Funnel lifted Rose's pendant triumphantly in the air, then slipped it around his neck to join its twin. The pendants pulsed alternately one darker than the other.

The young girl clapped, her face full of glee. Others mumbled excitedly.

"By Jingo. Incredible," Ormerod cheered.

"See! This is how strong the ancient magic is. You too can be powerful once we have completed the spell." Funnel pointed around the room and pulled up his sleeve, exposing the sun tattoo. "Our Shadow Lord, Verrulf, has chosen me – chosen us all. Are you ready to undertake the task he has set for us, brothers?"

Ormerod edged forward, pulling up his sleeve, revealing his own tattoo printed there. "I am," he exclaimed, kneeling before Funnel.

The others hurriedly copied Ormerod, until they all bowed at Funnel's feet.

Funnel sucked air in through his teeth and let his head fall backwards, as a further bolt rejuvenated him. "Your devotion strengthens me. Verrulf shall reward you all."

"Sir." Banks stepped forward. "It is fifteen minutes past ten o'clock. We must go to the West Pier, the planets align at midnight and we have much to prepare. Shall I dispose of the children?"

Dispose of us? Still handcuffed, Rose's eyes swung from Banks to Funnel and back again, realizing at that second that they wanted to kill her and Rui.

"Yes." Funnel glared at Rose. She trembled. "They know too much and the girl has a connection to the pendant."

"I could set fire to the house with them inside?" Snodgrass said snidely, glaring at Rose. His hand, where she'd bitten him, still oozed with blood.

Rui, whose cries were muffled by his gag, kicked out. Trickles of cold perspiration ran down the back of Rose's green dress. *Fire?*

Snodgrass continued. "They would roast like piggies." He flapped his fingers either side of his head like ears. "Oink, oink! And good riddance to them. He he!" His laugh droned like a whirring engine. But realizing no one else had laughed, Snodgrass stopped and his cheeks reddened.

"Enough, Snodgrass," Banks sniped. "You imbecile."

Snodgrass's shoulders hunched over; he looked like a scrawny hawk as he hopped away, protecting his injured hand like a broken wing, glancing distrustfully at the other men.

"Relax, Snodgrass, your loyalty will be rewarded, of course," Funnel countered somewhat half-heartedly. "No, house fires are messy, and too likely to rouse attention. Lock them up, the attic will suffice. Verrulf wants to question the girl." He gestured to Rose. "Once the black sun has risen, he and his Creeplings can decide their fate."

Creeplings? Verrulf decide my fate? Rose choked, her eyes welling up. She suddenly preferred the idea of the house fire. That way at least someone might see the flames and rescue them.

Funnel strode towards Missy and patted her head. Her china-doll face broke into an even grin, exposing two perfect rows of tiny teeth.

"And you, Missy," he said, "shall watch me become the man I was born to be. Verrulf has always had a soft spot for you, just as I do, my dark princess."

"Thank you, Great-Uncle," she replied with a sugared smile.

Great-Uncle? Rose scowled. Enna said the pendant had reacted strongly to her when she'd come to the house, and that was why *they're related*. Helpless, Rose's chest began to rise and fall, her sobs muted by the gag.

Funnel turned to the men gathered around him. "Tonight, my twelve brothers, we will unleash the black sun. After midnight, once the planets align and the spell is performed, the sun will turn black and this world will belong to Verrulf and his army of Creeplings. This will be the strongest spell performed on this earth for thousands of years. And we shall be rewarded with power and strength beyond our wildest dreams. To the West Pier!"

Funnel wobbled as a further surge of energy shot through his veins. Leaning on his cane he steadied himself. His eye rolled and a broad smile stretched diagonally across his thin face.

"And Ormerod, I trust you can transcribe the spell?"

Ormerod wedged his monocle over his right eye, clutching Mr Gupta's open journal. "The entire thing is written in a very ancient dialect." His voice quivered. "I have to admit it's not a type I am overly familiar with."

Rui looked up. Rose caught the flash of hope in his eyes.

"WHAT?" Funnel boomed.

Ormerod drew a quick breath. "But I am certain I can get by," he squeaked, removing his monocle and positioning it over the text like a magnifying glass.

"Very good," Funnel smirked. "Banks, deal with the children, and meet us at the West Pier when you're done."

"Yes, Sir," Banks replied.

He spun towards the others. "Shift them upstairs to the attic," Banks ordered. "Grobbs, take the girl. Graves, the boy and, Snodgrass, I trust you can manage the monkey?"

Still netted, Bahula shrieked as Snodgrass slung him over his shoulder like a sack of rags and bones. "Yes, Sir."

Grobbs's thick hands dragged Rose backwards across the carpet towards the door. Rui was pushed along behind her.

Missy looked on, twirling her ringlets around her finger, and then inspecting her nails. *However pretty she might be on the outside, she's got the innards of a viper*, Rose thought, her lips pursed. *I'd wipe that smile off her face given half the chance.*

Funnel's words carried from the room behind them. "In less than two hours the Black Sun will rise over us." He drew in a long breath. "The Creeplings will walk this earth tonight, our Shadow Lord, Verrulf, will become of flesh and bone and we will have the power we have dreamed of."

"Hear! Hear!"

"Bravo!"

"Long reign the Brotherhood of the Black Sun!"

Hot tears streamed down Rose's face. She knew she'd failed. The cause was…lost.

The Handcuff King

Snodgrass, Graves and the huge Grobbs hauled their captives up to Rose's attic room. Once there, Grobbs produced two more sets of handcuffs and bolted Rose and Rui onto the bars of the iron radiator that stood next to the bed, Rui at one end, Rose at the other. Tears trickled down Rose's face as she looked pleadingly at Grobbs, but his eyes were as cold as bottle tops. He clicked the handcuffs shut.

Bahula had stopped wriggling inside the net, and lay there shivering.

"Right," Grobbs said, dusting his hands together. "They won't be getting out of here."

"Just to be sure, I'll lock the blighters in too," Snodgrass whined, holding the door open as the other two men departed. "Hope you don't get too lonely up here!" He grinned as he walked out, shutting and locking the door behind him. "You'll have plenty of company soon enough," he whispered. "Of the shadowy type."

A minute later they heard the front door slam shut.

Rose frantically tugged at the handcuffs, which clanked against the radiator and sent an echoing clang of distress through the pipework of the empty house. But no one was there to hear it. It was useless; the handcuffs were so heavy that the more she pulled, the more they hurt.

The storm outside rattled at the window, throwing rain in gusty handfuls.

It wasn't even like Jack Billings would be nosing around. He was away, and there was no one who could save them.

She looked over to Rui, who had turned away from her, and was tugging at his coat trying to reach his pocket. *He can't even bear to look at me,* she thought.

Memories filled Rose's mind. Enna coming for her at the workhouse. Rui's excitement when they found the missing pendant. Mr Gupta's bulging eyes in the graveyard. The Creeplings… Verrulf. And then she thought about Enna trapped in the cellar of the tobacco shop all this time, when they could have saved her. The injustice of it all made her so angry. *We're not through yet.*

Rose turned her attention to her gag, jerking her jaw up and down repeatedly. With a purposeful tug towards her shoulder, it finally loosened. She spat out the ball of muslin.

"Rui!" she spluttered between gulps of air. He twisted his neck towards her, his eyes wide open. "Bring your head towards me," she panted.

Rose strained forward, latching her teeth on to the coarse cloth that covered Rui's mouth, and tugged and tugged. It fell.

"Thank you, Rose," Rui puffed. "I know I messed up – and I'm sorry. Perhaps I'm not as good a detective as I hoped." He looked down.

"Rubbish," Rose said. "Besides, you're a detective in training. You gotta get things wrong, so *next time* you can get them right."

"Next time, yes." His eyes flashed. "I think *next time* is already upon us. I have a brilliant plan, you see."

"You do!" Rose rallied.

"The handcuffs they've used to restrain us are Darby Cuffs; they have a single locking mechanism which, regrettably, is impossible to open without a key."

"Great," Rose sighed, knowing they didn't have one.

Rui continued. "You know, Harry Houdini, the world famous escape artist –" he didn't wait for Rose to answer

– "is also known as The Handcuff King. Nothing can contain the man – he is pure, slippery genius… I subscribe to his *Conjurers' Monthly Magazine*, of course."

Rui fiddled with something behind his back.

"Now, during my brief scuffle with Banks in the lobby downstairs, whilst trying to retrieve Mr Gupta's journal, I managed to remove something from his pocket – the only thing in there – it always pays to be resourceful in these situations."

Rose remembered seeing him slip something into his pocket before that Missy had turned on the lights. "The key to these handcuffs?" Rose leaned forward, a smile expanding.

"Alas, no."

Her mouth straightened.

Rui continued. "I suppose it would be no surprise that a man such as Banks, with greased-back hair and coiffured moustache, would have such a product on his person."

"What you on about?"

"Ballantine."

"Moustache cream?" *He's off his chump.* Rose scanned her sparse room for inspiration – anything that might help. *Nothing.* A deep sadness filled her. "I've turned out to be a pretty rubbish guardian. I lost the pendant to them, Rui," she sniffed. "And without that…I'm nothing."

"On the contrary," he corrected her at once, his hands still busy behind his back. "Without the pendant you remain Rose Muddle, my most tremendous companion."

Rose gave him a quick smile. "But the Brotherhood of the Black Sun have everything they need. They'll already be at the West Pier waiting for the planets to align. They've got Enna Lee trapped, and we're proper stuck here."

"I must disagree. You see, these particular cuffs were decommissioned due to one important defect: they are non-adjustable; one size supposedly fits all. They are heavy, cumbersome and, quite frankly, not fit for purpose when you have a lubricant...and hands as small and agile as mine."

There was a metallic clunk behind Rui.

He grinned.

"Now, if you wouldn't mind," he said standing free. "Wipe this on your hands, would you?" Rose looked down at his empty handcuffs, still attached to the radiator, her mouth ajar.

"You bleedin' well did it!" she spluttered. Rui helped smooth the cool lotion on to her hands. They slid free with relative ease. "Woo HOO!" she shouted, standing up and stroking her sore wrists.

Rui picked Bahula up, still trapped in the net, placed him on the bed and hurriedly released him. Bahula bounced free and jumped up and down on the mattress. Rose snuggled him into a warm embrace. Rui joined them, and for the tiniest moment Rose thought things might be all right.

"The West Pier!" She straightened suddenly. "They have my pendant!"

Rose and Rui stood face to face. "And the cup, and the journal and Mr Gupta's body." Rui ticked each off against the digits of his hand.

"And we have to rescue Enna Lee." Rose squeezed her hands into fists. "Let's get out of here."

"But, unfortunately, we are still locked in your bedroom."

Rose marched to her bedroom door and peered through the keyhole. "That Snodgrass is sloppy, he left the key in the lock," she muttered, a wry smile forming on her lips. "I have an old workhouse trick for this, and as that Funnel said earlier, you can't never take the workhouse out of this girl." She plucked a hairgrip from her head. A tuft of her auburn hair fell in front of her eyes; she blew it away.

Quick as a flash, Rose grabbed the brown paper packaging her new clothes had been wrapped in, squashed it flat and stuffed it under the door. Using her hairgrip, she poked out the door key, which chinked onto the paper beneath.

"Hey presto!" She grinned, theatrically pulling the

paper and key inside. "The key to my room, Master Rui."
She curtseyed, presenting him the key on her outstretched
palms.

Rui shook his head and smiled. "Tre-*mendous*!" he said,
unlocking the door and kicking it wide. "Open sesame."

Bahula hared out of the room and they followed him,
descending through the big house to the kitchen below.

Downstairs, Rose pointed at the kitchen clock in dismay.
"Look, it's gone eleven," she panted.

"Yes, and the spell will be performed at midnight.
We have less than an hour to get to the West Pier."

"But first of all we need to save Enna." Rose drew a
deep breath; she wouldn't let Enna down. "I ain't leaving
her trapped in the shop. Plus, we *need* her." Rose did up
her coat buttons. "Once we've got Enna, we'll head
seawards. The West Pier ain't that far. We can do it."

"Of course we can. Together we can do anything!"

Rain hammered against the kitchen window making
them feel like they were strewn on a boat far out on stormy
seas. Rose pulled on her gloves. "But the odds ain't in our
favour. Even the police are in on it. I've got nothing to lose
but you, Rui…" Rose trailed off.

"We must try and do whatever we can. That's what

Miss T would want: to fight the good fight. She would be spurring us on. Such a tremendous woman! And Mr Gupta too, they tried their best to stop these villains. But it looks like it's down to you and me now, Rose Muddle. You know." He paused for a moment. "I came here searching for adventure, Rose, and it turns out I found something far exceeding that: true friendship."

"Yes," she whispered, wanting to say more but not finding the words. *Friendship*. She realized in that moment Rui was the best friend she'd ever had. She felt a tear coming and looked up at the ceiling to stop it falling.

A clap of thunder shook the world outside.

Bahula sidled up to Rui's legs. "Oh! And you too are my friend – a brave and fearless comrade." Rui placed Bahula on the kitchen table, and bent down to eye level and spoke very softly. "May Hanuman, the monkey god, watch and guide you, tonight. We may have need of your cleverness."

Bahula stared at Rui, unblinking, as he spoke.

Rose rested her hand on Rui's shoulder. "Yeah. We all have to rely on each other now – it's all we've got."

"Right, well Godspeed." Rui pulled up his jacket collar, and Bahula jumped onto his shoulder. "Now, dearest friends – well, *only* friends," Rui continued. "The planets align in fifty-five minutes; we must together overcome the terrible evil the Brotherhood of the Black Sun plan to unleash. Ready?" He kicked the back door open.

A flash of lightning lit up the ugly night outside.

Rui turned to Rose. A moment of silence danced between them.

"Let's go get Enna!"

Two Halves

The storm cracked and shook the sky outside. Rui had wasted no time locating the wrench he'd found the evening before in the yard of the tobacconist's. Knowing the shop was empty, he'd forced open the chained padlock to the cellar, not caring if anyone heard.

Inside the cellar, rain lashed through the open trapdoor, splattering on the dusty flagstones. Rose found Enna's discarded shawl and held onto it, watching anxiously as Rui forced open the crate that Bahula had sniffed out.

The nails broke away from the frame with a groan. Rui dropped the wrench by his feet, and it clattered across the stone-clad floor.

The three of them peered inside the open crate. A flash of lightning spread a bright blue light over the cellar.

A frail body bound in gauze bandages lay scrunched up at the bottom. Sensing their presence, the head looked up.

"Enna Lee?" Rui croaked. The bandaged head nodded.

Tears stung in Rose's eyes. "Get her out!" she shrieked, as hot fury raced through her. "Them lily-livered cowards."

Helping Enna out, they unbound ream after ream of gauze from her face, until they could finally see her. Dark circles hung beneath her eyes; her skin was sallow and drawn.

"I need my waters…" Enna's chest heaved as she pulled away the remaining bandages. Her jewelled fingers gripped the crate for support. "Anthony Funnel," she hissed.

Rose explained all that had happened and the events that had unfolded. When they had finished, Enna turned to Rose, her tired eyes filled with sadness. "Rose, there is something you *must* know," Enna rasped over the knuckling rain outside. "Your two halves."

A shiver flew up Rose's spine. "Yes? What do they mean?" Rose stared at her unblinking.

"Emily Templeforth."

"Miss T's sister?" Rui asked.

Enna nodded, her dull blue eyes fixed on Rose.

"She's something to do with me, isn't she? I know coz

~ 272 ~

the pendant told me. Or tried to, but I just couldn't understand, and—"

"Anthony Funnel," Enna interrupted. She shut her eyes and drew a deep breath.

"Yes, Emily Templeforth and he knew each other," Rui interjected. "I remember in the library, the way Funnel looked at her portrait. I could detect a hidden history." He looked between the two of them.

"Emily and Anthony Funnel were childhood sweethearts," Enna stated. "Emily died quite suddenly at the tender age of twenty-one. We tried to get word to Anthony, who had left for India with the British Army. But some time later we received a telegram saying that he had died in a train fire," she spoke quickly.

"But as we know now, he faked his own death," Rui added.

Enna sighed. "I believe Anthony Funnel and Emily Templeforth had a child. A secret daughter, whom even Funnel did not know about. Following Emily's death, over forty years ago, Emily's father took that child to the workhouse…and left her there. That daughter was—"

A clap of thunder shook the room, followed by a blinding bolt of lightning. Rose stood firm.

"Elephas Maximus!" Rui stared at Rose.

"W-what? I'm not following this."

In truth, Rose was following every word, but she didn't like where it was leading.

"Your mother, Rose. She was the daughter of Emily Templeforth and Anthony Funnel."

"What? That…Funnel is my…grandfather?" She knew Enna was right, but the thought of it stung. "So that's why the pendant showed me the portrait in the library, then put me inside Funnel's head?" She squeezed her eyes shut. "It was trying to tell me all along."

"Your two halves, Rose," Rui said. "That's why it was so important. You share the bloodline of both brothers! Your mother was part Templeforth and part Funnel – which means you are too. That's why Verrulf fears you and why your power over the pendant is so strong."

Rose clenched her fists.

"Rose, the planets align soon. Then they will perform the spell." Rui tugged at her sleeve.

Enna pointed into the storm raging in through the trapdoor. "Go. Now."

"What about you?" Rose asked, wiping her wet hair from her face.

"I need to get back to the park and drink my waters; I need to revitalize, build my strength. I am no good to you this weak. *You* must stop Verrulf.

"If the spell performed is strong enough to open the

gateway inside the cup and let Verrulf out...we are in serious trouble." Enna stood up but stumbled, just managing to stop herself from falling.

Rose knew there was no way Enna could make it to the pier. It was down to them. Using the open crate as a launch, Bahula leaped onto Rui's shoulder.

Rui shot a look to Rose, his eyes fierce behind his long lashes.

"To the West Pier." Rose gritted her teeth. She grabbed Rui's hand and together with Bahula, they headed back into the storm.

40

The West Pier

The rain fell in sheets and the wind drove it towards them. Rose and Rui pushed on against it until, finally, the wrought-iron entrance to the West Pier loomed ahead. A fork of lightning highlighted the decked walkway beyond the gates, dotted with whitewashed buildings and pavilions. The waves of the English Channel crashed beneath it.

Rose picked up the heavy chained padlock on the towering gate and, shaking her head, shouted over the wind. "These gates are too high to climb, and this lock ain't going to be easy to break."

She peered through the iron bars, the icy metal biting

her cheeks. Rain pelted off the deserted boulevard like dancing gravel. "There ain't no one here."

"Rose," Rui called behind her. "Jack Billings said Mr Gupta's body was discovered *under* the pier, not on it!"

"You're right!" Rose ran past the entrance to the pier, and over to the waist-high railings stretching all the way along the sea road.

She leaned over the railings, wiping the loose strands of wet hair from her face. Several yards below she could see the pedestrian walkway which extended all along the seafront to Shoreham Harbour. The beach beyond formed a series of steep banks, pitting and falling down to the shoreline. The sea's frothing mouth dragged the shingle back noisily as the next wave pitched over it. The West Pier jutted out into the angry sea, supported by legs of iron.

"Do you suppose they are down there somewhere?" Rui shouted above the noise of the lashing rain.

Rose raised herself up onto the bar of the railing, and peered down towards the shadowy underbelly of the pier next to them. She spotted a distant light blinking within the cavernous blackness.

"I seen something, this way." She spat the salty hair from her mouth and grabbed Rui's hand. Together they rushed down the wide steps to the promenade below, Bahula scampering behind.

At the bottom, sticking close to the wall, they sneaked past the brick arches supporting the roadway. Bahula surged forward and grabbed something rolling on the ground. Turning, he held aloft his missing red hat.

"Look, Bahula's found his hat," Rui whispered. "He must have lost it down here, when Banks attacked poor Mr Gupta."

Grinning, Bahula strapped it back onto his head.

The wind whistled through the West Pier as they skittered between the tall iron columns. Thunder shook the ground. Rose looked up as the thick wires tying the structure together creaked around them.

Running from one iron leg to the next, they made their way towards the light, the storm masking the sound of their feet crunching the shingle. Bahula trailed above in the rafters.

The light now flickered twenty yards away.

"There are people over there," Rui whispered, pointing towards the shadowy figures ahead.

Ducking, Rose and Rui scampered to a discarded pile of fishing nets thick with seaweed. They crept along the back of the nets to the far end where a heap of lobster pots teetered in the breeze. Bahula swung down to join them as they peered over the top. The rain struck the walkway above them like a continuous round of applause.

Ten yards ahead, highlighted beneath a swinging lantern, the Brotherhood formed a wide circle. They wore hooded gowns which rippled in the wind. Rose picked out the spindly figure of Snodgrass, and the massive frame of Grobbs – but all the others were hard to tell apart. She gritted her teeth. She wanted to know which one was Banks.

In the centre, Funnel stood hands on hips. His outfit was different from the others: a hoodless black gown trimmed in gold. He spun around, revealing the black sun emblem embroidered on his back. Stepping to one side, he exposed Mr Gupta's body. The corpse sat cross-legged, kept upright by an iron rod forced down the back of his tunic. Funnel marched around the corpse, throwing his hands in the air and shouting.

"That's horrible." Rose swallowed. "Poor Mr Gupta." She squeezed Rui's arm.

"How dare they desecrate his body like this?" Rui murmured, his lips pursed.

Mr Gupta's swollen eyes stared, bloodshot, beneath the lantern, his mouth gaping and his turban balanced at an angle on his head, threads running free where the ruby had once been.

Bahula squeaked into his tiny fists and Rose squeezed him close to her.

Another bolt of lightning scattered blue light across the men, followed at once by a tremendous bang of thunder.

"Funnel looks decades younger now," Rui whispered.

Funnel's wrinkles had filled out, his scars healed, his lips were fatter, and his now brown hair waved around in the wind. But his missing eye, unashamedly absent, confirmed his true identity.

Rose shivered, not against the cold, but against everything. *Please let 'em fail,* she begged to anyone who might be listening. "What we gonna do?" She looked on in dismay. *Maybe Banks is right? What match are us two and a monkey against all them?*

"Why isn't this working?" Funnel whipped around and confronted Ormerod. "I can't see how pouring the water over a corpse can possibly be right!" Ormerod jumped back from Funnel's angry words, nearly losing his grip on Mr Gupta's journal. "I thought you said you could translate this! The alignment is already in place, man," he bellowed.

Rose and Rui peered through the lobster pots.

"I knew it! They can't translate it, Rose!" Rui whispered.

Ormerod flinched. "Try it again, but this time maybe let the corpse drink from the cup?" he shouted over the weather, his thin hand outstretched.

Funnel ducked out of view momentarily, then stood clutching the Amber Cup. A violent gust of wind suddenly swept through the moaning structure.

Funnel clicked his fingers, and a member of the brotherhood stood, and presented Enna's flask. It was Banks. His stony face flickered in the lamplight from beneath his hood. He popped off the crystal stopper and filled the cup with the red liquid.

"Enna's magic waters," Rose gasped, her eyes fixed on the cup, which started to glow as the brotherhood began to mumble strange-sounding words.

Banks hurriedly resumed his position in the circle with the others.

Thrusting the cup above him, Funnel's face illuminated under its glow. The cup's energy sent him stumbling towards the corpse.

The brotherhood's incantations carried on the wind; they chanted a language Rose didn't know.

The cup pulsed in time with their words. Funnel addressed the cup, repeating back the strange-sounding words that Ormerod spoke aloud for him.

"What's he saying, Rui?"

"He is saying: I am the bearer of the two pendants and I demand you to bring the Master of the Black Sun forth, his new body awaits. Rose, he's managing to translate it!"

The hollow sound of Funnel's laugh filled the air as black shapes emerged within the body of the cup.

The shadows, like a pack of hunting wolves, grew ever bigger. The grotesque projections radiated across the clearing and onto the hooded faces of the brotherhood. One electrical flash of lightning followed another before a rumble of thunder shook Rose's bones. It felt like the sky was cracking apart.

41

The Gateway

"KALA SURAI, KALA SURAI, KALA SURAI."
Banks's face shone in the light, unblinking and crazed. He repeated the chant, his mouth opening and closing in time with the others.

Rose covered her ears, her head throbbing. *Something terrible is coming!* She could feel it. Her skin crawled with its energy.

"Rui, we got to do something to stop them," Rose shouted above the noise, just yards away from the bizarre ceremony. She caught sight of her pendant flashing golden next to Verrulf's darker one. Trapped against its will, being forced to comply.

Rose heard a sudden rush of voices in her mind. "*Your two halves, Rose.*" Miss Templeforth's panicked voice cried above the others. Rose felt a warm rush through her heart. "Rui, I know what I gotta do." She flexed her fingers. "I need to get both 'em pendants. If I got both brothers' blood running through me, maybe I'm strong enough to stop all this?"

"But rushing in there now will just see us captured. There are too many of them," Rui insisted. "When the time is right, I will formulate a plan."

Rui was right. Rose had to trust him; a plan was more than she had just now.

Funnel's mouth twisted as he repeated aloud the strange words Ormerod whispered to him. Rose didn't need to know what any of them meant to feel a thick invisible ugliness that hung over the scene. She shivered.

"WE ARE READY FOR YOU, MASTER!" Funnel shrieked over the brotherhood's chants and the howling wind.

Funnel kneeled by Gupta's dead body and poured the cup's liquid into its open mouth. The ground beneath him rumbled, throwing him off-balance.

The whole pier shook with a metallic groan.

Bahula rolled around on his back, his hands grappling at the air above him.

"What's happening?" Rose breathed. While her heart was banging inside her chest, the rest of her was numbed with utter dread.

Everything froze. A vast, eerie stillness swallowed the space.

The noises of the crashing waves, the raking shingle and the howling wind all drew into a temporary vacuum. A moment so silent it pulled at Rose's eardrums.

Funnel stared at the cup, his lips trembling.

Slowly a wisp of blackened smoke drew up from inside the cup. Delicate and fragile.

The twelve members of the brotherhood gasped in awe.

Mesmerized, Rose watched the smoke dance around like a flame. Then it morphed into a crooked hand with elongated fingers that teased the air. It looked wretched. Rose's guts twisted as a choking fear flooded her body.

"It's him! He's coming." On Rui's words, a cloud of black matter exploded from the cup. It surged upwards and hit the platform above, before raining down to gather in a seething pool around Funnel's feet.

"It worked!" Funnel roared.

The thick, treacle-like mass licked about his feet. Funnel sniggered as it rose up, forming coils that curled up around him like a serpent. Funnel's smile dropped. The gunge wound higher up his body, roll upon roll until it reached his head. Terrified, Funnel's mouth opened to scream.

It covered him.

Silence.

ChhhhROARRRRRRRR!

The sound exploded. The blackness surged upwards into a giant column, twisting into the rafters, concealing Funnel and Mr Gupta's corpse.

The brotherhood stared calmly on, as if in a trance, their robes pulling them towards the swirling chaos.

"What's wrong with 'em?" Rose shouted. "Why ain't they trying to get away?"

Before Rui could answer, a streak of purple light exploded in the middle of the vortex. Rose steadied herself against the vibrating ground, but everything around them tumbled away. They were exposed.

Finding his balance, Rui dug his nails into Rose's arm and pulled her close.

"What have they started?" Rui breathed, his hair blowing forward.

"It's like the belly of hell has just ripped open," Rose muttered, holding Bahula close to her chest.

A whining noise thrummed from the cyclone and it spun round and round, howling, louder and louder. Funnel and Mr Gupta were still lost in its middle. Rose glimpsed a huge swirling face forming within the chaos, its mouth stretched wide, its teeth snapping, but by the next rotation it had been sucked away. Giant shadowy hands snatched out, trying to claw themselves free. Rose bent away in terror – the scene looked just like the picture Mr Gupta had detailed in his journal. The turmoil expanded and spiralled in every direction, until even the kneeling brotherhood were consumed by it.

Rui stepped forward, shielding his face from its force. Rose stood next to him, the hem of her dress drawing towards it.

"Let's see." Rui picked up a lobster pot and threw it inside the melee. The cage entered the cyclone, and getting sucked into its current, it spun higher and higher, faster and faster, until it was lost inside the black swirling mass.

"Deduction number one," Rui began. "We can enter the magic circle. "Deduction number two, if we do—"

"We're mincemeat," Rose said, with a swallow. Bahula gripped onto her leg.

"Correct."

A shrill sound filled the air. Rose held her head, the noise burning her ears. Bahula jumped onto Rui's shoulder and clung to his neck.

"This way, or we'll be drawn in." Rui pulled Rose over to the nearest iron column. "Hold on!"

They both clung on for dear life. Rose's knuckles turned

white. The force of the drag was so strong that she buckled her fingers together to resist it. Next to them, a lobster pot fell to the ground and tumbled along towards the vortex, followed by three more. The wind, the rain – even the oxygen it seemed – was ripped away from them.

The pier groaned, its structure shifting, and Rose's gaze turned upwards.

"This place is not going to withstand the pressure," Rui shouted. "We need to get out, Rose!"

And then in a heartbeat everything stopped.

Silence.

Rose heard a sudden rush of voices in her mind. "Your two halves, Rose," Miss Templeforth's panicked voice cried above the others. Rose's heart winged. She flexed her fingers.

Gravelly stones suddenly rained down on them, striking the iron structure like renegade bullets. Rose and Rui grabbed each other, shielding their heads from the falling debris.

The swirling black mist inside the circle calmed and gradually receded. At the heart of the circle Funnel lay in a crumpled heap. The cup rested upturned by his side. Opposite him a hulking black figure kneeled where Mr Gupta's body had been, his broad shoulders blanketed in a cloak.

The creature's giant stag antlers jutted from the top of his head, proud and otherworldly. The lamp had shattered and been replaced by a new mauve-coloured light source which radiated up from the ground inside the circle.

"Verrulf," Rose hissed.

42

HIM

Verrulf raised his hulking head and a sound like rustling leaves filled the air. He drew a rasping breath. His two glaring eyes pulsed red. Rose gripped her throat. "He's alive, Rui!"

"It's worked. The necromancy spell. Mr Gupta has been replaced," Rui said, his voice quivering. "By...Verrulf. He's free from the cup."

"And where have the rest of them disappeared to?" Rose whispered, staring anxiously around the iron column that they were now hidden behind.

Twelve unoccupied robes were heaped on the ground.

Above them a powdery blackness swam about. "They've gone!"

Verrulf's long black hair blew about around his youthful face. His chiselled cheekbones and strong nose glowed with a blueish-light, like moonlight. He shook his mighty antlers and stood.

Rose stared across at him, her mouth open. His branched antlers merged into the cavern of shadows above. Even without the antlers he must have been nearly seven feet tall. He wasn't at all how Rose had imagined he'd be. He wasn't all shadowy now, he looked more human instead. And young, and...handsome even.

Verrulf's cloak hung from his broad shoulders down to the ground, covered in squares of black-papery material, which rustled endlessly in the wind, like whispering voices. His thin lips turned down and his eyes blazed ever brighter behind narrowing lids.

"I brrreathe!" Verrulf's voice vibrated, deep and ugly. Verrulf studied his giant shimmering hands. "My human forrrm," he muttered to himself, his voice gravelly. "I will be so strrrong," he grunted, sniffing the air.

Funnel began to stir and stumbled to his feet. Tripping over his robe, he spun in a circle. "Where are my men?" he croaked, looking at the empty cloaks which writhed around as if each covered a nest of rats. Funnel doubled over, choking, blood spluttering from his mouth, his hair grey once more and his face sallow and drawn.

"Funnel's ageing again," Rose gasped. The pendants swung around his neck, no longer flashing, but as if they had no life left in them.

Verrulf's grin exposed broken gnarly teeth embedded into black gums. "You brrrought me back and the gateway is nearrrly fully open. My Crrreeplings are coming – and they arrre hungrrry!" Verrulf's navy-blue tongue ran along his thin lips. "Soon I will have strrrength to walk and then I shall HUNT."

"This is not what we planned and—" Funnel began, but his voice was swallowed by dark, unholy noises that swarmed around him. He looked about, trying to find their source. The brotherhood's robes shifted, rising up and down. Breathing. Funnel backed away. "What is going on?"

"You have serrrved yourrr purrrpose. You have my perrrmission to die." Verrulf's words shook around them. "So I can take the pendants for myself."

"Die?" Funnel cowered. "B-but I helped you, you're here because of me. You promised me riches. I command you to stop all this and return my men," he cried jutting out his chin.

"YOU WEAK HUMAN!" Verrulf boomed. The

~ 292 ~

ferocity of his words ricocheted off the metal structure. Funnel flew backwards, landing in a crumpled heap.

SSSSSSSSSssssssssssssssssssss.

Echoing voices hissed as one. Funnel shielded his face.

Rose's large grey eyes reflected the drama playing out before them like mirrors. "I ain't stopping here watching this, Rui. Somehow, I need to get both them pendants. And before that monster does. And I gotta put him back in the cup – just like Albion did." She sprang forwards, ready.

"Wait, Rose." Rui reached out to pull her back, turning to Bahula. "Quickly, Bahula, get the cup." He lifted the monkey up onto the iron column they were hiding behind.

The cup? Yes! Rose craned forward. With everything that had happened she had totally forgotten about it. She spotted it, now a natural deep red, camouflaged amid the darkness of the shingle. It pulsed once, as if winking at them. Bahula sprang silently away into the rafters.

"Once we see Bahula, we are going in. We need to create a distraction while Bahula removes the cup."

She knew her two halves still made her strong. Did it mean that she could control the cup if she could get both pendants? Would she be powerful enough? It was their only hope.

Almost immediately, a tiny silhouette scuttled down one of the iron stacks and into the magic circle.

"There's Bahula," Rose pointed.

"Now. Let's go," Rui said. Squeezing hands, they stood as one.

"Tally-ho," Rui said through gritted teeth as together they surged forward. Rose's heart thumped with fear and adrenaline. She knew they were doing the right thing. She had to stop Verrulf – or die trying.

They leaped over the inflating robes and into the middle of the circle.

Verrulf jumped back from Funnel. On seeing Rose, Verrulf's look of surprise turned into a grimace. "You!" he howled.

Rose stood tall. Rui stood with his back to hers, staring horrified at the blackness sweeping around the brotherhood's empty robes. The energy inside the circle felt electric with danger, outside of time, alive with the sound of hidden, whispering voices.

Blocked by Rose and Rui, Bahula grabbed the cup unseen.

"Rrrose Muddle! We meet at larrst."

"You fear me, Verrulf!" Rose shouted, surprised by the strength of her own voice. "I share your blood!" she continued, trying to hold Verrulf's complete attention while Bahula scuttled away up into the network of iron above, the cup gripped under his arm.

"Me – fearrr *you*! A human child!" His muscular frame dwarfed Rose and Rui.

Rose didn't budge an inch.

"*You* can't stop *me*," Verrulf hissed at Rose. "You arrre trrrapped inside this cirrrcle, you cannot leave. Welcome to your timely end, Rrrose Muddle!" Verrulf's voice sounded almost amused. "The gates to my worrrld arrre opening. Yourrr sun will be hidden by mine, and in that darrrkness the Crrreeplings will feed and *I* will rrrule suprrreme!" He spread out his arms making himself huge with his cloak.

"I CAN stop you. I share your blood and Albion's. I am the granddaughter of Emily Templeforth" – she pointed down at the body doubled over on the ground – "and Funnel. We figured it all out." Rose nodded, her nostrils flaring.

Funnel stopped still, then lifted his head to look at Rose. "My g-granddaughter?" She caught the mixture of shock and sadness register across his face. Funnel pointed at Verrulf. "You betrayed me!" he moaned. "You used me. LIED to me." He collapsed hard onto the shingle, without even the strength to contain his fall.

"Yes!" Verrulf sneered. "NOW DIE QUICKLY so I can take the pendants." He readied to lunge at Funnel.

"NO!" Rose blocked his path, tiny against Verrulf's

hulking form. He paused momentarily, taken aback by her grit.

Rose's heart banged like a caged bird inside her ribs.

"As you wish. I'll kill you firrrst."

"NO, WAIT!" Rui shouted, his hands raised. "We have the cup. And we'll put you back in it."

"Yeah!" Rose said. Though a nagging part of her was not at all sure they could.

Rui whistled up into the rafters and Bahula poked his head down before leaping to the ground to join them. He curled his limbs around Rui's feet and held the cup aloft.

Sssssssssssssssssssssssssssssssssssssssssssss.

Surprise flickered across Verrulf's face as he registered what was happening.

Verrulf cast his gaze over to Funnel, who still rolled about on the ground, writhing in pain. Still alive.

"On the contrrrarrry." Verrulf smiled at Bahula. "MY monkey has the cup." With these words, Verrulf's face softened and his eyes shut, opening to reveal the human eyes of Mr Gupta. Slowly, Mr Gupta's whole face appeared, replacing Verrulf's. He smiled at Bahula through a thick grey beard.

"He's shape-shifted!" Rui gasped. "Bahula, that's not your master."

"Mere pas ao mere mitra. Mere pas lao, tum chote se chatur bandar," Verrulf coaxed, but it was Mr Gupta's voice that spoke.

Bahula tilted his head

"Bahula, NAHIM! He's tricking you," Rui implored.

But Bahula scampered towards the sound of his old master's voice, taking the cup with him.

Verrulf laughed. "You cleverrr little soon-to-be-dead crrreaturrre you."

"Oh, Bahula. NO!" Rose begged him. But it was too late.

Bahula offered out the cup and grinned.

Verrulf bent low and retrieved it. As soon as he grasped the cup, Mr Gupta's face morphed back into Verrulf's and he let rip a greedy laugh.

Bahula flattened to the ground and cowered backwards.

"Rui, we're done for." Rose's hair blew across her face, her eyes fierce. She clung onto Rui's arm.

"What's this?" Verrulf squinted at the tiny cup, dwarfed by his big hands. He frowned.

"GRRRHHHHRRRAAAAGHHHHHHHH!" Verrulf's roar twisted through the iron structure of the pier. His eyes blazed red in their sockets.

What's going on? Rose strained to see.

"Look!" she panted, tugging on Rui's sleeve. "It's not the cup. Ha! Bahula's given him his hat!"

"His fez!" Rui grinned. "Why, Bahula is as brave as Hanuman himself," Rui whispered, his eyes darting every which way.

"Enough! I'm going to finish you once and forrr all," Verrulf roared at Rose. Hatred blazed in his eyes. He swiped at Rose with his massive forearm. She catapulted through the air landing heavily. The fall cut the breath from her lungs.

"ROSE!" Rui yelled rushing over to her side.

"Leave her alone!" Funnel whimpered at Verrulf, unable to lift himself from the ground.

"l'm going to rrrip yourrr granddaughterrr limb frrrom limb." Verrulf snarled at Funnel. "And you can watch."

Rui cradled Rose in his arms. But it was too late. Rose squeezed her eyes shut. Verrulf's head leaned back and he let loose an almighty cry. He charged towards them. They were done for.

43

Light in Growing Darkness

A ball of light vaulted over the brotherhood's robes, blocking Verrulf mid-leap.

"SssswAhhhghh!" Verrulf wailed. Stumbling backwards, he crashed to his knees.

Rose shielded her eyes, trying to see through the blinding white light.

Getting to her feet, Enna Lee blew the curls from her face. She stood proud and fierce, brandishing a stream of mirrored lamplight ahead of her, looking stronger than ever.

"Enna!" Rose's face lit up and she struggled to her feet. Again, she heard the words *TWO HALVES* channelling through her, as if the pendant was suddenly strengthened by Rose's renewed hope. She knew she had to get the pendants before Verrulf did.

"Rose, Rui, get behind me." They scrambled to Enna and the protection she offered. Funnel lay heaped by Enna's feet.

"This stops NOW!" Enna commanded. Her mirrored lamp projected a piercing light. She flashed it at Verrulf.

"Parandarrrh!" The word shuddered from Verrulf's mouth and he recoiled away.

Funnel moaned, as death took another swipe to control him. Enna spoke to him. "You fool, Anthony Funnel!" Enna's wild eyes glared at him. "What would Emily Templeforth think of you now? She'd be disgusted."

"I'm dying," Funnel said, staring at his hands, which were shrivelling back around the bone and sinew.

Keeping her eyes fixed on Verrulf, Enna replied, "The two pendants are killing you. No one person can wear them both and live. I suppose Verrulf failed to tell you that?"

"What?" Rose said.

"Rose!" Rui's eyes widened with terror.

A wave of horrible doubt filled her. *If I take them I'll...die?*

Enna stalked around Funnel in a circle, and Rose and Rui stayed close, her lamplight forcing Verrulf back into the darkness manifesting where the brotherhood had stood.

"That trrrick won't larrrst you much longerrr." Verrulf prowled slow and wolf-like, sniffing the air – waiting for a moment to pounce. "My Crrreeplings are already amongst us!" Dark unruly shapes thickened and swelled behind him. "You'rrre out...of...time!" Verrulf began laughing. "The gateway is open. Look arrround you!"

All at once, the cloaks in the circle shot into the air. Flapping in the wind, they towered around Verrulf, connecting to the ground with stretched powdery legs, their heads masked by the shadows above. Grotesque, withered arms ending in sharp pointy fingers grabbed the air, snatching at them.

"Rose!" Rui pulled her close.

"Fearrr them!" Verrulf hissed. "Fearrr is what they want, it excites them. Can you hearrr theirrr excitement?"

The scissoring gnash of teeth came at them from every direction. The Creeplings jerked towards Rose and Rui, moving in fractured pulses, as though passing through invisible films of water.

"Noooooo!" Funnel's wizened hands clutched at his head. He rolled over and began to shrivel before them, face crumpling, his eye disappearing into the folds of his brow.

His robes clung to the sharp edges of his shoulder blades. "Awwwwhhh!" His terrified howl cut through the night, but even his voice sounded aged and feeble now.

"He's dead?" Rose gasped, a strange mix of emotions surging through her. She dropped down beside him.

Funnel was evil, he'd become a complete monster, but he was family. Involuntarily, her hand outstretched to comfort him, but at that same moment, he suddenly stopped moving altogether.

Rui pulled her back, encircling her with his arm. "It's the pendants, they just...killed him!" Rui explained.

Enna's lamplight flickered and went out. They were unprotected.

Within the otherworldly light glowing inside the circle, one Creepling broke free of the others. Its face swung into view, its mouth shut, just its nasty polished eyes glinting. Keeping its distance, it sniffed them. Rose's heart buckled. Its snarl exposed blackened, pin-sharp teeth, stringed with slobber. The stench of rotting vegetation oozed from its mouth. It circled them on all fours, its body rising and falling. The others crept forward behind it, hissing.

"Destrrroy them," Verrulf boomed. "The pendants arrre finally MINE!"

"Rose," a weak voice groaned. Rose looked down to see Funnel handing her the two pendants. *He's still alive?*

His sunken eye glistened. "Take them...stop...him," he choked. "I'm sor—" Funnel collapsed, dead. A single tear trickled down his grey face. His fist gripped the two pendants, still offering them to her.

Verrulf's pendant hummed black then red. Hers shone in one piercing golden light – it wanted her back and she knew what she had to do. "Rui, if I share the blood do you think I can wear both pendants...and live?" she panted.

"No! What if it doesn't work? You'll end up like Funnel."

"I'm gonna find out." She dived forward.

"Nooooo. Kill them!" Verrulf boomed to the Creeplings. "Rrrip them aparrrt. NOW!" Verrulf lunged forward to take the pendants for himself.

"Oh no ya don't." She glared at him. Adrenaline and uncontrollable rage surged through her. "These are my friends and I'll protect them with my life." She pulled both pendants away from Funnel's grey fingers in a plume of ash.

"Rose, NO!" Rui shrieked.

A force like hot iron shot up through her body. She gripped both pendants in her hand.

The Creeplings squirmed around with double-jointed movements, fearing to come any closer.

Now what? She panicked. A distant memory of that first

evening in the library flashed into her mind – as though her pendant guided her. *Hold the pendants back to back, with yours on top.* Quickly she placed them one on top of the other, hers facing upwards. A tunnel of blinding light exploded from them. It worked.

Enna grinned. "You underestimated us *humans*…again, Verrulf."

Verrulf halted, and shielded his face from the new light. *SSSSSSSSSSSSSSSSSSSSSSSSSSSSSSSSSSSSSSSS!*

Squealing, the Creeplings bent away.

Rose felt impossibly strong. She drew a deep breath and turned.

"You hearrrd me. EAT THEM!" Verrulf roared, his eyes like furnaces. Screeching, Bahula belted up the nearest iron stack. He swung down above Rose and offered her the real Amber Cup. Without a second thought, she grabbed it.

Everything paused.

She and the cup locked together – outside of time, as one. A surge of energy coursed through her veins.

The cup lit up in a golden, throbbing light that matched the pendants. Rose gulped. Her whole body shone. The light was like an aura around her, sparkling and fizzing. She drew a deep breath, feeling the power travelling through her arms and right into her middle. She bonded as one with the cup's power: pure and invincible.

"She doesn't know what to do. She is just a child, a girrrl. Finish herrr. NOW…" Verrulf ordered, but his words were starting to sound drawn out…slow…distant.

The Creeplings screeched, still surging towards them, their robes thrashing about against the spindly bodies within. Rui spun in a circle, gripping Bahula in his arms. He shouted something to Rose, but she couldn't hear him. His words seemed to drag and she couldn't understand them. The Creeplings, too, moved in slow motion.

"Believe in yourself, Rose!" she heard Enna scream.

Rose gulped. She had everything; both pendants and the cup. *What do I need to do?*

Thoughts crashed through Rose's mind – her mother being left to rot as a baby in the workhouse; her true identity had been stolen from her, stolen from both of them… But the workhouse hadn't ruined her. No – Rose clenched her teeth – it made me stronger. Maybe she'd never known her mother's love, but somehow it beat through her still – a part of her.

"*What is it you want, Rose? It's up to you now. You alone command the cup.*" She heard Miss Templeforth's voice inside her mind.

She took one last look at the cup and, clasping both the pendants in her hand, she stood tall.

"Get back where you come from you bunch of…

COLLYWOBBLERS!" she screamed.

A crushing force surrounded her, whipping her up into the central point of a cyclone. The whole world broke apart in a tornado of black particles that writhed around her. Tortured moans raged in her ears. Black matter surged and tunnelled into the cup. She struggled to hold it steady.

RRRRRRRAAAAAAAAAAAH!

The roar engulfed her senses and the cup shook. Verrulf's huge face – blackened in his shadow form – twisted in front of her.

"I'm stronger than you," she shouted at him, as if it was just the two of them there, and everything and everyone else had washed away. "Stronger, coz I ain't all swallowed up with hate. I'm free. I've got love in my bones. Human love. And I…pity you." Tears streamed down her face.

Verrulf's mouth was open, eyes bulging. "This isn't overrr – I'll find anotherrr way. The spell opened otherrr gateways. I will find them and DESTRRROY you, Rrrose Muddle. RRRrraaaaaggghhhhh!" Verrulf yelled as the cup swallowed him down, antlers and all.

Black matter charged in after him, like thousands of wasps returning to their nest. Rose gripped the cup tightly, as if nothing else mattered. And both pendants glowed. "And shut this bleedin' gateway FOR EVER!" She shouted with all her heart.

The blackness at once turned into luminous white. The whole world broke into snowy particles, thrashing about, with her at the centre.

A beautiful woman emerged and swam towards her amid the current of white, her long sinuous hair swirling about her. Rose could barely believe her eyes. *Mr Gupta's wife!* Rose recognized her from the newspaper clipping – the memory of how she'd perished in the train fire all those years ago.

A translucent image of Mr Gupta formed. He smiled at Rose, resting his hands together as if in prayer.

"Mr Gupta!" Rose reached out to him, but he fell backwards into the woman's open arms, smiling. They spun together, her long hair twisting around his body. He ascended upwards in a spinning embrace, disappearing into the eddying white mists. Rose understood in her heart that Mr Gupta had been freed from the necromancy spell, and was being taken somewhere good.

Am I dead? Rose wondered, staring into the shifting white particles. The cup in her hand let forth a blinding light.

Then stillness.

The dragging sound of the waves on the shingle returned with the howling wind.

It all faded and she passed into it.

Carbolic Soap

Rose opened her eyes to find herself in a green room packed with rows of beds. The smell of carbolic soap snaked up her nostrils. "I'm back in the workhouse!" she panicked, sitting sharply up. "Where am I? Ouch." She gripped the thick bandage wrapped around her forehead.

Her mind fired into action. *The pier, the cup, the brotherhood, the Creeplings. VERRULF.* She tapped her throat, found her pendant hanging there and breathed a sigh of relief. "Rui! Enna...BAHULA!" she wailed. Her mind swam; she couldn't think clearly. Her head pounded beneath the bandage, as if it might explode.

"Ah, you're finally awake! You have concussion,

young lady." A podgy face loomed over her. "You are in the Brighton Royal Infirmary. I am Matron Wrigglesbottom." She spoke loudly and slowly, as if Rose was hard of hearing. "Now, it's the three R's for you. Rest, rest and more rest." The matron plumped up the pillows behind Rose's head and forced her back into them.

"There were shadowy things, from another world. An evil monster with antlers who wanted everyone dead, and—" Rose grabbed her pendant again. It pumped once in her hand to reassure her. *But where was Verrulf's pendant? I had them both* – she panicked, her heart racing.

"Enough of that nonsense, Miss Muddle, you are perfectly safe. It sounds rather as though the laudanum I administered has been giving you hallucinations." She tutted. "Shadowy things – antlers, whatever next!"

"But it's true..." *Ain't it?* She doubted herself for a moment. "I...we... W-where are my friends?" Rose stammered. "What happened? Is everyone safe? Are they... alive?" Rose tried to get up, but Matron gripped her shoulders.

"You will be going nowhere until I say so, Miss Muddle. But I can reassure you there's been quite a menagerie of visitors for you and they all seemed very much alive. The pushy little fellow in particular, claiming to be the nephew of the Maharajah of Jaipur! What front!"

Rose grinned.

"Then the infamous Gypsy Lee and the town's most respected lawyer, Mr Bartholomew-Smyth. And one of them even brought along a monkey! What company you keep!"

"Yes – that's them!" She sighed with relief. "Where's Enna Lee, Rui and the monkey? I need to see them all – NOW!"

"I sent them away. You've not been fit to receive visitors. Besides, the boy and his monkey have already returned to India."

"W-what!" Rose's heart plunged. "No! You gotta be wrong."

"Hush now." Matron lifted Rose's wrist, and consulted the fob watch hanging from her breast pocket. "He said his boat was departing yesterday."

"Yesterday? How long have I been here?"

"You have remained in a deep sleep for two days."

"Two days!" Rose's eyes brimmed with tears. *Rui!*

"Your pulse is high, Miss Muddle, and…"

Rose tuned out Matron's voice, and was lost inside her own thoughts for a while.

After everything that's happened he's…gone and left me. 'You come from nothing and you are nothing, Rose Muddle.' Miss Gritt's wicked words crept into her mind. But I wasn't a nothing was I? My ma and me, we was Templeforths all along. Things should have been better for her…for us. And what now? Rose knew Enna Lee would see her right, she'd promised she would. *But without Rui…how can anything ever be right again?*

"Can I go now?" Rose murmured, tears rolling down her cheeks.

"No, you must recuperate, Miss Muddle, which will take time. But I do have a letter for you, from Mr Bartholomew-Smyth, which he insisted you must read. It is on your bedside table next to the bell." Matron tucked in Rose's bed sheets so tightly they felt like constraints. "You may read it when you feel well enough. And not a moment before!" Turning, she waddled off, drawing the blue curtain around on the rail behind her. "I will check on you again shortly." Her footsteps faded away.

Rose rolled over and cried into her pillows.

Between sobs, she remembered the journey that had brought her to this point. Her excitement at leaving the workhouse to become a maid; meeting Miss Templeforth and learning about the pendant and then Rui arriving with Mr Gupta and Bahula. What a terrifying adventure they'd been on together. And yet somehow she'd overcome Verrulf and his Creeplings. Despite all this, she sat there feeling empty, alone and bewildered. *Without Rui, none of it's worth a fig.* She clutched her pendant, hoping to draw some comfort from it. It pulsed twice in her hand.

From the corner of her eye, Rose spotted the envelope. *The letter Matron said was delivered from some lawyer?*

Picking it up, she stroked the wax seal on the back. She opened it with little interest. The letter inside read:

Dear Miss R Muddle,

I write in haste, to inform you that the entirety of the Templeforth Estate, to include thirteen Sackville Road and all the contents therein, have been bequeathed to you. In addition, the princely sum of £100,000 sterling is awaiting your signature. The trustee to this arrangement is Miss Enna Lee of no fixed abode, Hove.

The official papers to finalize the transfer have been drawn up at my office, 34 Ship Street, Brighton. Please attend at your very soonest convenience.

With every sincerity,
G Bartholomew-Smyth

Mr Bartholomew-Smyth, Wills and Probate, 34 Ship Street, Brighton Town

Rose gasped. The letter dropped from her hands onto the bed sheets. Her eyes brimming with tears. Happiness, confusion, and about a thousand other emotions all welled up at the same time.

"I don't believe it," she sniffed, clutching her pendant. "I'm rich! Thank you, Miss T."

Why with that amount of money I can buy anything I want. Rui won't believe this when I— The emptiness returned. *But he's not here, is he... Without him what's the point in having anything?* she sobbed quietly to herself. *What if that's it, and I never get to see him again?* Tears streamed down her face. *I never got to say goodbye, or tell him how much I'll...miss him.*

A trolley rattled to a stop the other side of her curtain.

"Cocoa, Miss?" someone asked. "And some biscuits?"

"Nah, thanks," Rose managed, wiping her nose on the bed sheets.

"How about an adventure?"

Filthy Rich

The blue hospital curtain around Rose's bed lifted at the bottom, and Bahula's tiny, grinning face peered up at Rose.

"Bahula!" she whispered. He bounded onto her lap.

The curtain whipped aside, and Rui slipped in, wearing a tan caretaker's overcoat that reached his ankles.

"I am the master of disguise!"

"Rui," Rose managed, wiping away her tears. "They told me you'd gone back to India, and—"

"Ah, that, yes. The matron wouldn't let you have any visitors, so I told her I'd be leaving for India in order that I could sneak back undetected."

"I-I thought you'd gone without saying goodbye, and—"

"Never, Rose!" He sat beside her and took her hands in his. "Tremendous companions are not that easy to come by. Once you find one, you are advised to keep hold of them for as long as you can. My Uncle the Maharajah has asked if you are in the market for a job in the palace as my companion, back in India of course."

"Oh, Rui!" She held him at arm's length. "Yes, yes I am." Rose felt like she might burst with happiness as she pulled him close and held him as tightly as she could.

She clutched her pendant and remembered with a jolt that Funnel's was now missing. "The other pendant's gone, Rui. What happened to it? I was wearing both of them…"

Rui suddenly stood up and stuck his head through the curtains to check no one was coming, then he turned back to her.

"Well, at the end – and may I say, you were terrific by the way – there was an explosion of some kind. Probably caused by the force of Verrulf's world being sucked back into the cup. Debris lay everywhere. It was hard to see and by the time it cleared and I got to you, you were gripping hold of the cup – which had split in two, but you wore only one pendant. The other had disappeared somewhere amid the confusion."

"So it's gone!" Rose sat forward.

"Yes. Vanished. Enna's been searching for it. I am not sure whether she has had any luck. You can ask her when you see her. Now, how's your head?" he asked, inspecting her bandages.

"Better!" she lied. It still hurt quite a bit.

"Good. Because I need to get you to Enna." He drew the trolley inside. "With the other pendant still at large, Enna is worried for your safety. If you feel well enough, we should leave."

"How are we going to get past Matron?" Rose whispered though she couldn't hide her excitement. Swinging her legs around, she jumped down from the high bed, momentarily forgetting her sore, bandaged head. "Ouch!"

"I have a plan – of course." Rui tapped his nose with a finger, ignoring her pain.

Rui and Bahula began unloading the cups and saucers from the bottom of the trolley, and spread them across the middle of her bed.

Rose kept a lookout. She spotted Matron beside the bed at the end, flicking a giant needle, and grimaced.

Rui swept the bed sheets over the heaped crockery and admired the crude Rose-shaped bundle left beneath. Satisfied, he dusted his hands together.

"Your carriage awaits, Ma'am!" He pointed to the

cleared under-shelf of the trolley. Rose crawled in, giggling, carrying her bundle of clothes, Bahula and the letter. Rui draped a cloth over the top, concealing them inside. Then he flung back the curtain and set off, the trolley wheels spinning erratically on the parquet floor beneath. "Tally-ho!" she heard him murmur.

Together, they rattled out of the hospital ward to freedom.

Rose looked at the letter clutched in her hand – she hadn't even told Rui about it yet. *I've just inherited the whole of the Templeforth Estate!* She shook her head in disbelief. *But what am I going to do with ALL that money and that big old house?* she thought, gripping onto the shelf for dear life, as Rui took a sharp corner.

In truth, with everything that had happened at thirteen Sackville Road, it was the last place she wanted to live. *Besides, I'll have no need of it when I'm in India.* She grinned. *India!* Her mind filled at once with bright colours, sunshine, exotic-smelling spices and scented smoke. *Oh, and monkeys – the more monkeys the better!* she thought, cuddling Bahula even closer.

I'm so bloomin' lucky. Her thoughts switched to the workhouse and all the girls she'd left behind. *It don't seem right that I should have so much when they've got nothing at all.* Being filthy rich suddenly felt like a big responsibility.

She knew it was a life-changing amount of money. *Enough to make big changes...but what changes?*

Squeezing her eyes shut, Rose gripped her pendant, hoping it might help her. Deep in thought, the possibilities played out.

And then it came to her. Her pendant flashed and her grey eyes shone. A broad smile spread out, as the most excellent idea took shape.

46

The Truth's Out

MAYOR FOUND DEAD BENEATH WEST PIER

Mayor Cuthbert Stitchworthy was discovered dead beneath the footings of the West Pier in the early hours of November 1st.

Emerging reports suggest that an influential group of local men had stolen Hove's Amber Cup from the Museum in Brighton Town, and that Indian curator, Arki Ramesh Gupta, from the Jaipur Museum, had been murdered during his heroic attempts to stop them.

His Majesty King Edward has posthumously granted Mr Gupta the Order of Merit, the highest honour to be bestowed on any citizen of the commonwealth. Awarded, he said, for his outstanding bravery and in recognition of his services to archaeology.

The cup is now safely back in possession of the museum and is to be mended and and placed on display amid tighter security. The reinstated curator, Mr Thomas, made this statement: "This Bronze Age Cup crafted from amber and discovered beneath the giant burial mound once standing in the centre of Hove is a symbol of our ancestral heritage, and is now back in the museum where it belongs. It is the property of the People of Brighton and Hove."

Rui finished reading, and folded up the paper, placing it next to the skrying bowl as they waited for Enna in her caravan. He stretched back in his chair, his hands behind his head. "I simply couldn't have done it without you, Watson." He winked.

"Oi!" Rose elbowed him. "Well, I hope you ain't too disappointed that you don't get any mention in there?" She gestured towards the newspaper.

"No. Our actions are recorded over there." He pointed to the tapestry.

Rose looked over at her now-completed face, which showed her wearing both pendants. And stitched just behind her, Rui could be seen clutching Bahula, pulling the monkey away from the Creeplings. Her face broke into a grin. "We did it! We really did it."

Rui nodded enthusiastically. Bahula jumped up on her lap and snuggled into her. Rose cuddled him close. She was so glad to be back with her friends. The hospital reminded her of the workhouse – the smell of the place, all sterile and deathly.

Rose noticed Rui examining a giant ruby in the candlelight.

"That's Mr Gupta's, isn't it? You got it back?"

Rui grinned. "Yes."

"How? Tell me, what exactly happened to the brotherhood at the end?" she asked. "I thought they was all dead meat for sure."

"When the dust cleared they were all there again, as white as sheets, shivering and muttering about shadows. I think they were temporarily transported down to the abyss and replaced by Verrulf's Creeplings."

Rose listened intently as Rui continued.

"The brotherhood were so glad to be back in this world, that, when the police came, they begged to be taken to the station. They admitted everything." He chuckled.

"Snodgrass handed over the ruby to the authorities. I will return it to Mr Gupta's relatives personally."

"Good…your Mr Gupta, he really was a hero. Just like you always thought, Rui. Without him trying to stop Funnel, things could of turned out terrible."

The doors to the caravan swung open and Enna rushed to Rose's side.

"Dear Rose. How are you?" Enna cupped her face, before engulfing her in a mighty cuddle.

"I'm fine. Really."

Rose's mind flashed back to Funnel and all the unanswered questions. She looked up at Enna.

"I-I need to know about my ma, Enna. About Emily Templeforth, and about him, my grandfather…Funnel."

"Yes, Funnel." Enna sighed. "I never suspected him, or thought he would be capable of doing the things he has done. Verrulf's pendant possesses its bearers and so it is a potent force to resist."

"So Funnel weren't always bad?" Rose tilted her head.

"No, not bad, not back then, just ambitious."

Rose felt a strange sense of relief wash over her.

Rui sat forward. "Could the despair of losing Emily have driven him to take up the pendant?"

"Perhaps." Enna looked down. "Maybe we'll never know."

"And my ma?" Rose asked, her heart fluttering.

"Your poor mother. She was deposited at the workhouse by Emily's father, Mr Templeforth, as a newborn babe. Emily had died in childbirth – and to protect the family name, what with Emily being out of wedlock –" looking down, Enna arranged her dress with a sigh – "Emily's father, Mr Templeforth, covered this fact up, saying she died of sudden heart failure instead. He never approved of Anthony; he was from a lower social class. But I obtained your mother's birth records, which prove who she was. Emily's father had a breakdown after her death, you know. He lived out the last of his years in an asylum. Looking back, it must have been the guilt of letting your mother go."

Rose looked down and fiddled with her fingers. She just hoped that her ma had had some happiness in the years she'd spent with her pa outside of the workhouse.

"And the gateway inside the cup, is it sealed now?" Rui piped up.

"Yes, the cup is closed for ever – you saw to that, it broke in two after you banished them. Its magic has gone," she added with a quick smile that didn't reach her tired eyes. Enna ran her finger over the polished surface of the table.

"What is it, Enna?" Rose could tell she was holding something back.

Enna looked up. "I fear the dreadful spell performed under the West Pier during that planetary alignment has triggered something awful. How far across the globe it travelled is not yet clear, nor how it will manifest."

"What, you mean it's not over?" Rose sat forward, gripping her pendant, which pulsed, mirroring her fear. Verrulf's words to her as he got sucked back into the cup rang in her mind. *The spell opened other gateways. I will find them and destroy you, Rose Muddle…*

"So it opened other gateways, like the one in the cup?" Rose asked, a wretched dread inching through her.

"It may have done. Look, a powerful gridwork of energy and ancient magic once ran around this earth, though much of it is forgotten about today. Only a handful of people still know anything about it."

"Yes, Mr Gupta spoke to me about this," Rui said, leaning forward. "His journal was full of such ideas."

Enna nodded. "He was a good man."

"This earth energy is harnessed by geomancy. The ancient people knew how to access this power. They built monuments of stone, knew about the magic that existed in certain special places, like the red waters here. These powers have remained latent, but they can be awoken by magical forces – such as the pendants."

"So, the spell under the West Pier activated ancient energy across the globe?" Rui's green eyes glistened as he gripped the table.

"Yes, meaning other gateways could be opened – but only by using *both* pendants – and I know you would never let that happen, Rose."

Rose gripped her pendant and shook her head. "Never." She sat forward, fear rushing through her. "B-but, did you find out what happened to the other pendant, Verrulf's?" Rose could feel a swell of panic emanating from her pendant as she spoke.

Enna shook her head, her blue eyes trailing to the ceiling. "I have searched everywhere. Left no stone unturned, but it has vanished. We must consider it gone and remain vigilant lest it returns, for as sure as day follows night, return it will. It is a dangerous object that can neither be destroyed nor quieted. We must be thankful that the two of you have stopped them…for now."

"And Mr Gupta's journal? Where is that?" Rui asked. "It contained dangerous information."

"Destroyed in the explosion; there was no trace of it left."

"Phew." Rui's hand flew to his forehead.

"But enough of this. It takes time for darkness to amass. Who knows, decades maybe. And perhaps it never will." Enna threw her hands in the air but her eyes still looked cold with worry. "You both showed such bravery, we all owe you a great debt of gratitude. What plans are afoot for you both?"

"Well, Enna," Rui began, "Rose has accepted my uncle's job offer. She is to be my companion in India. She will be safe with me over there."

Rose's heart beat faster. *Me! Travelling to India.*

"I see." Enna tried to hide her sadness behind a smile. "Are you certain? You know I can't leave with you?" She looked down. "I have to stay here in Hove."

"I'll write though," Rose added, squeezing Enna's hand. "Every week."

"Well, you will be well provided for, thanks to your inheritance. As you know, the house and all the Templeforth's worldly estate is now officially yours. The paperwork is complete."

"Yes, about that." Rose sighed and leaned back in her chair. "The truth is, I don't much care for thirteen Sackville Road. I don't want to live there, that is. It gives me the heebie-jeebies after all what's gone on there. I've thought about it – and I now know what I want to do."

"Yes, Rose?" Enna said. "Miss Templeforth has made me the trustee of her estate. I shall do my best to carry out your requests."

"I want thirteen Sackville Road to become a home for all the girls left at the workhouse. Give them a chance like what I've had…like what my ma never had."

Rui stared at her open-mouthed.

Rose carried on, picking up pace. "And I want them each to have a room of their own…and I want the library filled with books about faraway places, and teachers there what are kind to them, so the girls can be trained up to be the best what they can possibly be. Oh, and Gritt is *not* to be allowed in." Rose shook her head, then grinned. "But Mr Crank can keep his job – it would do him good, I think. And I want it to be called, 'The Templeforth Academy for Brilliant Girls'. There!"

"Rose! Just…tremendous!" Rui said, puffing up with pride.

"Well, Albion's pendant always chooses one with a big heart," Enna marvelled. "And you, Rose Muddle, seem to have one of the biggest. A worthy guardian indeed. You make me *so* very proud. I will see that your wishes will be carried out –" she smiled broadly – "but I will make certain there is a generous monthly allowance remaining for you. I know Miss Templeforth would insist upon it. And should you ever change your mind, the house will always remain yours. You never know what the future may hold."

"Yep, all right," Rose giggled, gripping onto Rui's arm. *My future!* Sheer joy danced through her. She could hardly believe that she, Rose Muddle, was going to Jaipur to stay at the palace as an honoured guest – *and Rui's companion. Things are going to be just fine,* she grinned, *and who knows what adventures might await me there?*

Postscript

A girl sat in the back of a rattling carriage. Her destination: the docks at Shoreham Harbour. The ticket pinched in her fingers; it gave her passage on board the schooner *Carolina*, which, empty of its tobacco shipment, would shortly be embarking on its return journey to Guatemala. It would also stop en route in the Indian port of Bombay, to refuel and take on a new cargo of tea. The girl would disembark there and make her way overland to Jaipur, just as the voice in her mind instructed.

She stared out of the carriage window, as the sea lapped in silent waves against the shoreline. She looked down at the silver book resting on her lap, and caressed the enamel

eye on the cover with her fingertips. A tight-lipped smirk
flashed across her face. Her blonde ringlets bounced as she
drew back her silk neck-scarf and clutched the dark disc of
amber swinging there.

Great things were to happen in Jaipur, and her journey
had only just begun.

Rose

Rui

Bahula

THE ROSE MUDDLE MYSTERIES

continue in...

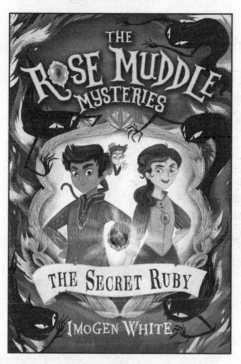

Rose and Rui set out for Jaipur to return Mr Gupta's ruby
to his family. But, unbeknownst to them, they are being
followed by a member of the Brotherhood of the Black Sun,
and dark secrets await them when they dock in India...

Coming 2018

I first moved to Hove – which sits on the south coast of England – many years ago. I immediately fell in love with the area; the spirit of the place, the people and the sea! And as I immersed myself in my new surroundings, I discovered that there once stood a huge Bronze Age burial mound right in the middle of Hove, which was flattened in 1856 during building works. It used to stand twenty feet high, close enough to the shoreline to have been seen far out to sea. This burial mound revealed a coffin roughly hewn from a hollowed-out tree trunk, and inside that, nestled amongst the bones and burial goods, sat a cup crafted from Baltic Amber – a cup that was over 3,000 years old!

Excitedly I told everyone about my findings – and was amazed that no one seemed to know anything about this mound, this cup – this forgotten chieftain once so important to the area. Even the place name itself – Hove – is derived from this monument. (The old Danish word "Hof" which means burial ground.)

I started imagining who this person might have been to be buried in such fine style. And what the significance of this small amber cup could have been? With each question, the germ of this book grew and grew. And with it, so did Rose Muddle – my heroine; a workhouse girl who is plucked from obscurity, only to discover that her future holds dangerous – and magical secrets...

I have borrowed many elements of *The Amber Pendant* from local history: there was a Chalybeate spring in St Ann's Well Gardens, renowned for its health-giving qualities. A Gypsy Lee really did use to tell fortunes from a wagon in St Ann's Well Gardens, and many of the geographical places you find in the novel can still be seen here in Hove today.

I hope this story inspires you to uncover forgotten secrets wherever you live – please let me know what you find!

The Amber Pendant is Imogen's debut novel and won a place in the 2014 Undiscovered Voices anthology. Imogen loves local history, and stories that aren't limited to beautiful countryside locations or secluded seaside coves.

Find out more about Imogen at *mysteryverse.wordpress.com*

I would like to thank my husband Dale who devoted so many hours to lovingly reading through my work. To my children, Oscar and Martha, for being so understanding and brilliant. I feel very lucky to have you all.

To my agent, Anna Power, who believed in my work and dedicated so much of her time editing this novel to ensure it reached publication. The ethos of her agency, Johnson & Alcock, is to be exactly the representative their authors need them to be and this has truly been my experience. My thanks to Anna for being the very best.

A big thank you to Davide Ortu for illustrating this stunning book cover. Also to Lenka Hrehova and Will Steele at Usborne for the original concept and finished design, and David Shephard for the map.

Team Usborne!! You really have held my hand through this whole process. Becky Walker, thank you for your boundless enthusiasm and editorial excellence. A special mention also to

Rebecca Hill, Sarah Stewart, Amy Dobson and everyone else at Usborne who has worked so hard to make this happen. I feel extremely fortunate

To the brilliant SCBWI Undiscovered Voices competition that I won in 2014 and which started me on this road to publication. Sara Grant and the team – you totally rock.

My writing group, the hugely talented Siobhan Rowden, Karen Moore, Astrid Holm and Shirley Archibald. Ladies, it's been such fun! Thank you for all your help and advice. You've been there through all the ups and downs. Big thanks also to Alex Caird, Saskia Wesnigk-Wood and Catie White. Also, Ambika – for letting me borrow all her family names!

I would also like to thank the libraries in Brighton and Hove, especially the local history sections, and the Brighton and Hove Museums for displaying the Amber Cup which is such a massive part of this book.

And finally, thanks to my lovely mum. You have been so supportive and excited – I'm glad you are proud! And to my stepdad Bobbie, to whom this first book is dedicated. The kindest and most generous of humans, who sadly passed away just a few months before I discovered this book was to be published. But I know how thrilled he would be now. He spent hours picking through those early (and very dreadful) first drafts. He always believed in me, even when I didn't. Thank you, Bobbie. X

Usborne Quicklinks

For links to websites where you can find out about the
places and people of Hove at the time when Rose Muddle's
adventures take place, see the real "Hove Amber Cup"
and other objects discovered in the burial mound, and find
out more about life during the first decades of the 1900s,
go to www.usborne.com/quicklinks and type in the keywords
"Amber Pendant". Please follow the internet safety guidelines
at the Usborne Quicklinks website.

*The recommended websites are regularly reviewed and updated but,
please note, Usborne Publishing is not responsible for the content of any
website other than its own, or for any exposure to harmful, offensive or
inaccurate material which may appear on the Web.*

For more spellbinding reads head to
www.usborne.com/fiction